Amid the Shadows

Michael C. Grumley

DEDICATION

To Mikayla and Amber, two perfect girls to whom I want
nothing more than to be your daddy.

And to Linda and Shannon, we miss you both terribly.

ACKNOWLEDGMENTS

Special thanks to Susan, Kim, Gail, Bryan, Dennis, Karen,
and Dan for all of your expert help.

New York City – 1871

They were being followed again. He could feel it. The man squeezed his son's hand and quickened their pace. He pulled his coat tighter, feeling the cold morning chill penetrate through his thick wool coat. Above them, the rising sun was obscured behind the thick layer of smoke from the sea of chimneys dotting the horizon.

The man looked over his shoulder and spotted the large figure behind them. He was getting closer. This was not the first time Dean Kelly had been threatened. His success as one of New York's largest merchants had made him and his family a common target by those less fortunate. This time was different though. Whoever this person was, he had been following Kelly and his son for some time and always watching them from a distance.

Behind Kelly, the dark figure quickened his pace as well and began to close in. He could feel his heart rate increasing rapidly, and his hands were beginning to shake. It was growing nearer. He kept his head down and mostly hidden beneath his coat's large collar. As he drew closer, his eyes narrowed. He splashed through a deep puddle without slowing. Fifth Avenue was busy with people walking back and forth, all trying to avoid the water-filled potholes in the dirt road. A large, horse drawn carriage passed unnoticed as the man's vision and hearing began to tunnel and zoom in on the Kellys ahead of him. What Dean Kelly did not know, however, was that it was not Kelly in whom he was interested. It was his young, eight-year-old son.

Kelly and his son walked faster. He knew the man behind them was getting closer. They neared a large construction site where dozens of men worked in the drizzling rain, shaping large stones for the foundation of a building behind them. The ringing of their metal chisels could be heard far down the busy road.

As they neared, one of the large men put down his tools and stood up. He spotted Kelly approaching by his dark hair combed straight back and, after locking eyes with him, Kelly gave a firm nod. The large workman put his hands inside his overalls and nodded back. He then turned and motioned to several men behind him, who all stopped and followed, heading for the road.

The shaking intensified as the figure was now within fifty feet of Kelly and his son. It was going to happen. It was time. He could feel his body flushing with adrenaline.

A large man dressed in work clothes suddenly stepped in front of him and put his hand up. "Ah, where ya goin' there laddie?"

The stranger pushed past him without a word but was stopped by the workman's hand around his arm.

"Hold on there, yeah?" Another man approached from behind and grabbed him from the other side. "You wouldn't be following the Kellys now would ya?"

The figure looked to each side and back to Kelly and his son. His crystal blue eyes widened as they began to move away from him. He pulled his arms free and tried to run but was caught again, this time by more men who crowded around him grabbing his coat firmly.

"We can't have that now." Without warning, the workman to his right slammed a fist into his stomach causing him to lurch forward.

But the stranger still barely acknowledged them. He quickly rose to his feet and surged forward, pulling the other men with him. His blue eyes now began to show signs of panic.

The other men were surprised by his strength and delivered two crushing blows to his back and kidneys.

The stranger fell again, this time onto a knee. The shaking in his hands became almost uncontrollable. He abruptly looked away from the boy and turned to the men around him. When he stood up, he did so with incredible strength, pushing the surprised men back in an instant. When they tried to grab him again, their hands now met a much greater force. The figure seized one of the arms around him and snapped it at the elbow, causing a large man behind him to scream out in pain.

The others instantly jumped on the stranger beating him savagely, but this time he did not fall, or even kneel. Instead, his body moved like a whip, spinning and kicking the largest man square in the chest, lifting him off the ground and sending him crashing into a nearby wheelbarrow. The stranger's arm lashed back and forth almost too quickly to see, striking one man in front and another behind him in nearly the same instant. Both men stumbled backwards with blood streaming down their face.

"Get his legs!"

Dozens more workmen were suddenly upon him as others fell to the ground. The figure in black spun again and two more men collapsed to the dirt beneath them, one unconscious and the other slowly dying from his smashed throat.

In a fury, Kelly's men crowded around, their constant blows raining down on the stranger but with little effect. Many of the strikes were blocked or missed entirely as the man in the middle seemed to move faster and faster. Flashes of metal were seen as long weapons appeared from under his thick black coat. They instantly found their targets and two more workers collapsed. Another shrieked and blindly felt for his eyes.

Finally one of Kelly's largest men launched himself at

the figure in the middle and struck him hard with a large heavy leather sap. The stranger reeled back, dazed, trying to find the weapon. Another sap was quickly pulled and slammed against his head, then another, and another. The stranger's vision began to blur, yet he continued taking his attackers down, one at a time. But the saps continued to find their mark. He stumbled and managed to grab one of the weapons and struck the sap's owner with it harder than any of them would have imagined, killing the man instantly.

More blows caused the stranger's vision to darken. He could barely make out Kelly and the boy in the distance. He desperately tried to push out of the circle and run after them. Just as he finally managed to get through the group of men, a gunshot rang out.

He lurched sideways as the bullet ripped into his side. A second shot immediately pierced his thigh, destroying a lateral wall of muscle and causing the stranger to fall onto his left side. His entire body was shaking now as his eyes desperately searched past his attackers for Kelly and the boy. He pushed himself up onto his right leg and managed to hobble two small steps forward when the next bullet dug into his back, toppling his body forward onto his chest.

Kelly pulled his son Ryan forward keeping him from looking back at the commotion, but when the shots were heard, the boy pulled away and turned back to look. He saw the strange man fall to the ground, his piercing eyes finding and staring straight at him. Their eyes locked for a moment as the man continued crawling forward with his hand outstretched toward Ryan.

Frightened, the boy suddenly stumbled backward over a large stone, slipping beyond the grip of his father and falling backwards into the crossroad behind them. "Ryan!" Kelly yelled, and reached for his son just as several passing horses snorted. The boy fell directly into their path and was trampled beneath them.

Seeing the boy trampled, the stranger, still trying to drag himself forward on the ground, let out a gut wrenching howl. His entire body convulsed and his eyes rolled up into their sockets. The eerie howling continued until the final blow to his head, and his body collapsed into the thick mud.

2

Saint Patrick's Cathedral was one of the largest and oldest in the entire city. Able to accommodate over 2,200 people, its decorated Neo-Gothic spires towered 330 feet above the street below. Inside, the *Pietà*, sculpted by William Ordway Partridge, was three times the size of Michelangelo's *Pietà*, and the cathedral's combined organs numbered over 9,800 pipes. It was also the seat of the archbishop of the Roman Catholic Archdiocese of New York.

The cathedral was a national historic landmark and a popular tourist attraction, bringing tens of thousands of visitors every year. The architecture was so impressive that few could resist taking a picture on the steps of its giant entrance and, with the warm spring weather, today was no exception. Hundreds of visitors milled in and out of the cathedral, setting off a continual stream of flashes from their digital cameras, then visiting the gift shop on their way out to take home a souvenir and a piece of the city's history.

Across the street, hundreds more stood back to snap pictures of the entire structure. Outside a nearby café, people dined on a late morning snack of scones and coffee while enjoying the view.

At one of the outermost tables sat a man in a suit taking in the scene. His hair peppered with small amounts of gray, he looked more like a local businessman than a tourist. Sitting calmly with his hand wrapped around a cup of coffee, he watched the mass of people entering and exiting the church.

A young, attractive barista with round glasses approached with a hot pot but seeing his cup was still untouched, she continued on to the other customers. She thought it odd that he had been sitting there for almost an hour and not even taken a sip. She gave him a curious glance before heading back inside.

A newlywed couple giggled and ran past the man's table. The young husband pulled his bride in for a quick kiss before they turned and trotted across the street, holding hands.

The newlyweds were soon followed by a small group of Japanese tourists who crossed to the other side where they stopped and took pictures of each other, beaming in front of the church.

The man looked down at his Rolex and calmly looked back up to the cathedral. He did not want to miss this.

At five minutes past eleven, the bombs went off. A deafening explosion could be heard from within the church, and smoke burst through the giant front doors. Everyone screamed and started to run when part of the ceiling began to collapse, and huge sections of the beautiful stained glass windows broke apart and fell onto the people below. The force of the collapsing roof pulled the west wall inward and down upon itself.

The screams were muted by a thunder emanating from the cathedral's enormous spires. One began to move, wobbling from side to side until cracks appeared and it too collapsed downward, pitching at its base and causing it to lean and smash into the second spire. Together they came down in a deadly heap of smoke, dust, and rubble.

People came streaming out of the café in horror, including the barista. No one noticed the well-dressed man stand up and walk to the corner. There, he continued to watch the carnage as people ran screaming in all directions, many of them bloodied and covered in dirt and ash.

Moments later sirens could be heard in the distance. The man took one last look and began to turn away when something caught his eye. He looked back to the smoldering building where, among the confusion, a mother was whisking her young daughter away to safety. But as she ran pulling her daughter behind her, the girl was not looking at her mother, nor the terrible scene behind her. The young girl was looking across the street and directly at *him*. He watched her for a long moment as the girl continued staring at him.

Suddenly feeling uneasy, the man turned and walked quickly down the street, disappearing into the chaos.

3

Detectives Danny Griffin and Mike Buckley pulled their sedan into the parking lot of the Marriott Hotel. Several patrol cars were already there and an ambulance was parked near the main entrance.

After getting out and slamming the car doors behind them, both men approached the area near the ambulance that had been cordoned off with yellow tape. As they passed an officer holding back a group of onlookers, Griffin looked up and counted the floors to the broken window; eight floors.

They reached two more officers in blue standing over the coroner who was kneeling down and examining the body.

"Jumper?" Buckley asked looking down.

The corner shook her head. "Hardly. She screamed all the way down." She adjusted her rectangular framed glasses and looked carefully at the victim's hands. "Got quite a bit of blood under the fingernails too." She wrote something down in her notebook and then turned her attention back to the body. "No, I'd say this lady put up quite a fight before going through that window."

Griffin popped a piece of gum into his mouth. "Where's Roberts?"

The coroner tucked a strand of brown hair behind her ear and made more notes. "Upstairs, room 811. Tell her I'll be up in a few."

Griffin nodded and looked around. He and Buckley scanned the group of onlookers for anyone who might be watching the crime scene with a little too much interest.

"Check out that guy." Buckley nodded toward a man standing in the crowd with orange hair and piercings covering his face. "He looks a little weird."

Griffin looked at him and shook his head. "That's Cleveland weird, not New York weird."

They backed up and surveyed the area, noting the basics: the glass, the distance from the building, and the position of the body. A few minutes later, they entered the hotel and headed for the elevators.

Cheryl Roberts was the lead investigating officer on duty. At five foot six with dark, shoulder-length brown hair, Roberts was known for being all business. She greeted Griffin and Buckley with a nod when they entered. Several other investigators were moving around the room, taking measurements and pictures. The detectives looked around the room and walked toward Roberts who had just finished with another officer. Virtually everything in the room was either broken or completely destroyed.

"What do we have?" Buckley asked, stepping over some broken glass and a large piece of a picture frame.

Roberts sighed. "Well, it's not a suicide. The other guests reported one hell of a fight, including gunshots." She pointed to bullet holes in one of the walls. "They said it sounded like several people and ended with someone screaming and the sound of breaking glass which, not surprisingly, we're assuming was the victim." She took a few steps over the debris and studied the couch laying on its side. "By then security was on their way up but found the room empty. Whoever did this left in a hurry."

Griffin got closer to the window and examined a piece of the broken edge. "This glass has to be a good quarter-inch thick." He knocked on it with his knuckle. "That must have been one hell of a push."

Buckley looked around the other side of the room. "Anything missing?"

"Not that we can see," replied Roberts. "Her purse still has her ID, money, and credit cards. Earrings and a watch are on the nightstand in the other room, but they're cheap."

Griffin noted more bullet holes on the far wall. "How much money did she have?"

"Forty-six dollars. She wasn't rich, that's for sure. We're doing a full rundown on her now."

Griffin looked at his watch. "So we have someone breaking in on what appears to be an average, middle-class woman at 1:30 in the morning for something other than a simple robbery."

"Even if it was a robbery," Buckley said, "they wouldn't have gotten downstairs before she called security. So at the very least, they had to know that she wasn't going to be in any condition to make a phone call when it was over." He raised an eyebrow. "Rape?"

Griffin shook his head. "The body was fully clothed on the pavement downstairs." He looked around the room. "I don't see fragments of clothing up here either."

Buckley looked at Roberts. "You got the ID?"

Roberts nodded and motioned at one of the officers. He was talking on the phone and holding up her driver's license. "Her name is Barbara Baxter. Lives upstate. We're guessing she was here on vacation."

Another officer stuck his head around the corner. "Hey, you guys are gonna want to see this." He motioned down the short hallway and all three followed him into the bedroom. He crossed the room to a large dresser and pointed to one of the lower drawers which was open. Inside were several pieces of clothing, neatly folded.

Roberts bent down and looked at the clothes. "These clothes don't fit a woman. They're for a child." She turned to the officer with a look of urgency. "Find out how many people checked into this room!"

The officer hung up the phone. "Two checked in, a mother and daughter. They guessed her age to be about six or seven."

"Jesus Christ," said Roberts, looking around the room.

"Search these rooms!" She got down on the floor and looked under the bed. They all quickly searched every nook of the small rooms but found nothing.

"Get downstairs and find someone who saw the girl. See if we can get a picture or drawing." The officer nodded and ran for the door. "And check the security cameras! See if they got a shot of her!"

Griffin watched Roberts' focus sharpen. She was a great investigator, but she was also a mother; and there was no greater instinct than that of a mother regarding a child.

"If she's not here," Roberts continued, "then they probably took her. I think that woman fought to protect her child, and lost."

Griffin could see her beginning to get angry. Roberts instructed everyone in the room, except Griffin and Buckley, to drop everything and search first the floor then the entire hotel. She also had the hotel's security team checking all footage from the cameras. A kidnapping was a different priority to cops. A kidnapping meant there was still hope.

"Get everything," Roberts said, "ballistics, tire marks, every fingerprint we can find, everything."

Suddenly one of the investigators burst into the room. "Come quick!" He disappeared back out into the 8th floor hallway with the others running after him. They ran down to the end of the hallway where a laundry cart sat next to one of the doors and another officer was waiting. They all came to a stop and looked at him expectantly. The officer calmly motioned toward an oversized cloth laundry bag. At the bottom sat a small blond girl, looking up, and scared to death.

4

Christine Rose parked her old, silver Honda in front of the 19th Precinct station on East 67th Street and climbed out from behind the wheel. She looked up at the five-story gray and red building and swallowed hard. Slowly climbing the half dozen steps, she reached for the large blue door and jumped back when the door suddenly flew open. She turned and watched an angry teenager storm down the steps. Being one of the nearest police stations to Central Park, the 19th was always busy and filled with *interesting* people.

She walked in and showed her ID to the sergeant behind the front desk who gave her a pen and slid a thick book in front of her for a signature. He then pointed her to the elevator and turned to help the next person. She walked gingerly down the hall and waited for the elevator, watching people pass back and forth. Christine took a deep breath when the doors opened and stepped inside. It had been over two years since she had last been there.

A few moments later, she stepped out onto the fifth floor. She peered through the double-glass doors and spotted the person she was looking for. She took a deep breath, pulled the door open, and walked through, crossing the room and stopping just outside the last office. Through the glass door, she could see Cheryl Roberts sitting next to a tiny girl and holding her hand.

"Christine?"

She turned to see Detective Griffin behind her. "Oh…hi Danny," she said, with a brief but nervous wave.

Griffin looked around with a confused expression. "What are you doing here?"

Christine took a breath. "Well, it's nice to see you

too."

"Sorry," he said, "I just meant-"

"That's okay." She looked at the little girl and then back at Griffin. "I, uh, was assigned this case."

"Really?" he asked surprised. "You're with Social Services now?"

Christine nodded and gave him a meek shrug. "I got reassigned. That's why it took so long."

"I see," Griffin said and looked over her shoulder at the girl. "Listen Christine. I'm not sure if you're ready for this. This little girl has gone through some serious trauma."

Christine fumbled for her purse and pulled out a folder. "I know, I read the report. How is she? They said it was a homicide."

Griffin sighed and shook his head. "It's hard to say. Roberts has been with her all morning, but she hasn't said anything. Looks like her mother was thrown out of a window, and she may have heard the whole thing. She hasn't slept all night."

"Right." Christine nodded, watching them. She suddenly remembered something and reached into her bag. "I brought her some food," she said, pulling out a small package.

Griffin looked at the package and frowned. "Donuts?"

"What?" Christine said innocently. "Kids love donuts."

Griffin's frown turned into a smirk. "I hope you don't have a soda in there too."

Christine didn't answer. Instead she looked at the man approaching from the other direction.

Griffin turned as Buckley reached them. "Oh Christine, this is my partner, Mike Buckley. Mike, this is Christine Rose with Social Services. She's here for Sarah Baxter."

Buckley shook Christine's hand. "Nice to meet you." He pulled out a small doll and handed it to her. "I found this in the lost and found. I thought maybe she'd like it."

Christine smiled and took the doll. "Thank you." She gave Griffin one more look and turned away, knocking gently on the glass door and cracking it open. She walked softly across the room, hoping her nervousness was not entirely obvious. When she got to the couch, Roberts patted Sarah's hand and stood up while Christine slowly sat down on the other side of her.

"Hello Sarah," she said softly. "My name is Christine."

Sarah looked at her apprehensively with big green eyes but said nothing.

Christine nodded to herself and looked at the other three standing outside watching her. She remembered the doll and held it up for Sarah to see. "Sarah, do you like dolls?"

Sarah stared at the doll and nodded. Christine held it out, and Sarah cautiously took it from her hands. *Okay*, Christine thought to herself. *Here we go.*

She cleared her throat. "Sarah, I work with these nice policemen, and we just want to make sure you weren't hurt."

Sarah did not answer.

"Sarah, I know you're scared, but I'm here to help you. Can you tell me if you were hurt?"

She remained focused on the doll. After a few moments, Sarah slowly shook her head.

"You were not hurt?"

Eyes still down, Sarah shook her head again.

"Okay." Christine put her hands between her knees and looked at Sarah's doll. "So you like dolls?"

Sarah nodded.

"Me too." Christine smiled, watching her begin to play with it. "Sarah, can you tell me how old you are?"

She held up six fingers.

"You're six?" Christine said with raised eyebrows. "You're…really getting to be a big girl."

Christine looked at Griffin outside and reluctantly

pulled the donuts back out of her bag. "Are you hungry? I brought you something to eat."

Sarah looked at the donuts and mumbled something under her breath.

"What's that?"

Sarah said it again a little louder. "I'm not supposed to eat that."

Christine frowned. "Ah, okay." She reached into her bag again and brought out a small juice box. "How about orange juice? Are you thirsty?"

Sarah looked up at her and then to the box. She nodded and took it when Christine nudged it into her hand. She carefully unwrapped the straw, poked it into the top of the box, and took a long drink. When she was finished, Christine took the empty box back and very gently placed her hand on Sarah's knee.

"Sarah, I want you to come with me so I can take care of you. Would that be okay?"

"Okay."

Christine smiled. "Okay!" She slowly stood up and reached for Sarah who also stood and placed her tiny hand inside Christine's.

Christine took a deep breath and smiled. She began to walk forward when little Sarah suddenly pulled on her hand, stopping her.

"Did my mommy die?"

Christine's smile promptly disappeared.

5

"So, *that's* Christine," Buckley said. They stood at the window upstairs watching Christine down on the street, fumbling with a car seat in the back of her Honda. She finally managed to get it right and buckled Sarah in.

"Yeah."

Buckley nodded. "She's cute."

"Shut up," Griffin replied, watching the car drive off.

Buckley turned from the window and looked at him. "So, what was the problem again?"

"She has…some issues."

He nodded. Both men turned around when someone called out for them.

"Phone call on line six!"

Griffin walked to a nearby desk and picked up the phone. "This is Griffin."

Buckley turned and watched a large television on the wall where several officers were following the coverage of the explosion at Saint Patrick's. All of the major news channels were onsite. As he watched, another officer approached and handed him a Post-it note.

After a few minutes, Griffin thanked the caller and hung up. He turned back to Buckley. "Do you know a Glen Smith over at FBI?"

Buckley shook his head.

"Said he was supposed to meet with Barbara Baxter today."

"About what?"

Griffin shrugged. "He didn't know. Says she wouldn't tell him over the phone." He paused. "What did she do for a living?"

"Secretary for a law firm."

"Right." Griffin looked out the window thinking.

Buckley held up his note. "We just got a message from forensics; looks like they found blood in the stairwell at the hotel. And it doesn't match the victim."

"Let's check it out."

In the forensics lab, Patty Eisendrath sat across the room on a stool, dressed in her usual white lab coat and staring into a large electron microscope. Eisendrath was arguably the best forensic scientist in New York state and, according to Buckley, one of the prettiest, too. So far though, his queries had resulted in zero dates. Which was just another reason why Griffin considered her about as smart as they came.

They walked up behind her and waited quietly.

"Good morning, gentlemen," she said without taking her eyes from the microscope lenses.

The detectives looked at each other. Before they could speak, she answered their question.

"It's Buckley's cologne."

Buckley, shorter and stockier than Griffin and showing the first signs of losing some hair, almost blushed.

Patty turned away from the instrument and held up a finger while she jotted down some quick notes. She looked up expectantly. "You obviously got my message. Did you check out the hotel?"

Griffin nodded. "We just came from there. Saw the blood in the stairwell. Looks like he made a run for it out the back parking lot."

"He and the others," she said standing up.

"Others?" Buckley asked.

They followed her to a large desk where she sat down and brought up a computer file, displaying several pictures of blood drops. "These are the blood samples we found descending the stairwell and out through the parking lot. Same blood type, same DNA, so one person was bleeding."

Griffin leaned in for a closer look. "You said others?"

Patty nodded and pointed to one of the drops. You can see a pattern here in this drop." She zoomed in to display a higher resolution image of shapes within the drop of blood.

"What is that?" Buckley asked.

"That's a shoe print."

"A shoe print?" he asked again. "It just looks like some random markings."

"Most of it is, but here," she highlighted an area of the screen, "you have a few impressions that are clearly part of a design from a shoe tread." She zoomed in on another large drop. "And here we have part of a tread again, but this one's a little different." She spun her chair to face them. "And since it's nearly impossible to step on your own blood drops while running, that means there was a minimum of three people fleeing the scene, probably at the same time."

Buckley raised his eyebrow. "So we need to start tracking down sole patterns of popular shoes."

Patty smirked. "No, I just thought you might find it helpful. There's not enough here to determine what kind of shoes they were. Besides, we would have to factor in additional variables such as speed of the run, the body's natural tendency to pivot the foot while running, and a host of other things."

"Okay," Griffin said, looking at her. "I'm guessing you didn't call us in to show us something that was just *helpful*."

Patty frowned. "Of course not. What I wanted to show you was the other sample, which is much more interesting."

"What other sample?" Griffin asked.

"They didn't tell you there was another sample?"

Both Griffin and Buckley looked at each other and shook their heads.

Patty smiled. "Well then, this is really going to cook

your noodle." She brought up another sample. This one was much larger. "The blood on the stairs was noticed first, which is why those were the first samples. However, when the investigators came back upstairs, they checked all the floors and carpets with Luminol."

Griffin and Buckley were both very familiar with Luminol. It was the crystalline agent used to make blood visible in a darkened room, primarily by reacting with the hemoglobin in blood. Every forensics team used it.

"When they sprayed the hallway outside the room," Patty continued, "it lit up like a Christmas tree!"

"So there was more blood in the hallway," Buckley surmised.

"Not just more blood," Patty corrected, "a *lot* of blood! And from a different person."

She brought up a picture of the hallway. "It wasn't noticed originally because the carpet is dark red. But judging from the sheer amount detected, this person stayed in that hallway for a long time."

Griffin looked at Buckley. "So someone else was injured, and they just decided to hang around?"

Buckley shook his head. "But security was there in a few minutes. How much could someone bleed standing in the hallway for three or four minutes?"

"Well, let's put it this way," Patty said folding her arms. "I've never seen that much blood without a dead person lying next to it. Whoever it was, I would say they had less than twenty minutes to make it to an emergency room, at the most."

The site of the Saint Patrick's explosion was somber, with only a third of the cathedral still standing. The rest of the area was leveled and covered in dust and rubble over twenty feet high. Every pane of glass, even from the walls that were still standing, was gone and now scattered in millions of fragments, some landing as far as two hundred yards away.

On three sides, the site was surrounded by emergency vehicles and construction equipment. Three days later, the crews were still finding bodies beneath the destruction.

Several bulldozers and backhoes belched smoke and picked through the rubble, lifting and moving the largest pieces so the search and rescue crews could comb below them. From a distance, hundreds of people watched and hoped for miracles, for another person to be carried out with a stretcher instead of a body bag.

Among all of the rescue workers, one individual was not looking for survivors. He was looking at something else. Carefully stepping through the large pieces of crushed stone, he examined the walls that were still standing. He looked at them thoughtfully, then turned and traced out where the cathedral's multiple alters had been located.

His tanned, bald head was covered in a light coating of dust as he methodically cleaned the debris from an alter and examined it. Flipping up a pocket on his khaki style shirt, the man withdrew a small camera. He zoomed in and snapped several high resolution pictures before standing up, pushing the debris back in place with his boot.

Christine sat at the table with the phone to her ear. While she listened, Christine watched Sarah slowly wander around the small living room looking closely at all the framed photographs. Most of the pictures were of Christine in her younger years and included what appeared to be her parents, always smiling with their arms around her. Sarah continued studying the pictures and noticed that her father was missing from a number of them. The more recent photos included only Christine and her mother.

Christine was speaking to Liz Iverson, a longtime friend and now her boss. Christine's old department had been disbanded due to budget cuts. Luckily Liz had been able to make a position available for her in her city social services department, in spite of her lack of experience.

"Okay, that's fine," Liz said through the phone's speaker, "but she'll need to see a doctor tomorrow."

Christine shrugged and looked across the room at Sarah. She kept her voice low. "I'll try, but she was really reluctant."

"That's normal. Where are you now?"

The pitch in Christine's voice changed slightly. "Um, my apartment."

Liz's sigh could be heard through the phone. "Christine, it's against policy to take them to our homes."

"I know," she replied. "But she fell asleep in the car, she wouldn't go to the doctor's, and she didn't want to go into the office. I didn't know what else to do." Christine watched Sarah bend down and gently pet the top of her cat's head.

"Alright, alright," Liz said. "It's not the end of the

world. Just get her into the office as soon as you can."

Christine nodded. "Okay, I will."

"Don't worry Chris, you're doing fine. I'll see you tomorrow." With that Liz hung up, and Christine pushed the button on her cordless phone to end the call. She sighed and looked around her tiny apartment. How did she manage to get herself into this? It was her first real assignment and it felt like she was already doing everything wrong.

She looked up when she heard her cat hiss. Sarah was grasping the cat by the tail, trying to keep it from going through the cat door.

"Oh honey!" Christine exclaimed and ran over to help. "It's okay, she's allowed to go outside." She grabbed Sarah's hand and gently pulled the cat's tail free. Sarah whined as the small calico quickly darted away, jumping through the tiny plastic door and leaving it swinging behind her.

"It's okay, she'll be back."

Sarah frowned and abruptly pulled away from Christine. It was hard to tell whether she was sad or irritated.

"Are you hungry Sarah?" she asked, standing back up.

Sarah nodded and lowered herself down on the couch.

"Do you like eggs?" Christine walked into the small kitchen and opened the refrigerator. "I think I have some cereal, or maybe…a piece of pizza?"

There was no answer.

She turned and looked back around the corner. "Sarah?"

Sarah was looking at the pictures again.

"Is this your mommy?" Sarah asked pointing to one of the pictures.

Christine walked up behind her. "Yes."

Sarah looked closer at another. It showed Christine's mother standing next to her wearing a white lab coat with her shoulder length brown hair put up. "Why is she wearing that?"

Christine leaned in and looked at the picture. "My mother was a pharmacist."

Sarah raised her eyebrows excitedly. "She worked on a *farm*?"

"No, no." Christine chuckled. "A pharmacist is someone who gets medicine for people."

"Oh," Sarah said with a hint of disappointment. She pointed to another, older photo. "Is this your daddy?"

"Mmm hmm."

Sarah looked up with her large green eyes. "What happened to him?"

"He's...in heaven." Christine frowned and changed the subject. "Hey, do you want to sleep in my big bed tonight?"

Sarah shrugged her tiny shoulders.

"It's a great bed, and I'll be right here on this couch. Just a few steps away."

Sarah nervously looked at the couch and then back at the bedroom door.

"And you know what?" Christine added. "My kitty cat Cassie likes to sleep in my bed. Maybe she'll sleep with you."

"She won't," Sarah said sadly, looking down at the floor.

"Well, she probably just needs to get used to you." Christine bent down and gave her an awkward squeeze around the shoulders. "Okay then," she said clearing her throat, "let me see what I can find to eat."

8

Griffin paid Lenny and picked up both hot dogs. Lenny Markowitz was small and boisterous, almost 70, and had been selling hot dogs on the same street corner in Manhattan for 43 years. And he was proud of it. He had survived recessions, natural disasters, and every kind of struggle life could throw at him, and he did it by selling hot dogs. That was perseverance. Griffin and Buckley liked him immensely and faithfully bought his dogs for lunch twice a week.

Griffin walked back to the car, where Buckley was leaning against the fender, and handed him one. "So," he said, taking a bite, "no hospital or clinic within ten miles reported having someone show up that night with a wound bleeding that badly."

Buckley nodded. "Apparently not."

"So if Eisendrath is right, and this person had less than twenty minutes to get help," he paused, "let's call it forty minutes…he would either have had to get help from somewhere else or left in a way that didn't involve hundreds of downtown traffic lights."

"Or both," Buckley added with a swallow.

"Or both," Griffin acknowledged. "Or they were not wounded that badly after all."

"But how could someone bleed that much if they weren't hurt that bad?"

"Exactly. Which means they *had* to be that hurt." Griffin took a bite. "I guess they just disappeared."

"What I don't understand," started Buckley, "is if there were three people running out the back, or at least three that we know of, why was the fourth still upstairs?"

"Maybe he was in the hallway before the other three

came down the stairwell, and he came down with them."

Buckley shook his head. "Then why didn't we see huge amounts of blood on the stairs or across the parking lot too?"

Griffin took a drink of his soda. "Maybe they bled out by then which means the other three would have had another body to carry…"

"Which slows them down, adds more weight, another source of blood droplets…all of which we don't see."

Griffin shook his head. "It doesn't work." He thought for a minute, absently watching a woman walk by with her dog. "Okay, let's forget the other three in the parking lot for the moment. Why would the person in the hall, who was hemorrhaging, simply be *standing* there?"

Buckley shrugged and downed his last piece of hot dog. "Deciding which way to run?"

"I don't think so. It doesn't take that long to pick a direction, a few seconds maybe. And even if he did, there was no other trail of blood downstairs or around the hotel."

"So where did he go?" asked Buckley.

"I don't know."

Buckley finished his soda and tossed his cup in a nearby trash can. "So, let me ask you something else, is it just me or are you wondering why it would take four guys, at least, to take down one single mother?"

Griffin folded his arms. "I've been wondering the same thing. And the amount of damage to that room was incredible. How much fight does one woman have against four attackers?"

"Or more."

"And when and how did little Sarah escape?" Griffin wondered out loud. He suddenly looked at Buckley. "What if the person in the hall was looking for Sarah?"

"And simply stopped looking because he was bleeding too badly."

"That fits." Griffin said. "But why would they *not* go

with the other three? Wouldn't that be their best chance at getting treatment somewhere? It still doesn't make sense."

Buckley reached into the car and grabbed his cell phone. It had a voice mail on it. He dialed the number and listened. With the phone still next to his ear, he looked at Griffin. "Roberts says she left you a voice mail."

Surprised, Griffin pulled his own phone out of his pocket. He frowned and rolled his eyes, holding it up for Buckley to see. "Damn thing turned off again. I think my battery is dying."

"You've got to get a new phone," Buckley said pulling out a small notepad and writing on it.

"What's the message?"

Buckley finished writing and hung up his phone. "She says they have an address for Barbara Baxter's work. Ready for a ride upstate?"

Albany, New York, was just over two hours away and had the distinction of being one of the oldest surviving colonies from the newly discovered Americas. First settled in 1614, it was located at the north end of the Hudson River and now served as the state capital of New York.

Griffin and Buckley arrived at Simon & Meyer, a small but prominent law firm, and were escorted to a conference room where they were joined by Aaron Meyer and Karen McClay, manager of the firm's support staff. The two were devastated when they heard the news about Barbara.

"Who on earth would do something like that?" asked Meyer incredulously. McClay sat beside him weeping.

"That's what we're trying to find out," said Griffin. He reached for a tissue box behind him and passed it to Karen.

"Can you tell us how long Barbara worked here?" asked Buckley.

"Years," replied Meyer, trying to think. "Five, maybe six years."

"Did she have any problems that you're aware of?"

Meyer shook his head. "At work? God no, she was incredible. She worked hard and was as sharp as a tack." He looked at Karen, who was still struggling. "I don't really know much about her home life. Karen might."

Karen looked up, but still couldn't stop crying long enough to get the words out. After a long time, she finally shook her head. "N-not that I know of."

"Do either of you know what she was doing in New York?" Griffin asked.

Meyer shrugged and again looked at Karen. She wiped her eyes and said "It was a last minute thing. A vacation for her and her daughter." Karen's eyes opened wide. "My god, is Sarah okay?"

"She's fine." Griffin nodded. "She's being tended to until we sort everything out."

Buckley cleared his throat. "Do you know if she was in any trouble? Anybody she was arguing with or not getting along?"

"No!" Karen shook her head. "Not a single person that I know of."

"Any boyfriends or bad relationships? Bad breakups maybe?"

"Not that I know of. As far as I know, she hadn't dated anyone in a long time. It was just her and Sarah. She was all Barbara cared about."

"Any idea if she was meeting anyone there?"

"Mmm…I think so. But you'd have to ask one of the other legal secretaries she worked with. They talked to her more often than I did."

Both detectives nodded and continued to write in their pads. Griffin looked up at Meyer. "Would you mind if we talked to some of the other staff?"

"Of course not."

Griffin turned to Karen. "Have you ever met her daughter Sarah?"

Karen looked surprised. "Of course I have. We all

have. She's a wonderful child, simply incredible."

Griffin looked at Buckley. "What do you mean incredible?"

She shrugged. "She's just about the nicest little girl I've ever met. Always polite, mature, and very perceptive."

"Perhaps we can see Barbara's employment records and a list of phone calls?"

Meyer managed a polite smile. "I'd like to detective, but I'm afraid we have some rather paranoid clients. You'd have to get a warrant for that."

He looked at Meyer. "How about a look at her desk?"

Meyer thought about it for a moment. "I'll tell you what, you can take as long as you like at her desk, provided I stand next to you and keep you away from any client related data that might be proprietary to the firm."

"That would be fine," said Griffin. "You do realize, however, that we *will* come back with a warrant."

Meyer smiled. "I certainly do. But for the sake of our business and reputation, we have to be diligent."

9

Christine and Sarah walked through the lobby of the Human Resources Administration building on 8th Avenue. They crossed the marble floor and found a long line forming in front of the elevators. Sarah spotted the stairs behind them and tugged on Christine's arm.

Christine looked at the sign on the door and smiled. "Okay, I probably need the exercise anyway."

They reached the fifth floor a little out of breath and found the cause of the delay. One of the two elevators was offline for repairs. A technician could be seen inside with his head stuck in an open panel.

Christine opened the door and Sarah walked in ahead of her, looking around at the giant open office area. They headed down a long hallway, turned a corner, and stopped in front of Liz Iverson's office.

Several minutes later, Christine was standing next to Liz. They both watched Sarah in the small room next door, sitting at an oversized table with a giant box of crayons.

Christine sighed. "I really didn't think she would come."

"I'm glad she did," Liz replied. "Let's see if she agrees to an exam." She handed Christine a small business card. "I made an appointment for you this afternoon at the Children's Hospital. Just in case."

"Thanks." Christine took the card and looked it over.

Liz looked at Sarah again. "How is she?"

"It's hard to say," Christine said. "She's talking and starting to open up a little bit." She looked back and gave her a nervous look. "I just feel like I'm fumbling a bit here."

"You're doing fine," Liz said, putting a hand on her arm.

Christine managed a grin. "Thanks."

"So listen, I spoke with Officer Roberts at the police department. They're trying to track down next of kin and find out if there was a will or trust that addresses her mother's wishes for custody. Has Sarah said anything about brothers or sisters, maybe aunts or uncles?"

Christine shook her head. "So far she hasn't said a whole lot of anything."

"Okay," Liz nodded. "Well, if she continues to open up, see what you can find out."

"I will."

"You might also see if you can find out anything about her father, like whether he is still in the picture at all."

Christine frowned. "Liz, what if there *is* no one or we can't find anyone?"

"We usually do, even if it takes some time. If it's a lengthy process, we will have to find a foster home or a temporary family she can stay with until we figure things out."

Christine said nothing and Liz knew what she was thinking. "Look Christine, it's normal to become attached. And to some extent that's okay. But we have to keep our heads here. The hardest part about our job is putting aside our emotions and personal interests to make sure we do what's right for these children. In the long run, that's the most help we can give them."

"I know," Christine replied watching Sarah. "You just feel so bad. I mean no one should have to go through what she has." She looked back at Liz. "We're going to get her some counseling right?"

"If the new guardians have no will or money to work with, then yes, we'll try to help."

Christine thought about that term, *new guardians*. It sounded so matter of fact, so detached. These children were so innocent and vulnerable, how could people detach themselves so easily? How could they just let some procedure or checklist determine the outcome? Maybe she had trouble with kids, but she sure wasn't heartless. Not that her colleagues were either, but where exactly was that line? How long did it take to eventually close off enough of your sympathy to function effectively in this job? And if they turn that off, how were they supposed to really feel and sense the kind of relationship the children might have with their *new guardians*? It wasn't just about finding someone who would take good care of them was it? Wasn't their job really about finding someone who would truly love these kids like they were their own? Or was that just a romantic vision that everyone new to the job brought with them, until they were finally beaten down by the reality of life?

Christine tried to sound professional. "So, how long…you know, do I…"

"How long do you look after her?" Liz asked.

"Right."

"Usually a few days. Obviously the sooner we get her into a positive environment, the sooner the healing can begin."

The *healing*. How long, Christine thought, does it take to heal from hearing your mother being thrown out of a window? Decades?

Liz gave Sarah one last look. "Okay, I've got to run. Stay in touch and let me know how it goes this afternoon."

"I will."

With that, Liz ducked back inside her office and grabbed her purse. She patted Christine on the arm once more as she passed and headed out.

Christine turned her attention back to Sarah. Watching Sarah sitting there coloring all alone stirred so many emotions. She looked so alone and vulnerable, and yet she also somehow looked strong at the same time. It was simply amazing how resilient some children could be.

Christine opened the glass door and quietly walked in.

Sarah remained focused on her drawing as Christine approached and stood next to her, peering down at what she was working on. It had a small, blue house in the middle and a bright, yellow sun in the upper left hand corner.

"What are you drawing, Sarah?"

"My house," Sarah replied without looking up.

"And who are these?" she asked, pointing to some stick figures.

"Me and mommy and kitty."

"Ah, very nice. And is this the sun here?"

Sarah nodded.

"And what are these?" Christine asked, pointing to small circles around the stick figures.

"Shadows. Kitty has one too but it's little."

Christine smiled. "It's beautiful Sarah." She looked up when the door opened and the receptionist entered.

"Christine, I have a call for you," the receptionist whispered.

"Who is it?"

"Not sure, she didn't give a name."

"Okay. Thanks Jen." Christine reached for the phone and picked up the line. She held the phone up to her ear. "Hello, this is Christine."

"Is this Christine Rose?" a female voice asked.

"Yes it is."

The caller was silent for a moment. When she spoke again, she sounded reserved. "I have some information about the Baxters…"

"Oh. You know I don't…I think you want to talk to the police, I'm not-"

"I don't want to talk to the police," the woman interrupted.

"Um, okay," Christine said. "Well you probably know-"

"I know about the other night, that's why I'm calling. This is not about Barbara, it's about her daughter…Sarah."

Less than two minutes later Christine was walking quickly down the hallway and back towards the elevators with Sarah in tow, barely keeping up. If she walked any faster, she would have been dragging Sarah. They reached the double doors of the elevators and Christine quickly pressed the down button.

"Where are we going?" Sarah asked.

"To talk to the policemen."

The elevator doors opened. Several people looked up at them and stepped back to make room. Christine took a step forward but was stopped. She looked down behind her. Sarah was pulling hard on the arm of her blouse.

"Come on, Sarah."

Sarah looked up at her and shook her head.

"It's okay, Sarah. Elevators are safe." She put her arm around Sarah's shoulders to help her forward but Sarah dug her feet in. "What is it honey? Have you not been on one of these before?"

Sarah shook her head even more and backed away.

Christine frowned. "Okay, we don't need to go that way. If you're afraid of elevators, let's take the stairs again."

Sarah ran ahead to the stairs as Christine apologized to the others and waved for them to go ahead. She trotted after Sarah as the elevators doors closed gently behind her.

"Hold on, Sarah. Not so fast." She grabbed the heavy stairway door that Sarah was trying to pull open.

Suddenly a terrible screeching of metal against metal sounded from the other side of the elevator doors, followed by a loud blast. The giant silver doors instantly bulged outwards, and a loud banging could be heard as the elevator car plunged five stories to the bottom of the shaft. Within seconds, the car smashed into the bottom floor.

Christine screamed and instinctively pushed Sarah into the stairwell and stared at the elevator doors. Sarah held on tight to Christine, looking into the stairwell with a frightened look on her face. Shocked and horrified, Christine stared at the elevator and covered her mouth with her hands. "Oh my god! OH MY GOD!"

Several people came running out of their offices. They reached the elevator just in time to see smoke and dust seeping through the twisted doors.

Griffin and Buckley left the small building and walked back toward their car. Other than a few pictures from Barbara Baxter's desk and a colleague thinking she was supposed to see someone in New York, they did not have much more than when they arrived.

As they reached their white unmarked car, Buckley's phone rang. He pulled it from his pocket and answered.

"Buckley here." After a moment, he mouthed the word *Roberts* to Griffin.

Griffin instinctively pulled out his own phone to find it dead again. "God dammit."

"Yeah," Buckley replied. "I'm with him right now…we're just heading back from Albany."

"What?!" he said, freezing with one hand on the driver's door handle. "When?" After a long pause, he replied with a simple "Okay." and hung up. He looked immediately to Griffin. "Get in the car, Danny!"

Buckley opened his door quickly and jumped in behind the wheel.

"What is it?" Griffin asked, peering through the passenger window. The sound of Buckley starting and revving the engine was all he needed to jump in.

Buckley floored it, and the car shot out onto the four lane boulevard.

"What? What the hell is it?" Griffin instinctively grabbed the siren, reached outside, and stuck it to the roof of the car.

Buckley was still accelerating as he wove in and out of other cars. "There's been an accident at the Human Resources Building on 8th." He looked at Griffin. "At Social Services."

Christine looked at Sarah's tiny figure and then returned back down the hallway. "She's asleep."

Griffin and Buckley nodded as she sighed and collapsed down onto her couch. She was dressed in sweat pants and a large Patriots T-shirt. Her hair was a mess and her eyes were red, betraying how exhausted she was.

"How are you?" Griffin asked.

Christine closed her eyes and shook her head. "I just can't believe it." She was quiet for a moment and then looked at Griffin, sitting across from her on a chair. "It was so horrible. Did they find anything yet?"

"They're still looking."

She shook her head again. "I'll tell you what, if it weren't for Sarah being afraid of elevators…I mean if she hadn't insisted we go down the stairs instead…god, it would have been us."

Both Griffin and Buckley looked at each other as she reached forward and picked up her tea cup. They were thinking the same thing.

"And Sarah." Christine made a halfhearted chuckle and leaned back on the couch sideways, folding her feet beneath her. "I can't believe what that girl is able to deal with. I mean look at me, I'm a total wreck. While she's six and already asleep."

Christine suddenly remembered something and looked around. "Where's Cassie?" She eyed the cat's food bowl which was still half full. "Have you seen her?" she asked the detectives.

They both frowned and looked around the room. "Uh no."

"She's a tough cat," Griffin said reassuringly.

Christine remembered how Griffin used to say that a lot.

Buckley took a step forward. "When we got here, you said you had something to tell us?"

Christine looked away from the food bowl as if coming out of a trance. "Yes, I do." She took another sip of tea and set the cup down again on the table. "Someone called me today, at the office. Someone who wanted to say something but was afraid of the police."

They both looked at her attentively. "Who?" Griffin asked.

"I don't know. She wouldn't say."

"She?"

"Yes, she," Christine repeated. "She said she was a friend of Barbara Baxter." She looked at Buckley who was already scribbling on his notepad. "She said they were friends and she had been worried about Barbara."

"Worried how?"

"She said Barbara had been acting weird lately, when she suddenly decided to take some time off."

"Jobs get stressful," Griffin said. "Maybe she needed a break."

"That's kind of what I said," Christine replied. She picked up her warm cup again and nestled it between her hands. "But she told me Barbara had done some things that didn't make sense. For one, she yanked Sarah out of school in the middle of the day. Then she disappeared with just a day's notice. The caller said that Barbara had never done either of those things before."

"Did she say anything else?"

"Yes," Christine said slowly. "And that is where it got a little weird."

Buckley stopped writing and looked up. "What do you mean?"

Christine took a deep breath. "She said that Barbara was afraid for her. For Sarah," she quickly clarified.

Griffin's brow furrowed. "Sarah's mother was afraid

for her? How close is this friend?"

"Pretty close, I think."

"How do you know?" Buckley asked.

Christine looked at him. "Because of what she said next." She glanced back down the hall and lowered her voice slightly. "She said there was something special about Sarah."

"What does that mean, *special?*"

"I don't know. The woman said that Barbara Baxter had brought it up a few times but would never go into detail. I got the impression that this wasn't something Barbara would share with just anyone. I could be wrong, but that was the feeling I got."

"A woman we met today at Barbara's work said something similar," Griffin said. "She talked about how wonderful Sarah was; how she was a such an incredibly nice little girl."

Christine thought about it and slowly shook her head. "I don't think that's what this woman on the phone was referring to." She shrugged. "It was a different...tone."

"What kind of tone did she use?" asked Buckley.

"I don't know. I can't really explain it. It's just one of those things you feel. I could be wrong. It was just a feeling."

Buckley's phone rang. He excused himself and walked into the kitchen to take the call.

While he was in the other room, Griffin leaned closer to Christine. "Chris, I'm getting a little worried, for you and Sarah. I think there might be something else going on here."

"What do you mean?"

"I don't know," he shrugged. "It's just a hunch. Something is not adding up."

Christine did not respond right away. Instead she mulled over what he said. Finally she looked at him. "I don't want to abandon her, Danny. I know that probably sounds weird coming from me, but right now she has no one else." She paused. "She trusts me. I don't know why and I'm not even sure I want to know. Maybe everything changes tomorrow. Maybe we find some family or maybe you find whoever did it and arrest them, but, for now, she *needs* me and it feels good to be able to help her." Christine stared down into her tea. "I know it sounds strange, but it feels like maybe I'm growing."

Griffin stared at her and smiled. "It doesn't sound strange, Chris."

Buckley could be heard hanging up the phone. He returned from the kitchen with a grave look on his face.

Griffin looked up. "What is it?"

Buckley looked at Christine and then back to his partner. "The investigation team says it was not an accident. The elevator was sabotaged. The explosion was not caused by a malfunction; it was designed to sever the elevator cable. And the emergency brakes had been disabled first, which was the screeching you heard."

Christine gasped and dropped her cup on the rug, spilling the last of her tea. She covered her mouth and looked at Griffin who was now standing above her.

"That's it," he said. "We're moving you."

Thirty minutes later they had three patrol cars waiting outside, and Christine had everything packed for several days. On Buckley's shoulder lay Sarah, half asleep. Griffin held Christine's bag and stood behind her as she looked over the apartment one last time. She looked at the three bowls of cat food on the floor, trying to decide if that would be enough. Her cat Cassie was still nowhere to be found, probably because of all of the recent visitors.

Christine closed the door firmly and locked the deadbolt from the outside. She turned around and looked at the others waiting for her. Three uniformed officers stood on the sidewalk watching the darkened street. She nodded to Griffin who turned and followed Buckley and Sarah down the short walk. As they neared the street,

Christine noticed something on the far side of the lawn area. Something under the hedge. She froze and her eyes opened wide. "Oh no! Is that-," she started to cry. "Is it…"

Griffin squeezed her arm. "Easy, it's probably not what you think it is. Let me take a look. Stay here." Sarah lifted her head off of Buckley's shoulder and watched Griffin cross the grass. When he got to the hedge, he knelt down to look at the object. The others watched from behind as he knelt motionless for several seconds. Finally his head dropped forward in disappointment. He slowly turned and looked over his shoulder, back at Christine.

"No!" she cried and ran toward Griffin. He quickly jumped up and raced back to stop her mid-way. Grabbing her arms, he worked to block her line of sight. "Don't Chris, don't!" He looked at her tenderly. "I think a dog got her. And you don't want to see that."

Christine had been pushing to get past him but now stopped and looked at Griffin, hearing what he'd said. She kept crying, but through her tears she knew he was right. That would be her last memory of Cassie and it would be more vivid than she could bear.

Christine lowered her head onto Griffin's shoulder and continued to cry. Gradually her breathing became less labored, and suddenly she felt something in her hand. She looked down to find Sarah standing next to her, her tiny hand inside of Christine's.

Griffin touched Christine's shoulder gently. "We've got to go."

12

The safe location was a nondescript house in a suburban neighborhood, forty minutes outside of Manhattan. The property was larger than usual for the area, and the half acre lot allowed most of the house to be hidden by a large group of beautiful Northern Red Oaks.

The two cars that transported them, now parked in front of the small house, were unmarked to avoid attracting attention from neighbors. Fortunately, it was late in the evening and few people noticed them come in.

Christine stood in the small living room looking like she was in a daze. In less than forty-eight hours, she had been assigned a young child to care for, been the target of a deadly attack, lost her twelve-year-old cat, and been forced out of her apartment and into a safe house owned by the city of New York. It seemed so surreal. She struggled to believe any of it had happened, let alone all of it.

"Christine?"

She shook herself out of her daze and realized that her name had been spoken several times. She realized Cheryl Roberts was standing right in front of her.

"Are you okay?" asked Roberts.

Christine focused on her and nodded. "Sorry…yes."

Roberts looked at Christine and then down at Sarah who was standing next to her, still holding Christine's hand.

"Look, I know things have been moving fast and that it's probably all a little disorienting for you. But don't worry, we're going to help you through this."

Help me through this? Christine thought incredulously. *What part exactly?*

Griffin came into the room from down the hallway. He had insisted on inspecting the entire house himself. "How you doin' Chris?" he said, falling in behind Roberts.

"Okay, I guess."

The small room was filled with old, but relatively clean, furniture. The carpet was about twenty years old judging from the color and shag, and on the far wall was a fireplace that looked like it hadn't been cleaned since the carpet was put in. A wide-open doorway led into the kitchen where a nice granite countertop clashed with the old kitchen table. Behind that was the back door with a window and faded curtains. Through the curtains, she could see the outlines of the security bars on the outside.

Roberts hoisted a small duffle bag up onto the old coffee table. She unzipped it and pulled out several articles of clothing. "I stopped at the store and got some things for Sarah." She fumbled through some of them. "Some pants, shirts, undies, and socks. There should be enough to last several days. I also got her a jacket." She pulled it out and showed Christine. "Since we don't know how permanent this warm weather is." Roberts looked down at Sarah. "Do you see any outfits you like, honey?"

Sarah just shrugged and moved further behind Christine.

Griffin came closer. "Listen Chris, I know this all seems crazy, but don't worry. We're gonna find out who did this." He motioned to the room behind him. "This is just to keep you comfortable and out of sight. Keep in mind that there's over a thousand safe houses in New York, which means if anyone's looking, you won't be easy to find."

Christine was sure Griffin's comment was supposed to make her feel better, but it didn't.

Roberts nodded. "That's right. And no one knows you're here, except us." She moved past Buckley to the front window and drew back the curtain. "You'll have two patrolmen watching from a car across the street, twenty-four hours a day. If you need them, just flick this switch near the door. It turns on the porch light. If they see that porch light come on, they'll be here in *seconds*." Roberts looked back to them. "You have nothing to worry about."

Christine thought again how every time someone talked about how safe they were, she felt more nervous.

After a few more minutes of instruction on how things worked, what they should turn on, and what they shouldn't turn on, the three officers seemed satisfied.

Griffin gave Christine's shoulder a squeeze. "Don't worry. We'll get this guy. Just stay here and relax." He looked down at Sarah. "And get to know each other."

With that they backed out and shut the door, waiting for Christine to lock the deadbolt behind them.

Once outside and back to the cars, Roberts turned to Griffin and Buckley. "Ramirez has an update on the technical investigation. You guys cover that, and I'll see if I can find any witnesses on the elevator job."

Michael Ramirez was a technical expert and one of the department's best in computer forensics. He had been with the NYPD for three years after moving over from a stressful consulting position in the private sector, culminating in a system meltdown which he had been warning his client about for months. He decided to try something a little more fulfilling.

At six foot one inch, with a barrel chest and shaved head, Ramirez did not fit the geek image by a long shot.

Griffin and Buckley walked into his lab, at almost 10 p.m., to find Ramirez at his desk with a hard drive connected to a thick cable. He was slowly and methodically "peeling back" bytes from the drive that had been written over several times in hopes of making the data unreadable, a common situation during financial corruption investigations. What he had been able to recover so far was not going to help the banker's case.

"Hey guys," Ramirez said, saving his progress and looking up.

"Hi Mike, appreciate you staying late. We were told you have an update for us on the Baxter case."

"I do indeed," he said and pushed his chair back from his desk. Ramirez spun around and slid a few feet over until he was in front of another keyboard and screen. "So I took a look at all of her stuff: credit card activity, financials, phone records, the whole thing."

Griffin and Buckley knew what Ramirez had done used to take days with a warrant, but now could be accomplished in hours or even minutes.

Ramirez logged into the second computer and ran down a list of cases, until he got to the one with Barbara Baxter's name. Typing in a few commands, he brought up a list of line items.

"This looks like a bill," said Buckley.

"It is. Her cellular bill actually." From the top he scrolled down several lines, highlighting a few. "I didn't spot anything unusual in her call records, but I noticed these lines in the carrier's system logs."

Griffin looked closer at the screen. "Those don't look like calls."

"They're not," Ramirez replied. He swung his chair around to face the detectives. "They're identification queries, or what you might call triangulation calls."

"What are those?"

"A triangulation call is when a carrier uses multiple towers to zero in on a cell phone's location." He shrugged. "You can think of it like a cellular search light."

Griffin looked at Buckley then back to Ramirez. "So what does that mean?"

"It means someone was looking for Barbara Baxter, as in her physical location." He turned back to the monitor. "Normally, I would not have caught that, but some strange characters in the logs got me curious. But that's not the best part."

"What is the best part?" Griffin asked for the both of them.

"The best part is when I asked the carrier for more detail, they didn't want to tell me, even though they have to. It was the first time I'd run into that. My guess is, whoever was requesting these queries wanted it kept quiet."

"Did the carrier reveal who they were?"

"They did." Ramirez slapped his enter key and printed out a few pages for them. "Care to take a guess who it was?" he asked with raised eyebrows.

Griffin and Buckley looked at each other and shook their heads.

Ramirez handed them the printout. "It was the State Department."

They were both surprised. "As in the U.S. State Department?"

"The one and only." Ramirez looked at both of them. "And there's something else. These queries only started a few days ago."

13

Cheryl Roberts stood inside the yellow caution tape examining the terrible scene where the elevator had smashed into the bottom of its shaft, almost at free fall speed. The bodies had long since been removed and taken to the morgue for identification and contacting next of kin.

The inside of the car was covered in gruesome amounts of dried blood, and most of the interior's metal walls had collapsed violently inward. What little of the car's outside that could be seen showed it to be deeply scraped, damaged on all sides and covered in dust and debris. It looked as though a giant hand had descended upon the car and crushed it like an aluminum can.

She took the stairs to the fifth floor and examined the small entryway in front of the elevator doors. The damaged doors were open, revealing the area above where the charges had been planted to sever the cables. The emergency brakes had been tampered with to prevent them from engaging when the cable gave way, but the team had not yet identified exactly how they had been disabled.

What they *had* discovered was the explosive was not set off by a timer; it was done by remote detonation which meant the person had to have been relatively close by.

Christine had told Griffin and Buckley that she and Sarah noticed someone working on the elevators that morning as they entered. But when they left, they had never actually gotten on the elevator. This suggested that the person with the transmitter had armed the bomb once he saw the two approach the open elevator and then quickly fled himself. It probably never occurred to him they might not get in.

After dozens of photographs, Roberts left through the front door. The Human Resources Administration building was still closed off, but a thin crowd of people watched intently from behind the police line. Roberts glanced around as she walked toward her car. She never noticed the bald man watching her from across the street.

Once back at the 19th Precinct, Roberts put her things down and attached her phone to her computer which began downloading the pictures she had taken. She sighed and leaned back, watching them display one after the other as each file was copied.

After making a few notes in her folder, she got up to get a cup of coffee from the break room when she heard someone call "Chaplain" from the adjoining room. Roberts poked her head in and spotted the department's Chaplain, Douglas Wilcox. She smiled and strode in carrying her Styrofoam cup.

"Hiya Chaplain," she said, catching his attention. Wilcox turned his thick head of white hair in her direction and smiled when he saw her.

"Well hello, Cheryl!" he exclaimed.

Roberts smiled broadly and gave him a hug, prompting him to move a thick folder from under his arm and put it down onto the table. A few years back, they had worked together on a number of cases and developed a tight bond. She still smiled when thinking back on how hard it was keeping up with him, even though he was twice her age.

The chaplain leaned back and squeezed her shoulders in both hands, as a father might admire his grown child. "It's been a while now, hasn't it?" he grinned. "You look as spry and pretty as ever."

Roberts gave a playful roll of her eyes. He was always so complimentary. "What are you doing here at the 19th?"

"Well," he said, "I've been helping over at Saint Patrick's after the bombing, and I thought I would stop in to see if one of the investigators were here." He looked around. "Unfortunately, it looks like I missed him."

Roberts grimaced. "Oh right, Saint Patrick's. Its been all over the news. How's it going over there?"

The chaplain shook his head. "Rough, I'm afraid. But we're making progress. And what about you? What big cases are you working on?"

Roberts shrugged. "Primarily a homicide, and a strange one. In fact, the more we dig, the stranger it gets."

"Well, I hope you don't have as many cooks in the kitchen as we do at Saint Patrick's. Things are starting to turn into a bit of a mess."

She looked down at his thick folder lying on the table. "What are you working on there?"

"We're piecing together what was recovered of the cathedral's registry, so we can identify anyone else we might still be digging for and to contact others who were there that day. A lot of people fled and may still need some counseling." He frowned sympathetically. "We're trying to be proactive. Terrible events like this often take a far deeper emotional toll than most realize."

"I'm sure they do," Roberts replied. "Any decent leads on who did it? Earlier they had some experts who were suggesting it was part of an attack by Muslim extremists."

"Ah yes," the chaplain sighed, "the *terrorist* theory."

Roberts tilted her head inquisitively. "Something tells me you don't agree."

The chaplain exhaled and hesitated for a moment. They had gotten to know each other well during their time working together, and he always found her to be surprisingly objective compared to the other officers. It was one of the reasons they had such interesting conversations. She reminded him of himself when he was younger. "Well, I suppose I find the terrorist theory rather...convenient."

"Meaning?"

"I don't know," he said. "It just doesn't feel like it fits. There are details about the attack which don't seem to make sense under a terrorist plot. Terrorists or extremists, call them what you like, usually want to cause the most damage possible, to really upset the enemy's psyche and hopefully shake their belief system. You see it's not just about the deaths, it's about damaging the belief system itself."

Roberts continued listening. She remembered the chaplain had degrees in both Theology and Philosophy. He was, of course, a man of deep faith, but he was also curious and genuinely interested in understanding other faiths outside of his own. *"We're all God's children,"* he used to say to her. *"We often just have different explanations."*

"What's different about Saint Patrick's," he continued, "is if the attackers wanted to achieve the most damage possible, then their timing was very poor. They attacked on a quiet Saturday morning. If it was really about damage and terror, anyone else would have attacked during mass. Which makes me wonder whether timing was a real consideration."

Roberts leaned back, sitting on the edge of the desk and listening.

"That's just one puzzle. Another was where the bombs were located. Again, if the death toll were the real objective, the bombs should have been placed in the center of the church where most people tended to spend time and take pictures. But these bombs were almost the opposite. They were placed along the walls and set up in series, which means they didn't go off at the same time." He looked at her. "There is another group of people I can think of who set off bombs in series like that. They do it to complement each other."

Roberts shook her head slowly and raised her eyebrows. "What group?"

"Demolition teams," he answered. "The teams that are tasked with taking structures down."

"You see," the chaplain said, now with a deliberate tone, "Jihad, or a religious war, is usually just that, a war or *struggle* for a religious or secular cause. But that doesn't seem to be what this is about. Instead of targeting the individuals or the believers, it almost seems as though the target was the church itself."

"So you think it was someone unrelated to terrorists?" Roberts asked.

He shrugged again. "Well, if it *was* someone else, would it not be more useful to have it blamed on a more convenient enemy?"

"I suppose it would."

The chaplain suddenly smiled. "Ah well, I'm sure I'll prove myself wrong in the end, but I'm always a little leery of a group consensus." He looked at his watch with a start. "And I'm afraid I just remembered that I need to catch someone before they leave for the night. So if you will excuse me."

"Of course," she said, standing and hugging him goodbye. "Can we please have lunch the next time you're around?"

"I would like that very much." With a wink, he hurried across the room and turned down the hallway back toward the stairs.

Roberts stood there, thinking about what he had said. Objectivity was always the straightest path to the truth. She wondered if she was being objective enough in her own case.

She looked down and realized that he had forgotten his folder still lying on the table. "Oh no, Chaplain wait!"

Roberts turned to run after him but fumbled and accidentally knocked the folder to the floor, spilling the papers everywhere. "Dammit!" she yelled under her breath. She looked up hoping he had heard her, but he was gone. Roberts franticly worked to gather up the papers and put them back in the folder. Several pages were filled with columns of names from the church registry. She was trying to quickly put them back in order when she suddenly froze.

In her hand was the second page in the list, and her eyes instantly recognized a name near the bottom. A name she had been looking at in her own file just a few minutes before, *Barbara Baxter*.

14

Ron Tran was one of the best computer hackers alive. He sat quietly in a small internet café, drinking a latte in downtown Beijing, dressed in jeans and a faded T-shirt with a Pepsi logo on the front. While Tran waited, he watched the rows and rows of teenagers glued to their giant computer screens, each playing one of the many popular, virtual world computer games. Some of whom were still in their seats from the day before.

Tran smiled to himself. He resembled at least half of the males in the room; intentional, yet none of them had any idea who he was. He was known to the hacking community as *GtheWhite*, yet his official identification showed him to be an accountant at a small fertilizer company living in a small apartment with seven other friends. As far as anyone knew, he was saving money to buy his first car and had aspirations of starting his own accounting company someday.

In reality, Tran had become extremely disillusioned with the reality of the world around him. The Chinese government ran the country with a stranglehold grip on over a billion citizens who only seemed to stop and ask questions when their television or internet service was interrupted.

Yet, the other major countries were no better. They were simply controlled by other secret groups, oligarchs, or bankers. They merely manipulated and controlled their citizens through different languages, different constitutional loopholes, and from beneath different colored flags. They all lied and they all obfuscated.

What made Tran different was that he despised the *herd*. Opinions and conventional wisdom were nothing more than affirmations for each other. They were barely aware of each new squeeze on their collective throats. They were cattle being driven straight toward the slaughter house, but some of those cattle knew the truth and he was one of them.

Ron Tran hated what the world had become. The core of human existence was now deeply corrupt. It needed to be changed from the inside out, and he was one of the few who had the skills to do it.

He continued watching the herd in front of him, imperceptibly shaking his head. Not only did they not know who he was, but they didn't know why he was there either. Just a fellow gamer waiting for a friend to drop by with a new game.

Finally, the person he had been waiting for walked in and looked around. He ignored everyone's face and hair color since he didn't know what GtheWhite actually looked like. Instead he looked for a T-shirt with a Pepsi logo.

The man spotted Tran and approached casually. He was also dressed in jeans and a T-shirt, but being a government official, he wasn't pulling it off quite as well. Nevertheless, he sat down next to Tran and handed him a DVD case with a picture of a popular game on the cover.

"Here you go," he said in broken English.

"How is it?" Tran asked.

"It's great," the stranger said. "You'll love it."

"Awesome." Tran raised his voice just loud enough to be heard by some of the others. "Are you going to stay and play?"

"No," his friend said. "I have to get back to the restaurant. My father needs me. I'm already gone too long."

"Okay. I'll play for you." Tran laughed out loud and handed a second DVD back to him. "In the meantime, try this game. You'll like it."

"Cool, I will." His friend nodded, then got up and

gave him a friendly departing wave.

Tran flipped over the cover, pretending to take interest in the description of the game. Instead he was just wasting time, waiting for a machine to become available.

More than an hour later, Tran finally got an available computer. He was glad to see that it was far toward the back as he collapsed into the chair and pushed his black hair out of his eyes. Inserting the DVD into the computer brought up a big splash screen, displaying the game's artwork. Like many modern games, there was a deep back story to this one, and Tran let the computerized animation play out. What no one around him noticed, however, was the small window he opened and moved to the bottom corner of the screen.

He immediately started typing, opening up a connection to another machine over the internet and several cities away. Once he was on the second computer, he opened up another connection to a third, then to a fourth and a fifth. From those five he launched a small computer script that automated the process and created new connections in every direction and many levels deep, connecting to more and more computers in more and more countries, until he had taken control of over a thousand computers in less than thirty minutes. One by one, each of the remote computers proceeded to route themselves through encrypted proxy servers which would protect him behind a very complicated and confusing wall of misidentification. If anyone tried to trace his connections, they would end up in Kenya before they would end up in Beijing.

What the thousand computers then proceeded to do, was nothing. Their primary instruction was simply to wait until they received a special command. For now, he would let the scripts run on each new computer, which would then quietly reach out and connect to even more.

Tran closed the small window on his screen and looked

around. *Had anyone noticed?* No, they were so engrossed in their games, they probably wouldn't notice if he was wearing a pink dress. Satisfied, Tran removed his disc and stood up. He took one last look at the sheep around him. *They had no idea what was coming.*

15

Christine woke up on the couch, still in her clothes. She looked down to see Sarah lying against her with her head nestled against Christine's arm. From the window, a thin sliver of early morning light beamed across the small living room and lit up part of the wall behind her.

She winced and carefully adjusted her neck, then looked at her watch. It was almost seven thirty.

The room looked different in daylight and quite a bit dirtier. She wondered how long ago it was last used. She grabbed a small pillow from the floor and slowly pushed it behind her head. Staring up at the dusty ceiling, she went through the last couple days in her head. Her feelings were a jumble of worry and confusion, but strangely not as much fear as she would have expected.

She looked at the light switch near the front door, the switch that Griffin told her would bring two officers running if she turned it on.

Sarah began to stir, taking a deep breath and slowly looking up from Christine's arm where her small head was resting.

Christine smiled. "Hey there, girlie."

Sarah made a tired smile and looked around, stopping at the clothes on the table that officer Roberts had given them. She looked back at Christine and then lay her head back down gently.

Christine reached down and gently stroked her hair. "How did you sleep?"

Sarah nodded without raising her head.

"Are you hungry?" Christine asked softly.

Sarah paused for a moment to think about the question, then nodded again.

Christine waited a moment, then slid Sarah off to the inside of the couch and got up. She walked into the kitchen and looked around. There were some folded grocery bags on the counter, and opening the small refrigerator revealed a jug of orange juice, eggs, bread, and some other basic staples. She walked back and looked at Sarah, who was sitting up and examining the room.

"How about toast and orange juice?"

They both sat at the small metal table in the kitchen which reminded Christine of the table they'd had when she was a little girl, back in the late seventies. Along with the chairs, the set almost looked retro if she hadn't suspected they were originals.

Sarah quietly made quick work of the toast and juice, all the while peering outside through the small window at the large trees. She looked at Christine. "Are we going to be here for a long time?"

Christine frowned and shook her head. "I'm not sure."

Sarah nodded and kept looking around the room. "Is that your phone?" she asked, pointing to the object on the counter.

"Yes." Christine only now remembered Griffin's instructions from last night to keep her cell phone off. He had turned it off and placed it on the counter in front of her for effect.

"Are you scared?" Sarah asked shyly.

Christine thought about her question and finally nodded her head. "A little bit. Are you?"

Sarah nodded too. "A little. Are we safe here?"

"I hope so." Sarah trusted her, and Christine had decided to be as honest as possible. The last thing she needed now, on top of everything else, was lies.

Sarah seemed to accept her answer and continued looking around. She spotted an old doggie door at the bottom of the kitchen's back door. It had long been rusted shut. Sarah frowned and looked back to Christine.

"I'm sorry about your kitty."

Christine gave a painful nod. "Thank you, honey."

"I tried to stop her."

"I know."

Sarah's face saddened. "But you wouldn't let me."

Christine nodded. "I'm sad, but I guess it was just one of-" She suddenly stopped and looked at Sarah. "Wait, what?"

Sarah shrugged innocently and looked down at her bare feet.

"I don't-" Christine stuttered. "What does that mean? What were you trying to stop, Sarah?"

"It was happening. Her shadow was black."

Christine looked at Sarah with a puzzled expression. "Her shadow was black? You mean Cassie?"

"Mmm hmm."

Christine still wasn't following. "I don't understand. Where was her shadow?"

Sarah looked back at her shyly. "All around."

Christine remembered the picture Sarah had drawn the day before at her office. She quickly got up, went to the counter to dig through her purse, and pulled it out. On it were the three figures with circles around them. The circle around the small stick figure cat was colored black.

"You mean these shadows, Sarah?"

"Yes."

Christine studied the picture for a long moment. "What does a black shadow mean?"

Sarah looked up from her picture to Christine. "It means you're gonna die."

Christine was speechless. She stared at Sarah trying to decide if she heard her right. "Did you say *die*?"

"Uh huh." Sarah looked at her empty plate and was considering whether to ask for more.

"Do you see other shadows?"

"Yes," Sarah answered. "Everyone's."

Christine felt a tingle run down her spine. "You see

everyone's shadow?"

"Mmm hmm." She nodded again.

"Are other people's shadows black?" Christine asked.

"Sometimes, like the people in the elevator."

16

Christine sat frozen at the table, trying to comprehend what she had just heard.

"What?" she said quietly. "What was that about the elevator?"

Sarah looked at her innocently. "Their shadows were black. The people inside."

Christine thought back to what had happened. "You're not afraid of elevators?" she asked.

Sarah shook her head.

"Not at all?"

Sarah shook again.

Christine found herself searching for some other explanation, but couldn't find one. *Was it possible? Could she really see what she claimed?* "So you knew something was going to happen to those people?"

"Yes."

"Did you know *what* was going to happen to them?"

"I was just scared something was going to happen to us too."

Christine could see the fear in Sarah's eyes. She reached out and covered Sarah's tiny hand with her own. "You did good, honey."

After breakfast, Christine sat on the couch looking at Sarah's picture again. She looked curiously at the little girl who sat in front of her playing with an old set of Legos she'd found in one of the closets. She hummed quietly to herself while she pushed the pieces together, then reconsidered and pulled them apart again, searching for another in the box.

Christine leaned forward with the paper in her hand.

"Sarah?"

"Mmm hmm." Sarah replied, still sifting through the old cardboard box.

"Do you see anything else when you look at people?" When Sarah turned and looked at her, she held up the picture. "You and your mommy have different colors in this picture."

Sarah looked at it again and then back up at Christine. "I see lots of colors."

"Besides black?"

Sarah nodded.

"What do the other colors mean?"

She pointed to the small stick figure which had a light colored circle around it. "Kids are always white. But grown-ups are different colors."

"And what do the colors mean?"

"Yellow means good," she said. "And orange means a little bad. Red means really bad. A lot of grown-ups are orange."

Christine looked back at the picture and at the stick figure that Sarah claimed was her mother. There was a large yellow circle around it. "Your mommy was yellow?"

Sarah nodded again.

Christine took a deep breath. "Sarah, what color am I?" She realized she was suddenly afraid to hear the answer.

"You're yellow. Like mommy was. Until the bad men came."

Christine felt her heart sink. She thought about when she first met Sarah at the police station. "Honey, is that why you came with me, because I was yellow like your mom?"

Sarah was back to playing with her Legos, but she nodded. "Mommy said I could trust yellows."

"Are there a lot of yellow grown-ups?" she asked.

"No." Sarah said, adding another block to her Lego house.

17

Griffin exited the store and let the glass door close slowly behind him. He walked across the small parking lot where Buckley was leaning against the side of the car, waiting. They had hit the morning commute traffic in Baltimore about three hours into their four-hour drive from New York to Washington D.C. Since they still had a couple hours before their appointment, they decided to stop at a cellular phone store in Baltimore to kill some time and wait out rush hour.

"You all set?" Buckley asked, taking a sip of his coffee.

Griffin held up his new phone. "Yep. Guess it takes a little while to move my number over to the new carrier. The good news is that I now have access to over ten thousand applications that I will never have time to use."

Buckley laughed. "You can always quit your job." He put the cup down and folded his arms across his chest. "So listen, I've been thinking. Barbara Baxter suddenly took her daughter out of school and time off work…at the same time that someone was trying to find her."

Griffin nodded. "She was running. We already talked about this."

"Right," Buckley replied. "She was probably running and came to New York to see someone. Maybe someone who could help her, like that Glen Smith at the FBI."

"That's the most logical explanation," Griffin agreed.

"But," said Buckley, "what if she *wasn't* coming to see someone?"

Griffin paused and thought it through. "Then why come to New York?"

"Exactly. Just for the sake of argument, let's assume she wasn't coming to see someone. Why else would she run and come into the city of all places?"

He saw where Buckley was going. "Because it was the most densely populated location available to her."

"Right." Buckley nodded. "So either she came to New York to meet Smith, *or* she came to hide in one of the largest crowds on the planet."

"Okay, I'm with you," Griffin said. "So why all this talk about a plan B?"

This time Buckley held up his own phone. "Because while you were inside, I called the FBI office in New York. There is no Glen Smith. In fact, they only have two Glen Smiths in the entire bureau. One in Texas and one in California."

Griffin's eyes narrowed.

"Now I'm really hoping she came here to hide," Buckley continued. "Because if she didn't, then she may have ended up walking right into the arms of the very person who was tracking her down."

"That could explain her going through the window at the Marriott. She and Sarah show up and Smith, or whoever he is, is waiting for her with a few friends." Griffin gave Buckley a disturbed look. "Maybe there is a Glen Smith working at the State Department."

Buckley stood up and walked to the driver's side. "Well," he said, opening the door, "I guess we'll find out."

The US State Department is the federal department responsible for all international relations. It was the first federal department, established in 1789 under the country's new constitution. The original responsibilities of the State Department included management of the U.S. Mint, being keeper of the Great Seal of the United States, and acting as the depository of more than 200 multilateral treaties.

In essence, the State Department advances U.S. objectives by implementing the President's foreign policy, and it also supports the foreign activities of other departments such as the Department of Defense and Central Intelligence Agency. With an annual budget of more than $50 billion, the State Department's global reach was massive, operating in over 270 locations, 172 countries, and conducting business in 150 currencies.

Located just a few blocks from the White House, it took Griffin and Buckley almost two hours to drive from Baltimore, through traffic, to reach the Harry S. Truman Building on C street where the Department had been located since 1947.

Housing over 1.5 million square feet of usable space with a roof over 7 square acres in size and over 4,000 windows, the giant buff-limestone building gave off a look of raw power and influence.

It was a little after 11 a.m. when the detectives were escorted into the Deputy Secretary's office. Many claimed the Deputy Secretary actually ran the department, as opposed to the political figurehead appointed as Secretary whose job consisted of little more than photo ops and golfing with other government elites.

Even the Deputy's office was massive, decorated in an old turn of the century architectural theme with a view overlooking much of downtown D.C. It was clearly a position of appreciable power that most people knew little about.

Griffin and Buckley turned away from the giant window as William Zahn walked in with his aide. At six feet three, Zahn was an atypical bureaucrat. He had a muscular build, was exquisitely groomed, and had a focused look on his face that was all business. His aide was similar in size, but with shorter hair, and appeared to be of middle eastern descent.

Zahn looked at the detectives and crossed the room. "Hello gentlemen, you must be the detectives who wanted to see me." He reached out and shook their hands. "This is my aide, Kia Sarat." Sarat nodded and silently extended his hand as well.

"Thanks for your time. I'm Dan Griffin and this is Mike Buckley. We're detectives with the 19th in New York."

Zahn raised his eyebrows. "New York? That's quite a long way. What brings you down here?" He glanced at his phone and walked around his large desk.

The detectives approached from the other side. "We're investigating a homicide," Buckley said.

"I see. And how exactly does this homicide bring you here?" Zahn smoothly sat down in his chair, motioning for them to use the chairs in front of his desk. His aide, Sarat, moved to the side and remained standing.

"Actually, we were hoping you could tell us," Griffin said, filling his seat.

"I'm not sure what I can do, but I should warn you, I have to leave to catch a plane in a few minutes." Zahn extended his arm and looked at his watch. "So what is it about your investigation that involves the State Department?"

"Well," Griffin cleared his throat. "A woman was thrown out of an eighth-story window just days after she suddenly left town with her daughter."

Zahn looked at Sarat and then back at the detectives, spreading his arms in a curious gesture. "I'm sorry to hear that. So what does that have to do with us?"

Griffin leaned forward. "During those few days, it looks like someone was trying to locate her. We spoke to the phone company and someone had instructed them to track the victim's location through her cell phone. That instruction came from your State Department."

Zahn looked confused. He remained quiet, thinking. "Perhaps there is a connection between this woman and some investigation we have underway."

"Perhaps," Buckley said. "It just strikes us as a little odd, since the Department of State is an international organization, not domestic. So why would the department be following, or trying to find, a woman who has never traveled outside the country?"

Zahn shrugged. "I'm afraid I don't know. Again, perhaps she was involved in something or with someone that -"

"She didn't have a criminal record either," Griffin interrupted. "And while it's possible that she was involved in something or with someone who did, in our experience that's pretty uncommon. People who stay out of trouble generally tend to have relationships and friends who also stay out of trouble."

Zahn shrugged again. Griffin noted that he was beginning to look a little irritated. "Well then, perhaps she was romantically involved with someone who she didn't know very well. We do have an office in New York. Maybe she was involved with someone within our employ and things did not end well." He shook his head and looked at his watch again. "I'm sorry detectives. I cannot even begin to imagine the range of personal or professional issues that my thousands of employees might have. My schedule is extremely busy and I'm afraid I'm just not briefed in the details of everyone's lives within this department," he added with sarcasm.

"We understand," Buckley said. "And we know that you are very busy. It would be helpful if we could have a look at some of your phone records to see if we might learn who it was that made the call." Buckley tried to maintain a non-threatening tone. "Of course, this can be a little tedious, so we're happy to do the grunt work to ensure we don't waste anyone's time."

Zahn gave a coy smile. "Well, I appreciate the offer Mr. Buckley, but as you can imagine, communications within the department are frequently of a confidential nature. You can understand the challenge it would pose for us, turning over internal information without first reviewing it."

Back in New York in the forensics department, Mike

Ramirez sat in front of his computer looking through the telephone company's phone logs. He looked closely at the digital entry that had originally launched the searches for Barbara Baxter's location.

There were some special characters included in the record details that he did not recognize. He looked at the byte count, or size of the record, and noticed that it was significantly larger than the rest of the log records. Ramirez thought to himself, tapping his nose with his index finger. It looked like some kind of *attachment* to the actual record. He looked at the initials of the person who had added the entry. It read KL.

Ramirez picked up the phone and dialed a number. It only rang once before it was picked up. "Hey Steve, this is Ramirez again. So listen, I'm looking through the logs you sent me, and I see that the person who entered the search instruction has the initials KL. Does that ring a bell?"

After a pause, Ramirez's contact at the cellular company replied, "Yeah, that's Kelvin Lu. He was a manager, but he doesn't work here anymore."

"Hmm…," Ramirez sat thinking. "It looks like this record has more data to it. Like something appended; like an attachment. Can you open it up?"

On the other end, Steve started typing quickly and fell silent. After several seconds he came back on the line. "Unfortunately, I can't get access since he was a manager. You'll need to send a formal request to his replacement to have a new password applied to Kelvin's account. And that usually takes a couple weeks."

Ramirez grimaced. They didn't have a couple of weeks. He needed it now. "Any chance we can break into his account?"

Steve lamented, "You didn't just say that."

Ramirez smiled on the other end of the phone. "Say what?"

Ramirez suddenly noticed something show up in the chat window on his computer. It was from the same person he was speaking to.

Can't say on the phone. Chat is encrypted and safer.

Ramirez cleared his throat and spoke into the phone again. "Okay, thanks Steve. Hey you want to go to the game next weekend?"

"Sorry can't," Steve replied. "Maybe next time."

"Sure, I'll catch you later then." Ramirez hung up, put down his phone, and immediately typed a reply.

What system are these requests accepted from?

After a few moments, a reply appeared on the screen.

System is called nadcsub01. That's all the help I can give you. Am now deleting these messages.

Ramirez smiled. That was more than he needed. He immediately went to work trying to resolve and find the server in their giant network. Once he had it, he closely examined the server and discovered existing security vulnerabilities in the operating system that had not been patched. He was not surprised. Few if any companies kept their network systems perfectly up to date. When a computer team is responsible for maintaining and troubleshooting those servers, the common mantra was "If it's not broken, don't fix it". As a result, almost every system server had patches that were waiting to be applied until the computer team was sure the upgrade would resolve their issue without creating technical problems at the same time.

Where Ramirez was really lucky was in the particular vulnerabilities this server had. There was a little known cheat to gain control of the operating system by using a command to fool the machine, making it believe Ramirez was the authorized administrator, and then resetting the password for him. It was an old vulnerability and an old hack which made him wonder how many other servers had been neglected.

Once he was in, it took less than thirty minutes to find the old user account for Kelvin Lu, reactivate it, and then reset the password to something that Ramirez could actually use to log in. Finally, the last step was finding the right record he was looking for. When he did, he opened it up in the system and looked at the attachment. It was a letter from the State Department, and it was signed by the person who had ordered the search for the Baxter woman. Ramirez picked up his phone. Griffin and Buckley were going to owe him *big* for this.

Zahn's time was up; he had to catch his plane. He stood up and straightened his jacket. "I'm sorry detectives. I simply do not have time for this as I must leave. Rest assured, I will submit an inquiry on the matter and see if we can get an answer for you."

At that moment Griffin's cell phone chirped loudly. He reached into his pocket and pulled it out, looking at the text message that was sent to him. It was from Ramirez.

The person who signed the request for Baxter's searches was the Deputy Secretary. His name is William Zahn.

Griffin stared at the text message, not believing what he had just read. He realized his eyes had opened wide, and he tried to quickly regain his composure. He turned to Buckley and showed him the message. Buckley had a similar reaction.

In front of them stood Zahn, standing behind his desk and watching. He was watching them closely, observing the sudden change in their positions and ease.

Zahn looked up at Sarat, then slowly back down to Griffin and Buckley who were still seated. He calmly reached over to his desk phone and pushed a button. A female voice answered immediately.

"Yes, Mr. Zahn?"

Zahn spoke, never taking his eyes off Griffin and Buckley. "Dorri, hold my plane."

"Yes sir," she answered.

Zahn ended the call and stood up straight. He continued looking at the detectives until a smirk appeared. His aide, Sarat, moved back a few steps as Zahn came around to the front of his desk. He stopped and sat on the edge between the two detectives, just a few feet away.

"You may not know this, but my aide, Mr. Sarat, is one of our top liaisons for our middle eastern allies. He's also one of many experts on the countries that are not so friendly to us. Iran for example. He even knows some extremists personally, though most of us western nations call them terrorists." He glanced at the ceiling. "It is, of course, a little more complicated than that." He looked back at the men. "But one thing they have in common, the one thing that seems to run through all Persian blood, is they can be extremely ruthless."

Both Griffin and Buckley looked at him with confusion. Zahn raised his eyebrows and motioned for them to look at Sarat. Both detectives turned around to find Sarat standing six feet behind them, pointing a gun at Griffin's head.

Both men jumped in their seats. "Jesus Christ!" Griffin said. "What the hell are you doing?!"

"I wouldn't do that," cautioned Zahn, as Buckley's hand instinctively moved around his hip.

Buckley withdrew his hand.

"Mike Buckley," continued Zahn. "Born on April 3rd, 1978, in the Bronx to a plumber and teacher. Graduated high school with a B average in '96 and applied for the New York Police Department two years later. Now divorced with a young eight-year-old daughter. Tell me Mr. Buckley, how is your daughter enjoying the second grade at Kennedy Elementary?"

Buckley looked at him with eyes wide, completely stunned. He slowly turned and looked at Griffin with a mix of shock and fear.

Griffin was already watching Zahn. "You can't be this stupid. We're police officers!"

Zahn frowned. "And only marginal at best as I understand it."

Griffin's mind was racing. He was trying desperately to keep his wits and think, but panic was quickly overwhelming him.

"Do you have any idea how much trouble you're about to get into?" he tried reasoning. "Look, I think we have a major misunderstanding here." He turned slightly to see if Sarat was still in the same position. He was. "Just put down the gun and let's figure out what happened!"

Buckley nodded desperately in agreement.

Zahn looked at Sarat. "The detective feels we have a misunderstanding Kia."

"Listen to me!" Griffin said. "Don't take this any further. Look, we can work this out! If we don't, things are going to escalate and then it will be out of our hands. Christ, our people know where we are!"

Zahn looked amused. He reached for the phone again and pushed the same button. "Dorri, get me the New York Police Department, 19th Precinct."

"Yes, sir," she replied.

Zahn raised his fingers to his lips instructing the detectives to remain silent. As an extra incentive, Sarat took a step forward and lined his gun's sights with Griffin's right ear.

Zahn's secretary transferred the call and it began ringing.

After four rings, a voice announced, "Police department, 19th. Can I help you?"

"Yes," Zahn said calmly. "I'm calling from the State Department in Washington D.C. I had two detectives, a Mr. Griffin and Mr. Buckley scheduled for 11 a.m. It looks like they are no shows. I'm afraid they will have to call back and schedule another appointment."

Griffin's eyes widened.

"Uh, okay," replied the loud voice on the other end. "I'll let the Lieutenant know."

Zahn calmly returned the phone to its receiver and hung up. He looked at Griffin. "You were saying?"

Griffin still could not understand what was happening, but he could feel his heart about ready to jump out of his chest. "What the hell are you doing? What do you want?! We're just working a goddamn case here!"

Zahn watched him silently for almost a full minute. He was enjoying the look on their faces. "How did she do it?" he asked simply.

Griffin shook his head. "What?"

Zahn sighed. "Don't test me Mr. Griffin. I want to know, *how did she do it?*"

Griffin quickly looked at Buckley who was as confused as he was. "What are you talking about? How did who do what?"

Zahn stared at him. Finally, he sighed again. "I was hoping it wouldn't have to come to this."

"Wait, wait!" Griffin blurted. "Don't…do anything crazy. Just tell us who you're talking about. We'll tell you whatever you want to know."

Zahn watched him carefully, trying to decide if he was being sincere. He finally replied. "The girl," he said, "Baxter's daughter."

If the detectives looked confused before, they looked completely baffled now. "What?"

"The girl!" Zahn said, raising his voice. "Sarah Baxter!"

Griffin began shaking his head. *Sarah? How did he know about Sarah? What in the hell did she have to do with this?* "I-I don't understand-"

Zahn lunged forward. "She *saw* me! How did she do it? Did someone tell her?"

"What do you mean, 'she saw you'? I don't-" Griffin still could not comprehend what Zahn was saying.

Zahn was watching him, waiting for an answer.

Griffin and Buckley looked at each other again. Neither of them were following any of it.

"At the cathedral...she saw me, didn't she? Was it the mother?"

Griffin shook his head again. "What cathedral? When?"

"Saint Patrick's," Zahn said. "She spotted me. When no one else did. Someone must have told her!"

In that moment, it began to dawn on Griffin. *Saint Patrick's Cathedral was the one that was blown up. Was Zahn there? Was Sarah?* "You were there?" Griffin asked.

Zahn leaned back with a look of disappointment. Neither one of them knew. He looked at Sarat who had not moved an inch. "Hmm...," he said, thinking. "Well, I suppose if you don't know, then there's really only one thing you can tell me. *Where is she now?*"

Now Griffin's expression changed from fear to terror. *He wanted to know where Christine and Sarah were.* He could see Christine's face in his mind. *He had to warn her.*

Zahn watched Griffin and then turned to Buckley. "You know, I don't think he's going to tell me. But I think *you* will."

Buckley slowly shook his head.

Zahn smiled. "Ah, don't play hero, it doesn't fit you. You see, Mr. Griffin is single, never married. But my dear Michael, you are a father."

Buckley immediately stopped his head, nervous. At that moment he could feel the tip of Sarat's gun touch the back of his head.

"Yes," Zahn continued. "You love your daughter don't you? Of course you do. Daddy's little girl." He crossed his arms. "So...Michael Buckley, father to Amanda Buckley, do you want your little girl to grow up without a father? Or would you rather she not grow up at all?"

Buckley didn't reply. He didn't say anything. Instead he just sat there and stared at Zahn, as tears began to well up in his eyes.

18

The New York City Public Library was the largest public library system in the United States, founded over a hundred years earlier in 1895. It hosted over 51 million items, all contained within 58 different locations throughout the city. Some of the system's historical treasures included Columbus's 1493 letter announcing his discovery of the New World, George Washington's original Farewell Address, and John Coltrane's handwritten score of "Lover Man."

Cheryl Roberts ran up the four short steps of the Yorkville branch, barely a dozen blocks from the 19th Precinct station. She swung open one of the heavy doors and quickly ducked inside. She walked briskly, but quietly, through the library's Palladian-inspired décor, looking around the lower level for the person she was supposed to have met there twenty minutes ago.

There were dozens of people in the lower level, silently reading or browsing through books and magazines. Near the back, she spotted the person she was looking for and hurried over.

Wilcox was sitting at a long table with a few books spread out before him.

She bent down and surprised him with a hug from behind. "Sorry I'm late, Chaplain."

"Ah, that's alright there lassie," he said with a smile. "I was just doing some reading."

Roberts circled to the other side and sat down, then dropped her purse on the table and scooted her chair in.

Wilcox grinned. "So what is it you wanted to meet and talk about?"

She took a deep breath and looked around. "I wanted

to talk to you more about what we were discussing last night. About Saint Patrick's."

"Ah," Wilcox said leaning back in his chair. "Well remember, that's just a theory. The ramblings of an old man really."

Roberts smiled, acknowledging the comment as his standard *clause* for what came next, being "just his opinion". She cleared her voice. "You said you thought this may not be a terrorist attack, which is the story all the news channels seem to be trumpeting."

The chaplain made an innocent gesture. "I have my doubts. Primarily for the reasons I explained last night."

"Right," she said with a small nod. "You said terrorist attacks target the highest number of people, but the attack on Saint Patrick's was the opposite."

"More or less," acknowledged the Chaplin. "Terrorism is about damage, or retribution. The terrorist attacks on the World Trade Centers in 2001 is an example. A truly horrifying event, but the attack was largely in retribution over a long standing level of oppression and control over their sovereignty, as a country and as a people. In essence, we had military bases and a presence that were allowing us to take their oil, which was pretty much their only natural resource of any value. The point is, the attacks targeted a very large number of people for a very dramatic result. Something that would truly scare, or terrorize, their enemy. Of course, the reason they used airplanes was because they did not have any weapons that could come close to the arsenal the United States had. Therefore, they made do with what they could. The bombing of the USS Cole is another example," the chaplain went on, "They wanted to achieve the most visual and emotional damage possible. They wanted to make a statement."

"And what statement was that?" Roberts asked.

The chaplain shrugged, "Leave us alone."

"I thought they hated our freedom?"

The chaplain almost laughed. "Please. I am not a

believer in the Muslim faith, but the literal words of the Qur'an share many values and principles with our Bible. And while many see the Arabs as being backwards, which they're not, they are certainly not stupid. In other words, they don't travel halfway around the planet to attack a way of life that doesn't affect them. They don't do that unless, of course, it *does* affect them. Which means, unless we are doing something to them."

"Like stealing their oil," Roberts answered.

"Correct."

"So you're saying they had no reason to attack Saint Patrick's."

The chaplain sighed. "I'm saying, that if they were making a statement, it's pretty unclear what that is. And if they really were trying to achieve the most damage, to gain the most attention and sympathy to their plight, why wouldn't they wait another twenty-four hours, when they could hurt or kill three times as many innocent people?"

"And this is why you think the target may have been the church itself?"

"It might make more sense, but only on the surface." He turned one of the books around which showed an older, full-sized picture of Saint Patrick's Cathedral. "Why travel all this way to destroy a church? If they wanted to destroy a big church, there are dozens, *hundreds*, of other candidates that are much bigger and much closer. And it would be far easier than here in the United States. Why this one?" he asked rhetorically. "Saint Patrick's holds no historical or religious significance above the others. The only real significance is that Saint Patrick's is the seat for the archbishop of New York, but a lot of churches serve as seats for archbishops."

Roberts looked at the picture in the book. She turned the page and then another and another. Page after page showed pictures of other giant churches and cathedrals around the world. "Maybe they were after the archbishop."

The chaplain shook his head. "He hasn't been there for weeks."

Roberts sat silently, considering what the chaplain had said. He was right, the terrorist angle did not make much sense. Without a motive like self-preservation or revenge, it simply did not fit with an extremist mindset.

Roberts had a thought. "What if this is not the end? What if more are coming?"

"So instead of attacking the cathedral, the attack may be one in a string against the establishment?"

"Possible?" Roberts asked.

He continued thinking it over. "That's a frightening thought. It's a little too reminiscent of the crusades."

"The Crusades?" asked Roberts. "You mean *The Crusades?*"

Wilcox nodded. "Yes, the two hundred year war between the Muslims and Christians with their ultimate goal of retaking Palestine."

"My god," Roberts whispered. "You don't think this could be the start of something...like that."

"It's possible," the chaplain replied. "But if it is, it could be far worse."

"What do you mean?"

"The battle between the Turks and the Franks, as they were known, was gruesome and unrelenting. But it was largely between Europe and the Middle East." He took a breath. "Today the Christian and Islam faiths are much, much bigger and they span the entire globe. They are now the two largest religions in the world. The warring that surrounded The Crusades was, for the most part, geographically localized. Today it would be global."

"So," Roberts said, "I guess we hope that this attack is not part of something larger."

"Not hope, *pray*," he replied.

"And we still don't know who did this, or why?"

"Correct."

Roberts fell against the back of her chair and thought

to herself. *Nor do we know what this has to do with a six-year-old girl.*

19

Christine turned on the small table lamp in the living room to give them some light. The sun was down, and they were trying to remain distracted. She taught Sarah how to make a paper airplane which had kept her busy for the last hour, and Sarah was now making her most colorful version yet.

Behind her, Christine moved through the rooms and double-checked the doors and locks. She had to admit some doubt was beginning to creep in on how much danger she was really in. Things had been incredibly quiet since they got there, and she was wondering if some of this had been an initial overreaction.

She certainly didn't know why Sarah's mother was killed or under what circumstances. Was it possible that she had some terrible skeleton in her closet? Maybe she had made the wrong person angry, or maybe she had an ex that was jealous or crazy. Even in her old job, Christine had seen so many life tragedies first-hand that she didn't think anything could surprise her at this stage, including what Barbara Baxter might have had in her history.

And what about the elevator? That horrible memory would keep playing itself out in slow motion if she let it. The police were sure it was sabotaged, but...could it have been sabotaged for someone else? There were other people on that elevator. Was it possible that she and Sarah were just in the wrong place at the wrong time, and Sarah's gift had saved them?

No. She shook her head. Chance didn't work like that. A homicide and a near-homicide that close together could not be an accident. And Danny was sure they were in danger. He wouldn't have moved them to a safe place unless he was really worried. She had to trust him. She may not have romantic feelings for him anymore, but she sure as hell remembered how smart he was. She wondered where he was right then.

Christine turned after she was hit in the arm by what looked like a flying rainbow. She faked a troubled look at Sarah and reached down to pick it up. Just as she stood back up and pointed the paper airplane back at Sarah, she heard something outside followed by a loud knock on the door.

They both jumped and stared at the front door. She motioned at Sarah who quickly ran around the couch and stood behind Christine. They both remained frozen wondering who it could be. *How could someone just walk up to the front porch?*

The knocking came again, this time louder. Christine and Sarah did not move.

"Ms. Rose?" a man's voice called. "Ms. Rose, are you in there?"

She slowly looked down at Sarah, and then back to the thick brown door. She took a deep breath. "Who is it?"

"Ms. Rose, I'm from the FBI. I need to talk to you."

The FBI? That would explain how he made it to the porch. "Who are you?"

"My name is Glen Smith," he shouted through the door. "Ms. Rose, I just need to ask you some questions."

"About what?"

"About Barbara Baxter," he replied loudly. "She called me before the accident."

Christine glanced down at Sarah at the mention of her mother's name. She just stared back up at her with her left hand clinging to Christine's pant leg.

"Ms. Rose, I can show you my ID. Just look through the peep hole."

Christine slowly approached the door. When she reached it, she instinctively put her hand on the deadbolt handle to make sure it was locked and turned as far as it would go. She glanced back at Sarah one more time and slowly put her eye to the small hole. "Okay, show me."

On the other side of the door, a badge came into view.

Christine studied it, but it was too small to make out any details. The picture looked blurry and far away, but she thought it showed someone with light brown hair.

"Please, Ms. Rose," he said. "I just need to get some information on what you know. We're trying to find out who did this, and you might have some details that can help."

Christine did not reply. Instead, she stood still thinking. The badge did look official, and she'd seen enough to remember generally what they looked like. Reluctantly, her hand moved to the deadbolt.

Suddenly, Christine heard something behind her. She quickly turned and looked through the kitchen at the back doorknob. It was *moving* back and forth. A moment later, the deadbolt higher up on the back door could be seen turning from the other side, slowly unlocking itself.

Christine gasped and instantly flipped up the light switch on the wall next to the door. *The warning signal.*

Standing on the front porch, Glen Smith shielded his eyes when the bright light came on.

Just over a hundred feet away, the unmarked police car sat silently in the dark. Inside, the two officers sat in the front seats, each with a trickle of blood running down their neck and pooling around their collars.

Christine backed up, away from the door, and waited to hear the running footsteps from outside. She kept waiting and reached back to grab Sarah's arm, feeling her way down to her tiny hand. There was still no sound of the officers running toward them. *Christ, how long could it take?!*

Christine turned to see the deadbolt on the kitchen door finally complete its turn. Next the doorknob moved again, but it was locked too. The knob was quietly being turned from the other side, but this small lock was preventing it. It stopped turning. Then it began to shake. Someone was trying to break it.

"Oh god!" Christine cried and pushed Sarah into the corner. "Somebody please help!"

Just then the back door burst open, and four men dressed in black rushed through. They scanned the kitchen in a fraction of a second before spotting Christine at the far end of the adjoining room. They covered the distance quickly, raising assault rifles to their shoulders.

Suddenly without warning, a figure came crashing through the front window of the living room, sending glass in every direction. Before hitting the floor, he fired from a large gun in his right hand, and the first two shots hit the lead attacker approaching from the kitchen. The black-clad figure crumpled to the floor in front of the other three.

The man in the living room jumped out of the way as bullets tore into the floor where he was kneeling, and pieces of wood and carpet jumped into the air after him. Bullets continued to follow the man across the room as he crossed the floor and ducked into a corner, out of direct sight of the kitchen. In a blur, he took advantage of the momentary safety and raced to the edge of the wall where the men in black were simultaneously trying to step over their dead friend as well as swing around the large door jamb to get another clean shot at him. The second attacker, now in front, came around quickly but saw two flashes before he could squeeze off his own shots. He fell face first next to his lifeless friend.

Christine screamed and dropped to the floor, pulling Sarah down with her. She grabbed the girl's small frame and quickly pushed her back behind the large sofa.

Three more shots went off. She could hear the sound of powerful punches landing and things getting smashed. It sounded like the whole kitchen was getting demolished. Christine flinched when she heard something huge crash against the floor on the other side of the couch. She kept her head low and frantically grabbed Sarah's arm. In one quick motion, Christine pushed off of her knees and they ran for the front door. She grabbed the doorknob and quickly unlocked both it and the dead bolt, flinging the door wide-open just as she heard a grunt behind her. Someone fell to the floor with another thud.

They were out and running! Christine came to a sudden stop on the grass and looked around. She spotted the unmarked police car and sprinted towards it, still pulling Sarah behind her. "Where were you?!" she yelled, reaching the driver's side and yanking the door open.

She shrieked when she saw both men sitting in the front seats, dead. "Oh god!" She looked back at the house. More gunfire could be heard inside. She shuddered and grabbed the driver. Cringing and with her eyes half closed, she pulled him out and let his body fall with a crunch onto the hard pavement.

Christine quickly ran to the other side of the car while Sarah hid behind the driver's open door. With a disgusted look, she pulled the second officer out and onto the ground. "Get in!" she cried to Sarah.

They both jumped into the car and crawled over each other to the opposite sides, where Christine grabbed the keys still in the ignition and started the car. Instantly, without seat belts or even closing the doors, she dropped it into gear and punched the accelerator.

With a giant surge, the car lurched forward with both doors slamming closed from the momentum. Spinning tires left long skid marks as Christine peeled out, sideswiped a nearby truck, and sped away.

20

The large, thick door buzzed and slid open, allowing Cheryl Roberts to step in from the lobby outside. She held up her ID and badge and lay them on the small table in front of her. The officer before her, dressed in body armor, scanned the ID. He then typed in her badge number and waited to see if the photo in the database matched.

Roberts looked around the large room where two more armor-clad officers stood by watching her carefully. Behind them, the rest of the room looked more like a common office than the first floor of an ultrahigh security building.

The nondescript, gray building was the new electronic and security nerve center of New York City. All computers, security systems, phones, and electronics for the largest police department in the world came through this stronghold.

Most people, even residents, did not know that New York had more than 6,000 security and surveillance cameras installed throughout the city, monitoring tens of thousands of citizens daily. They also had thousands of microphones planted in public buildings, airports, bus stops, and many other places where groups of people formed. The microphones were constantly listening and feeding the audio back to the nerve center which searched every stream for patterns of words that were considered *interesting*.

A young man approached Roberts. With red hair and light freckles, he looked like someone new to both the uniform and the workforce. In fact, he barely looked out of high school.

"Officer Roberts?" he asked.

"Yes."

"Hi, my name is Justin Fischer. I'm your tech."

"My tech?" she asked.

He nodded. "Everyone accessing the cameras is assigned a tech for assistance."

"For assistance or supervision?" she asked.

He grinned but did not reply.

"Okay." She reached out to take her identification back but was cut short by the officer behind the table.

"We keep these until you come out," he said dryly.

"Both?"

"Yes." He finished typing and clicked his mouse, then turned to retrieve a printout. He lay the paper down in front of her and handed her a pen. She looked it over, surprised how much of her information was on the form. After signing, she looked at Justin who was waiting patiently with a slight slouch.

The larger officer picked up her paper and filed it. "You get your ID and badge when you leave."

She rolled her eyes and shrugged. "Okay." She walked past him to where Justin was standing. "I guess I'm all yours."

Justin smiled politely. "Follow me, please," he said and led her down a long hallway to the stairs. After descending two floors, they wound their way through a series of twists and turns. As they walked, they passed several large rooms each with walls completely covered with hundreds of video screens. In front of the screens sat a dozen team members watching as the views automatically switched from street to street.

"Wow," Roberts mumbled, passing their fourth giant room. "This is amazing."

Justin stopped at a red door labeled simply with a number 6. He opened the door and waited for her to walk in first. Inside was a huge desk with three giant monitors in front of the keyboard, all displaying dozens of small windows from different street cameras. "So, you said you needed to look at a specific camera," Justin commented as he sat down. He motioned for Roberts to sit down next to him.

"That's right," she said, taking the seat. She looked at the images. "I can't believe how clear the pictures are."

"All cameras installed in the last three years are high def," Justin replied. He typed in his ID and password and brought up a map of the city. "Where are we looking?"

Roberts squinted and looked at the map. "Between 5th and Madison."

Justin typed in "Madison Street", and the map quickly zoomed in. An older picture of Saint Patrick's Cathedral was easily recognizable from the top. Justin looked at her. "Saint Patrick's?"

"Mmm..hmm," Roberts answered, studying the map. "Do you have a view of the north side?"

Justin zoomed in further. "Well, we have a camera here on the corner of Madison and East 51st." He used his mouse to bring up a separate window with a list of all connected cameras. He then entered the two street names which displayed an icon on top of the map. Clicking the icon instantly filled the right hand monitor with the live video feed from the Madison intersection.

Roberts was impressed. She stared closely at the picture, trying to get her bearings. "Which direction is this facing?"

Justin pointed to a small compass display in the right hand corner. "This is facing east."

Roberts looked disappointed. "So it's facing the wrong way?"

"Not necessarily. They're bidirectional." Justin said, moving the mouse. "Let me see if we can view the opposite direction." He clicked another button, and it switched the view to west. "Most of these cameras are actually quad units which means we can view each of the four directions." They both watched the camera feed switch to a disturbing view of a black and smoldering block of rubble.

"What time and day?"

Roberts looked at him. "Saturday morning at 11:00 am."

Justin began typing in the date when he stopped and looked back her. "The time of the attack?"

She nodded.

"Some of us have spent a lot of time with the FBI going over these feeds." He entered the date and waited several seconds while the video picture changed.

The picture switched to an older video feed showing the giant cathedral still standing tall and majestic in the morning sun.

"Can you freeze that?"

Justin clicked his mouse and froze the picture. Roberts leaned in over his shoulder and looked closer at the screen.

"This is five minutes before the explosion."

"Correct."

"Can you roll it forward in slow motion from here?" she asked.

"Yep," he replied and adjusted the video speed.

They both sat silently watching the scene slowly unfold. The crowd outside the cathedral consisted of several groups of varying sizes, most likely tourists, and many more individuals looking, talking, and pausing for pictures. Just as the timer on Justin's screen approached 11:05, he slowed the video further until they were viewing almost frame by frame.

A black and gray cloud of smoke suddenly burst from the giant double doors which stood wide open. Giant pieces of debris followed in the same instant, showing what looked like large chunks of rock and wood. One piece moved through the video screen so fast that Roberts had no idea what is was. Another giant piece right behind it was clearly a large piece of a pew bench.

Many of the figures standing in front of the church

before the explosion disappeared into a cloud of debris that enveloped everything. When it began to clear, Roberts felt a sick feeling in her stomach when she saw how many of the people were no longer there.

The scenes were awful. Watching in this level of detail made her feel like it was happening all over again. She wanted to close her eyes and turn it off, but she was afraid she might miss something crucial. Then finally, after several painful minutes of watching frame by frame, she saw it.

While dozens of people ran back and forth, two figures caught her eye. They were running down the steps, away and toward the outside edge of the camera's coverage. It looked like a mother and daughter. What was strange was that while everyone else was running away, these two figures suddenly stopped and remained still for a few seconds before continuing.

"Can you zoom in on those?" she asked.

Justin complied, and the computer isolated the frames from the camera and zoomed in, self-correcting for pixilation at the same time. He zoomed in as far as he could, and even though the picture was stretched due to the angle of the camera from down the street, Roberts could clearly make them out. It was Sarah and her mother.

Justin froze on the clearest frame while Roberts studied them. It looked as though Sarah was tugging at her mother, and yet she was not looking at her. Sarah was looking at something else, something out of camera shot.

"Can you determine what angle this little girl is looking at?" Roberts asked.

"Hmm," he said. "Maybe." He brought up a new window and began typing in it. To Roberts, all computer syntax looked like Greek. "If we can correct the angle of the picture," Justin said, watching as the computer squared the dimensions, "then we can overlay our cardinal points of direction." Next, the video screen was covered with four lines labeled north, south, east and west. "And if we can approximate the direction the girl's head is facing…". He typed more lines and the computer then zoomed out to an overhead view of the street, with a red line approximating the angle that Sarah had been looking in the frame. "It looks like she may be looking about…here," he said. He pointed to the street corner almost directly across the street from the cathedral.

Roberts frowned. "But we can't see it."

Justin shrugged. "Well, not on this camera. But we might be able to see it from the camera facing the opposite direction one block down."

After another ten minutes of angle adjustments and computer enhancements, Roberts could see what she believed Sarah had been staring at. A tall man, in a dark suit, standing on the corner watching the chaos unfold. Unfortunately, she could not see his face. What was very strange to her though was that everyone was running or reacting to the carnage of the explosion, even people on the other side of the street. Everyone *except* this man.

Roberts collected her badge and identification and signed out. She walked purposefully across the lobby and through the double, sliding glass doors, and was crossing the parking lot when her cell phone rang. She immediately recognized the extension from the 19th Precinct and accepted it.

"This is Roberts," she answered.

"Cheryl, this is Deborah from the station. I was told by the deputy to give you a call."

"Hey Deb, I was just on my way back, what's up?"

"Cheryl, there's been an incident."

Roberts' pace suddenly slowed. "What incident?"

"Darlington said you were using one of the safe houses."

Oh no, thought Roberts. She closed her eyes and took a deep breath.

Deborah continued. "There were shots fired. We're

on the scene now, but I don't have a lot of detail yet. You might want to get over there."

"Oh god!" she said, ending the call and running for her car. She fumbled for the keys as she ran. When she got to her car, she swung the door open and quickly jumped in, jamming her key into the ignition.

In her rush, she did not notice the dark figure crouched down in her back seat.

21

Liz Iverson stood in her kitchen cooking dinner for her husband, who sat in the next room in a large recliner, watching a rerun of Hogan's Heroes. She turned the steak over in the pan and turned her attention back to the small pile of mail on the large granite countertop. She spent a few minutes flipping through an advertisement for the local supermarket. As she turned and dropped it into the recycle bin, her cell phone rang.

Reaching inside her purse, she pulled the phone out and looked at the number.

"Hello?" she answered.

"Liz!" yelled Christine through the phone. "Liz, thank god!"

"Christine? What is it, what's wrong?"

"Liz!" Christine cried. "They tried to kill us! They tried to *kill us*!"

"What are you talking about?" she asked. "Who tried to kill you?" Liz looked through the doorway at her husband who had overheard and was now staring at her.

"I don't know!" Christine said, still frantic. "They came to the house! I think it was the FBI!"

Liz's brow furrowed. "The FBI? Why on earth would they want to hurt you? What happened?"

"They came to the house! But when I turned the emergency light on, they didn't come! They were dead Liz, they were both dead in the car!"

Liz was utterly confused. "Who was in the car? And what emergency light? You're losing me, I don't understand what you're saying."

"I know," Christine said anxiously. She tried to slow her breathing. "I'm just scared and I don't know what's happening."

"Christine, take a deep breath and tell me exactly what happened." Liz spoke slowly into the phone as her husband approached and stood behind her.

"Okay, okay." Christine took a deep breath, and then another. "They came to the house. Someone knocked on the door and said they were the FBI. I didn't want to let them in but more of them broke in through the back door, with rifles! And then the FBI person on the porch smashed through the front window. But then they started shooting at each other, so I don't…I just grabbed Sarah and ran out." She took another breath. "But when we got to the car, the two policemen inside, they were supposed to be guarding the house, but they were dead. They were dead in the car."

Dear god. "Okay, take it easy." Liz said. "The first thing we need to do is call the police."

"No!" yelled Christine, suddenly excited again. "I mean, I just…I just don't know who to trust. They killed the police before they could even get out of the car. The ones that broke in, they all looked like professionals, like killers or something. I mean what if someone in the police is in on this?"

Christine was scared, but she had a good point. Liz's husband whispered something in her ear. "Is Sarah okay?"

Christine looked at Sarah who was standing inside a McDonald's restaurant, just inside the glass doors, to keep warm. "Yes."

"Good. Listen carefully Christine, my husband is a retired police officer, remember? Let us come get you. Until we know what's going on here, let us come and get you and bring you someplace safe. He has friends that he can trust, they will all help keep you safe."

Christine thought it over briefly before replying. "Yeah, okay, but hurry!"

"Okay," Liz said. She grabbed a pen and paper. "Now where are you?"

Christine looked around. "We're in Quakertown," she said. "At a McDonald's. I see a road called West Broad Street."

"Okay," Liz said, writing it down. "We'll find it." She quickly turned off the stove and followed her husband down the hallway toward their garage. He grabbed coats for both of them. "Christine, stay right where you are. You'll be safe in a public place."

Christine hung up and walked toward the entrance. People walked in and out of the restaurant, barely noticing either one of them. Was anyone looking at them strangely? As she opened the door, Christine looked back at the unmarked police car with a damaged right fender. At the very least, she thought, someone would be looking for that car.

Christine sat in a brightly-colored, plastic chair while Sarah quietly sat next to her, eating French fries. The restaurant was filled with loud and obnoxious children running up and down the aisles while their parents appeared oblivious and went on with their conversations.

Christine tried not to jump every time the door opened, slumping with disappointment when she saw it was not Liz. She tried to distract herself by watching the customers, marveling at how many did not even have to look at the menu, but instead had their order memorized in what she considered a sad display of social repression.

She watched an unusually large woman order several items of food and a diet soda. She looked down at Sarah who was watching the other children. Sarah looked up and smiled.

Christine smiled back. "You doing okay, honey?"

Sarah nodded. "Are you scared?"

Christine frowned. "Yes."

"Me too," said Sarah. She turned and looked at the front door. "Is your friend going to be here soon?"

"Yes." Christine forced a smile and patted her leg.

"She should be here any minute."

Sarah nodded again and looked over to a child screaming at another table.

They both turned when they heard the sound of screeching tires. Outside, Liz and her husband jumped out of their Jeep Grand Cherokee and ran for the door.

Christine grabbed Sarah's hand and turned anxiously to face the door as Liz stepped inside and scanned the large dining room. She spotted Christine and immediately crossed the room, barely avoiding a customer with a large tray of food.

"There you are!" she said, approaching. She looked from Christine to Sarah and then back again. "Are you two okay?"

Christine took a deep breath and nodded. She smiled quickly at Liz's husband who walked up behind her.

Liz sat down across from Christine. She reached out and held her hand. "Okay, we're just going to wait here for a few minutes until Tim's old partner shows up. And then we'll get you someplace safe."

Christine nodded.

Liz then looked at Sarah. "How are you, dear?"

"I'm okay," Sarah said. She finished the rest of her orange juice through the straw and sat back in her chair. With a timid look, she peered up at Liz's husband standing behind her. She noted his large belly sticking out beyond his jacket and the slight bulge of his gun underneath, on his hip.

"Have you eaten anything?" Liz asked Christine.

Christine shook her head. "Not really hungry."

"When *is* the last time you ate?"

"A while," she said with a shrug.

"Okay well-" Liz was interrupted when her husband Tim looked outside at a pair of headlights screeching into a parking space on the other side of the large dining room.

"Steve's here," he said, patting Liz's shoulder lightly. He watched the large man pass along the windows outside and enter through the far doors. He waved Steve over.

"Christine," he said. "This is my old partner, Steve McCaullah. We've been friends for more than twenty years."

McCaullah nodded and looked at them. He then looked carefully around the dining room. "We'd better get you girls out of here."

Liz smiled and stood up next to her husband. "You two ready?" As Christine began to stand, Liz turned to lead them out.

Christine was suddenly stopped by Sarah's hand on her arm. She glanced at Liz who was already starting to walk away and then looked back down at Sarah.

Sarah was leaning in close to her with a scared look on her face. "He's a bad man," she whispered.

Christine froze halfway off the chair. "Who?"

Sarah whispered again, quieter. "Him." She motioned to McCaullah who was watching the Iversons walk away from him. He turned his attention to the glass doors as three darkly dressed men walked in.

Sarah gasped. Peering back at Liz and her husband, she watched both of their shadows change from orange to black.

"What is it?" Christine said, and then followed Sarah's fearful gaze to Liz. "LIZ WAIT!"

It was too late. When Liz and her husband turned back around, they found McCaullah pointing his gun at them. A confused look on their faces were just forming when McCaullah pulled the trigger repeatedly, firing two bullets into each of them.

Dozens of customers screamed and ran for the doors in a panic. Some made it out while others tried to hide behind something or searched for their children, screaming at them to get down or out of the way. Liz was killed instantly, but her husband desperately ran his hand underneath his coat as he fell. He barely managed to withdraw his weapon but fumbled it onto the floor. The gun was quickly kicked out of the way by one of the three men approaching behind him.

Tim Iverson struggled on the floor and turned onto his back. A thin line of blood began seeping through his lips. As he was trying to speak, McCaullah leaned down over him and pushed his gun into his chest. "Sorry Timmy," he whispered with a disappointed look. "This is bigger than both of us."

Iverson was still trying to move as McCaullah fired two more bullets into his heart.

Everyone was still screaming. Some parents had managed to get to their children and were now trying to force one of the emergency doors open to get out. Christine grabbed Sarah and looked around the restaurant, but there was no way to get past them, much less to an exit. She squeezed Sarah tighter and tried to think of something to do, anything, but she was stopped when McCaullah stepped in front of her and reloaded his gun.

"A lot of people have been looking for you two," he said, putting the used magazine into his jacket pocket. "We couldn't find you, and then, imagine that, Tim calls me from out of the blue." He smiled at the other three standing to the side. "With that kind of luck, I should be playing the lottery."

He looked curiously at Christine. She didn't seem as frightened as he would have expected. She was obviously afraid, but there was also a hint of determination as she kept Sarah behind her. *Pity.* He pulled the slide back on his gun to verify the chamber was loaded. He then released it and held the gun in his right hand with a relaxed grip. "So the question for you is…do you want to come with us, or not? I have to warn you," he said with a smile, "the second option may have some bad results."

McCaullah gripped the gun and began to raise it when the wall of glass suddenly exploded and a large car drove through it. One of the few areas of empty seats ripped from the floor and tumbled forward in front of the car's bumper, and a giant wave of glass slid down, and then off of the hood. Just before it stopped, the front of the car struck McCaullah hard, and his body disappeared from where he was standing.

The man that Christine saw at the safe house, who identified himself as Glen Smith, stepped quickly and calmly out of the driver's side as McCaullah's three friends took a few steps back and pulled out their own guns.

Behind them, the screaming got even louder with people pushing through *any* possible exit, even the open wall of glass. Behind the car, Smith's movements were fluid and fast. He shot two of the three before any of them got a single shot off. The third opened fire forcing Smith to duck down. In a panic, the man unloaded his entire magazine, with most of the bullets missing completely and shattering another set of windows at the far end of the room. Smith waited for him to run out of bullets and then dropped him with a single shot.

He scanned the restaurant and then looked outside. Satisfied, he swiftly stepped over the debris between himself and the girls. He looked down at Sarah and then to Christine. "We need to leave, get in the car."

Christine was shaking, looking as though she might be in shock. Slowly she blinked and looked up at Smith. "Why…what…" she shook her head and grabbed Sarah's hand again. "What in the hell is this?" she cried. "Who are they…who are *you*?"

"Glen Smith," he answered calmly. "I was the one standing outside your front door."

"What…happened?" She looked around the dining room. Several innocent people were lying motionless on the floor. "Why are they doing this?" She looked back toward the front, and her eyes fell on Liz's body. "My god! They killed Liz!" Her eyes began to well up. "Why? Tell me why!"

Smith watched her and holstered his gun beneath his jacket. "I'm sorry, this is not the time for questions. We need to leave."

In stunned silence, Christine did a full scan of the restaurant and thought she could hear the faint sound of sirens in the distance.

Smith heard them too, glancing in the direction from which they were coming and then back to Christine. He looked at Sarah again, then took a few steps over some twisted bench seats and opened the passenger's door. "Getting arrested by the police will not help. It will make things far worse." The sirens grew louder over the sobbing of people outside.

Christine turned to Sarah and whispered, "Is he *red?*"

Sarah shook her head no.

What was she supposed to do? Christine thought. No one in the police department had been able to protect them. They still didn't have any answers. And Smith was the only one offering protection now. It had to be protection, didn't it? If he wanted to kill them, he would have already.

The sirens were getting closer.

"Okay," Christine said meekly. She rose slowly and pulled Sarah with her to the car. She scanned the inside, both front and back, and pushed the seat forward, letting Sarah into the back. "Put your seat belt on," she said with a trembling voice.

Christine watched Smith circle back around to the other side of the car and slide in. He closed his door and looked at her. With reluctance, she closed the passenger door and continued to watch him.

Smith quickly started the car and dropped it into reverse, then drove backward until he could turn around. He turned off his headlights and headed east on the main street, away from the approaching lights and sirens.

"Are either of you hurt?" he asked, looking over his shoulder. They both shook their heads. "Good." He continued to drive, watching the rearview mirror. After several minutes of silence, Smith turned to Christine. "Can you drive?" he asked.

"Yes," was all that came out.

"Can you drive *now*?" Smith asked again. "Are you hurt, are you tired?"

"No." Christine frowned. "Why?"

Smith leaned forward and looked carefully out the window for a place to pull over. "Because I'm about to lose consciousness."

"What?"

Smith pulled into a dark parking lot behind a convenience store. He put the car in park and turned off the engine, then reached down gently and pulled open his blue jacket. The left side of his torso was covered in blood.

Christine's eyes widened. "Oh my god!"

Smith grimaced slightly when he pulled his shirt up; some of the blood was already dried. The bullet had gone straight through. He blinked twice and turned to her. "Listen carefully. I don't have much time." He pulled his jacket off and reached across Christine, opening the glove compartment. He pulled out a roll of duct tape from the inside.

"What's that for?" she asked, watching him rip off a large piece.

"It's for repairing ventilation ducts," he answered dryly.

She frowned sarcastically. "I know that. I mean what-" she stopped when he stuck the tape to the steering wheel and then pulled his shirt off and ripped it lengthwise. He folded one half of the shirt a few times and pressed it against the wound while securing it with the tape. He ripped off more tape from the roll and did the same to the wound on his back.

When he was done, Smith turned and looked at Sarah who stared nervously back at him from the rear seat. He turned back to Christine. "Where is your phone?"

"It's right here." She looked in her purse and pulled it out. "Why?"

"Turn off your cellular signal," Smith said. His

breathing was beginning to sound labored. "They can find you that way. Do you know how to turn it off?"

"Yes." Christine nodded and fumbled with her phone, finally turning off the signal.

"Just…use the GPS." Smith said. He reached back into the glove compartment in front of Christine and pulled out a piece of paper and pencil. He wrote something on it and handed the paper to her. "Use your phone's navigation to get to this place…as quickly as you can."

Christine took the paper apprehensively and looked at it. On it was scribbled a set of numbers. "Is this an address?" she asked.

He took a deep breath and shook his head. "They're GPS coordinates. Just type them into your phone." He blinked again, longer, then turned and focused intently on Sarah. "Get to that location. Your lives depend on it."

He managed to get the last words out before losing consciousness and sliding with a thud against the driver side door.

22

Zahn exited the jet and stepped out into the arid Dubai morning air which was already approaching ninety degrees. A large delegation waited for him at the bottom of the stairs. Several photographers stood in front, while the black limousines could be seen behind the crowd. He descended the stairs and waved with a perfect smile. When he reached the black tarmac, he bowed to the Arab diplomats before him, continuing down onto his knees and kissing the ground, symbolizing his respect for their sovereign land.

It took over an hour for the photographs and respectful exchanges with nearly a dozen sheikhs. Zahn finally continued with his small entourage to the limousines and climbed into the back of the middle car. A few minutes later, the three cars rolled forward, away from the crowd, circled the west end of the terminal and headed for the large metropolitan skyline in the distance.

Dubai was originally established in 1833 by Sheikh Maktoum bin Butti Al-Maktoum when he persuaded 800 members of his clan to follow him from present day Saudi Arabia to the Dubai Creek. Since then, and due to the advantage of its strategic, geographic location, the city had grown from an important trading hub into a major international and cosmopolitan center for the Middle East.

Zahn peered out of his tinted window at the hundreds of skyscrapers that had come to symbolize the wealth of Dubai. All funded by the United Arab Emirates' untold billions in oil money, it was a city that was now one of the most expensive in the world.

He looked at his watch. He was ahead of schedule. His next meeting with Mohammed bin Manal Al Maktoum was not due to begin for another hour. But it was the very last meeting that he was thinking about.

The man that sat across from Zahn lowered his cigarette and exhaled the last of the cigarette smoke. Being Iranian, he was not a sheikh, but closer to an ayatollah with one important difference: Ra'ad was a warrior. He had long since rejected the path of a religious scholar and instead maintained a humble existence, fighting for his people and more importantly for his God.

Zahn sat two hundred miles north of Dubai and across the Strait of Hormuz in a dark underground complex inside the Iranian border. His entourage patiently waited for him in a downtown Dubai skyscraper, maintaining the illusion that Zahn was still there, deep in discussions with various heads of state in the Middle East, all of whom had secretly left hours earlier.

Ra'ad put his cigarette out in the ashtray and looked to his men, one on his left and one on the right. Unlike most of the "scholars", Ra'ad's English was perfect. He took Sun Tzu's code of *know thy enemy* very seriously. "So we have come to it at last," he said.

A smile crept across Zahn's lips. "Finally."

"I will admit," Ra'ad said with a grim smile of his own, "I did not trust you. Until the church."

Zahn shrugged. "Words prove nothing."

Ra'ad nodded in agreement. From his demeanor, not to mention his worn turban and clothes, no one would believe the power the man wielded. After all, most Muslims believed his reputation to be more akin to a ghost than a man. And it was a distinction that no one ever wished to find out.

Ra'ad studied Zahn as he always did. He would never have imagined that a westerner would come to him with this kind of a plan, and certainly not a bureaucrat. Never in his lifetime would he have thought it. He put his hands together in front of his chapped lips. "You are sure he will come?"

Zahn smirked. "Of course he will. There will be no choice." He watched Ra'ad light another cigarette. "When will your men arrive?"

"Two days," Ra'ad replied, dropping the match into the ash tray. "And then they will be yours, for whatever you need."

Zahn understood Ra'ad and, more importantly, he understood his men. They were not trained in silly desert camps using wooden planks and jungle gym equipment. Instead, Ra'ad's men were converts of the deepest kind. They were all trained in a special forces group before being turned. All highly trained, thoroughly disgusted with the evil western empires of greed and sloth and now happy to share every piece of their expert training with those willing to take a stand. More importantly, they believed in Ra'ad, a man who rejected every form of self-indulgence, ate the rotten rice that his men ate and drank the same dirty water. He knew the history and struggle of his people almost verbatim. He knew the difference between taking a side and taking a *stand*. And Ra'ad was about to take the ultimate stand.

Yes, Zahn trusted Ra'ad and his men. He knew what they were capable of. After all, his man Sarat, who was sitting to his left, used to be one of Ra'ad's best.

Zahn smiled again at Ra'ad, who was still watching him very carefully with his dark eyes. His rough and leathery face was a testament to what he was willing to endure for his people. Zahn admired the man's determination, his righteousness, his faith. What he had promised Ra'ad was going to shock the world, and it was a promise he fully intended to deliver upon. Yet if Ra'ad could see deeper into Zahn's eyes, if he could only read his mind, he would never have imagined what was to come after that.

23

The New York Archives stood less than a mile from the Simon & Meyer law firm that Griffin and Buckley had visited in Albany. Established in 1971, but not open to the public until 1978, the massive building housed 200 million public records dating all the way back to the 17th century which meant it held nearly the entire history of New York state on microfiche.

The man sitting in front of one of the microfiche machines slowly moved through the images, the large monitor creating a dull glow that reflected off of his tanned, bald head. On the table next to the machine were twelve large boxes of the special film and a small laptop with its screen displaying a list of historical documents.

A young clerk walked by with an armful of books and glanced over at the man again. It didn't look like he had moved since she started her shift almost seven hours ago. The clerk wondered what he was looking for. Usually people asked her for help on a topic, but this man simply kept asking for more boxes of film. She shrugged and kept walking.

The man at the table suddenly leaned in and studied the screen carefully. He wrote something down and then turned to his laptop, bringing up a new window filled with names and dates. He scrolled carefully down the long list until after several minutes he spotted what he was looking for. He held a finger to the computer screen and looked back at the microfiche data. He compared them both several times and then jotted more down on a piece of paper.

The man removed the microfiche from the machine and looked around. He gently slid it back into the small storage box, putting it into the middle of the deck. Stacking all of the microfiche boxes neatly together, he shut down his laptop and put it back in his bag.

As the man walked to the exit, the clerk glanced up and watched him leave. *Strange man*, she thought. *I wonder what kind of a name Bazes is.*

The man named Bazes approached a black Mercedes in the parking lot and pressed a button on his keychain to open the trunk. It was late in the evening. He casually removed his coat and placed it into the trunk alongside his laptop. When his phone rang, he removed it from his shirt pocket and answered it.

"Yes?" He listened for a few moments. "What happened?" He continued listening and looked around the parking lot, which was almost empty, and glanced at his watch. "Where?"

"I'll be right there." He reached up and slammed the trunk closed. He walked forward and slipped the phone back into his pocket as he opened the driver's door, then slid in behind the wheel. As the engine roared to life, he pulled the door closed and dropped it into gear.

24

Christine slowed the old Dodge Charger, looking back and forth between her phone's navigation system and the dark road in front of her. A dark forest surrounded her on all sides making it impossible to see anything that might give her even a clue as to where they were. Even the stars were completely blocked by the giant trees.

She turned and looked at Sarah in the back seat, curled up and asleep. She gazed over at Smith who she had barely managed to push into the passenger seat after he passed out. She stared at his chest looking for movement. His breathing was very weak, but he was still alive.

What the hell have I done? She thought to herself. *Some guy shows up, gets himself shot, tells me to drive to god knows where, and I just say yes?* Well, she hadn't just said yes. The fact was that she sat contemplating what to do before getting behind that wheel. She had no idea who he was or how he had found them, but he did save them. Had he not arrived just in time, and twice now, she was sure they both would have been kidnapped or dead.

She snuck a peek again at Sarah who even in an uncomfortable position looked like an angel. Her blond hair was covering part of her face with her tiny hands resting together under her cheek.

Even as innocent and helpless as Sarah was, now many hours later, Christine's anxiety was really beginning to set in. It had been years since she'd been around kids, much less in charge of one. Slowly but surely, the emotions were beginning to flood back, and it was becoming increasingly difficult to contain them. But Sarah needed help. She was all alone, and even if it wasn't her, the poor girl needed *someone.*

Christine peered hard past the bright glow of her phone but could barely see anything. Her phone's navigation program was telling her that she had arrived, but she had no idea where she was or what she was looking for. She looked at the fuel gauge. Less than a quarter tank left.

Exasperated, she finally stopped the car and turned off the engine. She pushed the button forward and killed the headlights, then turned the screen off on her phone. After letting her eyes adjust, she quietly opened the door and stood up on the old, gray, asphalt road. She looked around for anything -- a driveway, a mailbox, a sign -- anything that might give her some comfort that they were not lost or, worse yet, in another dangerous situation.

She heard a noise on the far side of the road and froze. She heard it again. Something was moving through the brush under one of the trees. It sounded like it was something large and moving slowly. It also sounded like it was moving directly toward them.

Christine ducked down a little closer to the door and gripped the steering wheel with her right hand. She shifted her weight and got ready to jump back inside the car.

Just as she was about to launch herself back into the seat, something appeared out of the darkness. It was the barrel of a gun.

She froze again. The barrel inched forward until the outline of a man's face appeared. His short white hair and face eased slowly out of the darkness followed by his body. He was holding what appeared to be a scary looking shotgun.

"You alone?" he asked in a low voice.

She nodded, careful not to move anything except her head. She continued to remain still, watching as he approached the car and the passenger's door. The man shined a red flashlight into the car and spotted Smith's still figure.

"What happened?" He looked surprisingly calm.

Christine spoke quietly. "He's hurt."

The man gave her a sarcastic frown. "I can see that. How hurt?"

"Bad," she answered. "He's been shot."

The man looked at Sarah, asleep in the back seat. "Is she hurt?"

Christine shook her head.

He finished looking the car over and turned back to her, placing a finger over his lips for her to be quiet. He looked back down the dark road and stood very still.

After a long silence, Christine realized that he wasn't looking for something, he was *listening*.

Satisfied, the man lifted his Mossberg shotgun and slung it over his shoulder. He leaned against the car door and released the handle, letting it open quietly. He then reached in, pulled back Smith's jacket and examined his makeshift bandages.

He placed a hand on Smith's right side and let the door swing fully open. "We need to get him inside quickly." He motioned to Sarah. "Get the girl." With that, the man grabbed Smith's arms and pulled him out in a rolling motion. In one quick movement, he ducked down and pulled Smith over his own shoulder, lifting him up and away from the car.

He looked at Christine who was watching with wide eyes. The man looked like he was in his sixties or seventies and yet he put Smith's body over his shoulder with little effort. "Are you going to get her?" he asked, standing motionless with Smith.

Christine blinked and nodded nervously, then circled the car. Through the open passenger door, she flipped the seat forward and pulled Sarah forward into her arms.

The old man waited and when Christine was ready, he turned and peered down the dark road once more before leading her back the way he came. "Be careful," he said and slipped back into the shadows.

She could barely follow him through the darkness, even with wisps of moonlight fighting their way down between the thick forest of trees. She stumbled several times and began picking her knees up higher with every step. After several minutes of tromping through knee-high grass and with her arms beginning to ache, Christine spotted a small lit window in the distance. As they got closer, she could see the larger outline of a cabin, and when they reached the front door, she leaned against the railing for support.

The old man checked over his shoulder and quietly opened the door. He stepped inside and waited for her as she took a deep breath and lifted Sarah again. She walked into what appeared to be a dimly lit living room and moved to an old couch set against the wall. With her arms beginning to shake, it took all she had to set Sarah down smoothly.

Christine looked back as the man pushed the door closed. His leathery face told her she was right about his age, but he still seemed barely uncomfortable carrying Smith.

"I need to get a look at him. With a lot of rest, he may make it." He locked the door. "I'll go back out to hide the car when I'm done." He nodded toward a cedar chest against the wall. "There are blankets in there. You should both be able to sleep comfortably on the couch. In the morning we'll talk."

Christine instinctively began to nod but suddenly stopped. "Wait." She glanced around the old living room and noticed the kitchen off to the side. "Where exactly are we?"

He was headed for the hallway when he stopped and turned back. "Someplace safe."

Christine awoke with a start when she felt something brush her arm. She opened her eyes to a dark room and the old man leaning over Christine. He was quietly laying a blanket on top of her. She looked down to see Sarah curled up against her, breathing easily and quietly. He removed her tennis shoes and pulled the end of the blanket over her feet.

"How is he?" Christine whispered.

The man stood up and gave a sigh of relief. "He'll be alright. Thanks to you. If you hadn't driven him here…"

Christine wasn't sure if he could see her grimace. "I almost didn't." She stared at him for a moment. "I still don't know what the hell is going on."

"Well, you had the right instinct."

She glanced down again at Sarah to make sure she was asleep. "Why are they after her?"

His head shook in the darkness. "I don't know."

She thought about his answer, then changed the subject. "I don't know your name."

He smiled. "Sorry. The name is Avery, Jonathan Avery."

She smiled back and carefully wiggled her hand out from under the blanket. "Christine Rose."

He shook it gently with his rough hand. "Pleased to meet you Christine Rose." He smiled down at Sarah lying against her. "You've done well."

Christine almost scoffed. "I don't know about that. All I've been doing is running without any idea what I'm doing."

She could see Avery shake his head again in the dark. "No, Ms. Rose, what you've done is keep that little girl alive."

Christine looked down again and gently stroked Sarah's head.

"Is there anything I can get you?"

Christine smiled. "How about a couple toothbrushes?"

Avery chuckled quietly. "My pleasure, young lady." He leaned down and patted her leg. "Now get some sleep."

25

Chaplain Wilcox looked out the window as the 737 banked and began its decent into Washington D.C. A sickening feeling welled up inside him when he saw the smoke visible, even from twelve thousand feet up. The sun was rising in the east and casting an eerie shadow across most of the city. Only as they dropped further could he begin to see the site clearly.

Within just minutes of each other, another two cathedrals had been attacked in the middle of the night, and like Saint Patrick's, they had been utterly destroyed. The first target was the Washington National Cathedral in Washington D.C., one of the largest and most historic cathedrals in the world and a national icon that had hosted many U.S. memorial services.

The second collapse was the Old Saint Mary's Church in Philadelphia, the second oldest Roman Catholic church in the city. It was founded in 1763 and had a particularly significant history as a frequent meeting place of the Continental Congress.

Both attacks, just days after Saint Patrick's, had instantly set off a panic among the public that was already spreading across the nation as people woke up to the horrifying news. Fortunately, the loss of life was again small, but even the dozen or so casualties were enough for the media to latch onto. The news channels were quickly billing this as an attack against Christianity. A generalization that the chaplain feared may be too narrow and premature.

With the panic spreading quickly, Wilcox was one of a dozen chaplains asked to help assist in trying to bring any comfort possible to the scene and to the community.

As the plane continued its decent, the chaplain thought about Cheryl Roberts. She had not returned his phone calls, and he was beginning to grow concerned. It was not like her. He hoped he would have a message waiting on his cell phone when he reached the ground.

There was no message waiting, but Wilcox was quickly distracted when he and four other chaplains were whisked away upon landing. Their first stop was an early morning mass at a nearby church where several public figures were giving speeches, including the vice president. This was the first time he had welcomed having politicians at the scene in a long time. The public desperately needed to be calmed.

When they arrived at the nearby Saint John's Church in Lafayette Square, it was a little after 9:00 am, and the place was already a zoo. Located across from the White House, both H and 16th streets were completely blocked off. Over a hundred police officers tried to keep the crowd orderly with barricades while dozens of television reporters and their crews were already set up and broadcasting.

The chaplains were quickly ushered out of their van and into the church's side entrance where a sizable group of parishioners had already gathered and were overflowing through the double doors in front. Many of those inside were sitting in the benches, crying and holding each other while pastors moved through the large crowd hugging and consoling as many as they could reach. Chaplain Wilcox jumped right in.

Hours later, reinforcements arrived and gave some pastors a chance to take a break. Several, including Wilcox, volunteered to go to the National Cathedral to look for anyone else.

When he arrived though, Chaplain Wilcox was dumbfounded. He climbed out of the van and stood staring at the site from a distance, thunderstruck. If he thought Saint Patrick's was horrible, then the National Cathedral was beyond words. In New York, the damage to Saint Patrick's was truly terrible, but here the damage was *total*. It was gone, the entire cathedral was simply gone, leveled completely to the ground.

Everything was smoldering and a thick cloud enveloped everything and everyone within a two block radius. Everyone except the search and rescue teams met and operated out of a large plumbing and parts warehouse four blocks away.

Wilcox sat and held parishioners who had come to see for themselves. Most broke down immediately into tears. He held their hands and prayed, quoting many verses in the bible explaining that God was still watching over them. More than anything else, Wilcox sat and listened.

Eventually, he was able to visit what was left of the Cathedral itself. The smoke rose into the air in giant thick columns, then slowly widening and spreading out overhead. Unlike Saint Patrick's, where some of the walls had remained standing, nothing at the National Cathedral was still vertical. Considered to be the national house of prayer for all people, nothing was left standing at all. Both the famous Gloria in Excelsis Tower and Pilgrim Observation Gallery were reduced to mere rubble.

Wilcox thought about the enormity of the National Cathedral and guessed that it must have taken three or four times the explosive power of Saint Patricks' to do that. The nauseating feeling in his stomach suddenly grew worse as he realized that the attacks were much more powerful this time which meant the possibility that this was *escalating*.

He slowly walked around the perimeter, unable to believe the destruction, even after Saint Patrick's. As he walked around the outside, he watched the rescue crews slowly and methodically turn over pieces of wreckage. It was then that he noticed something. Not far from where he stood, near the remains of the altars, was a man who looked oddly familiar.

Wilcox had a keen memory for faces, but it was not trigged by the man's middle eastern look or his bald head. It was what he was doing.

The chaplain looked around and spotted a man behind him that appeared to be one of the crew's supervisors. He walked over to the man and introduced himself.

"What can I do for you, Chaplain?" The man was polite but curt.

The chaplain pointed back the way he came. "That man over there, near the back. Do you know who he is?"

The man glanced up briefly and squinted his eyes. "Uh…no," he said, looking back down at his clipboard. "Some special investigator I think."

The chaplain nodded, still watching the man. "Did you catch his name?"

The supervisor stopped for a moment and raised an eyebrow. "Mmm…I think his ID said Bases or something. I can't remember exactly."

The chaplain nodded again. "Did he say what he was looking for?"

"Nope."

The supervisor was clearly busy. The chaplain thanked him and walked back toward the wreckage, watching the man. He was sure it was him. He had seen him at the wreckage of Saint Patrick's a few days ago. He remembered the face, but what really seemed curious was why both times he'd seen the man digging in the same area of the church's remains.

26

The sound of running water woke Christine. She slowly opened her eyes, squinting at the ray of sunshine peeking through the dark curtains. Sarah was asleep on top of her again with her tiny hand laying across the bottom of Christine's face. She slowly removed Sarah's hand, trying not to wake her, and set it softly on her own tiny stomach.

Ever so gently, Christine rolled off the couch and onto a knee, standing up and stretching. She followed the noise into the kitchen where she found Avery washing out a dishcloth.

He spoke quietly over his shoulder. "Sorry, I was hoping that wouldn't wake you."

"That's okay," she said with a yawn. "What time is it?" she asked, peering around the two darkened rooms.

"A little past two."

"Wow." She couldn't remember what time she had fallen asleep, but she sure didn't think she would sleep that long.

"How's Glen?" she asked.

Avery smiled. "He's better. Still needs more rest though." He turned off the water and hung the cloth over the faucet. "Would you like some tea?"

"I would love some," she said. She eyed the smaller kitchen window and walked over to it, pulling back the curtain a little. She looked outside at the dense wall of giant pine and cedar trees. Outside and directly beneath the window was a large wooden deck with two chairs and a small table. On the other side of the table was a large pile of firewood. Christine let the curtain fall back over the exposed window and looked closer around the dimly lit kitchen. The place looked rugged and void of any frills, highlighted by the wire rack on the counter with dishes drip drying. To the right was an old gas stove, and next to that was a refrigerator that looked even older. It reminded her of the small, rounded looking fridge her grandmother once had.

In front of her and next to the window was a small wooden table with four matching chairs. She quietly pulled one out and sat down with a creak.

She watched Avery pour the water into a tea cup and wondered where he had gotten the hot water. She didn't remember hearing the whistle of a teapot, and there was certainly no microwave. She could not have been that tired.

He walked across the small room and put her tea down in front of her. Avery then sat in the chair next to her and took a sip from his own cup.

"So," Christine started, curling her fingers through the handle. "What exactly is going on here? Why is everyone after us?"

Avery put his cup down. "They're not after you. They're after Sarah."

Deep down Christine knew that. "She's six-years-old, what could they want with her?"

Avery looked at her curiously. "You tell me."

"I-I don't know," she said looking baffled.

Avery watched her with a dubious look. "I see."

Just then Sarah appeared near the open doorway. Christine waved her over. "Hi Sarah. Come on in."

Sarah walked quietly over and sat down in the chair next to Christine.

"Sarah, this is Mr. Avery. He helped us last night."

Sarah smiled shyly and gave him a polite wave.

He grinned, revealing deep dimples in his old cheeks. "Did you get a good night's sleep Sarah?"

"Yes," she said quietly.

"Would you like something to eat?" he asked.

Sarah glanced at Christine and then back to Avery. "Yes, please."

Avery rose and opened the refrigerator, withdrawing a bowl of fruit. "Here you go." He placed it on the table in front of her.

Sarah grabbed some grapes and started popping them into her mouth while she looked around the room curiously.

They both watched her eat for a minute before Avery spoke again. "Sarah, I was just about to tell Christine that you are both safe here. We're here to help you. So don't you worry, okay?"

"Okay," Sarah replied again politely as she reached for more grapes.

Christine smiled, marveling at Sarah. She had such good manners, better than she'd seen in a child for a long time.

Avery turned to Christine. "Can I get you something?"

She shook her head. "No, thank you, I'll just nibble on some of this fruit."

"Okay then. Let me check on Glen again." With that Avery left the kitchen and strode down the hallway toward the back of the cabin.

Christine remained still, surprised at how happy she was just watching Sarah eat. After a few moments, she broke the silence. "Is Avery a nice man?"

"Mmm hmm." Sarah said with a quick bob of her head. "Very nice."

Christine nodded with relief. She decided to change the subject. "Sarah, are you missing school this week?"

"Yeah," Sarah replied. "My mommy took me out of school. She said we'll have to do a lot of homework to catch up."

"I see." Christine put her cup down and leaned toward her a little. "Sarah, did your mommy tell you why she was taking you out of school?"

Sarah took a break from chewing. "Because of the bad

men."

"What bad men?"

Sarah looked at her innocently. "The bad men that tried to get into our house."

Christine tried to suppress her look of surprise. "They came to your house?"

"Yes. Just like they came to the hotel and the hide house."

"The hide house?" asked Christine. "Oh, you mean the place we were hiding at, the *safe* house?"

"Yeah," she said. "But the bad men keep coming."

Christine sighed. "I know honey." She patted Sarah's hand and was struck by how natural it felt. "But I think we're safe now."

She wanted to get back off the subject. "So, do you have a lot of friends in school?"

"Yes," Sarah said, picking the last grape off a small bunch. "Muna is my best friend. She's black."

Christine's eyes grew wide. "What? She's black?"

"Yeah, her mommy and daddy are black too. They're from South Africa."

Christine laughed a little in relief. "Oh, you mean black. As in, their skin is black. I though you meant…oh never mind."

Sarah looked curiously at Christine. "Do you think I'll be able to go back to school soon?"

Christine felt her heart sadden but forced a smile. "I sure hope so."

Together they finished the fruit in the bowl, and Sarah put it carefully into the sink. They went into the living room and opened the curtains a little, allowing more sun in. Together they folded the two blankets and stacked them neatly on the end of the couch.

Christine looked at Sarah's clothes and then her own. "I guess we're both dressed already."

Sarah giggled and nodded.

They found the remote control to a small television in

the corner of the living room. Christine managed to turn it on and flipped through a few channels with some reception before stopping on a relatively clear cartoon show which Sarah was very excited about. She quickly dropped down and sat on the floor.

Christine stood back and grinned again at the thought of Sarah being able to be a kid, if only for the moment. Christine absently brushed a strand of hair out of her face and realized how dirty her hair felt. She needed to freshen up.

She peered curiously down the hallway. There was a light under one of the doors which she assumed was the room that Glen Smith was resting in. It was across from the bathroom she had used in the middle of the night. Quietly, she stepped inside and closed the door, this time noticing behind it a tub and shower. She was surprised at how clean it was.

Christine turned on the light, and stared into the large mirror above the sink. She looked terrible and needed a shower badly. She turned on the sink faucet and pooled some water in her hands, rinsing her face off several times. She then took the band out of her thick, dark, red hair and let it fall forward. There was no brush, so she did her best by running her fingers through it and pulling it tight into a ponytail, doubling up the band to secure it.

She already felt better, but this wasn't the time for a complete overhaul. She reached for the door but stopped when she looked at the mirrored medicine cabinet on the side wall. She looked around instinctively and then reached for the cabinet door, gently tugging it open and waiting for a loud squeak that never came. Curious, she looked inside to find it almost empty. Only the bottom shelf had anything on it: a razor with blades, a few sticks of deodorant, and some aspirin. Strangely disappointed, she began to shut it when a noise outside in the hallway made her jump. It sounded like the other door had been opened abruptly. She quickly closed the cabinet and double-checked herself in the mirror. She then casually turned the door knob and pulled the door open.

She saw that the other door was cracked open. She looked up and down the hall curiously. Avery must have already reached the kitchen.

Christine quietly stepped across the hall and positioned herself in front of the small opening in the second door. She leaned in and put one eye close enough to look through.

She gasped! Inside, she could see the figure of Glen Smith, and he was standing up. Christine slipped and pitched forward, accidentally pushing the door open, and realized she had been helped by Avery who had silently appeared behind her in the hall. She abruptly stumbled into the room to find Smith standing in front of a mirror, wearing a long sleeve shirt which was unbuttoned down the middle.

If Christine had been startled at seeing Smith on his own two feet, what she saw when he whirled around truly frightened her. The skin on his side looked smooth and showed no sign of injury, much less a bullet hole.

"Oh my god!" Christine cried, trying to back up. "How? How?" She bumped into Avery who was still behind her.

Avery put his hands slowly on her shoulders. "Easy, Christine," he said in a calm voice. "Take it easy now."

Christine was petrified. She kept staring at Smith and slowly tried to back up and around Avery. "My god, w-what *are* you?" She turned and realized that Avery was between her and the door. It didn't look like he had any intention of letting her out.

Avery spoke again. "Easy. It's not what it looks like."

"No?!" Christine shot back. "Well, it looks like he was shot and bleeding to death last night, and now it looks like he's pretty...*unshot*!"

Smith stopped trying to hide his abdomen and straightened.

"Okay, well maybe it *is* what it looks like," Avery said with a weak smile, trying to break the ice.

Christine turned and made a deliberate effort to get past him and through the door, but Avery stayed in front of her.

"Don't do anything rash, just let us explain." He looked in her eyes. "There is a lot for *everyone* to explain here."

Christine gave him a suspicious look. "What is that supposed to mean?"

Avery shook his head. "I mean there's a lot happening here. Let's not freak out." He held his hands up in front of himself as a calming gesture. "You're in no danger here."

Christine stared at him and then at Smith. She held a finger up and motioned to the door. "Just let me say something." Avery stepped aside while Christine called down the hall. "Sarah, are you okay out there?"

"Yes, I'm fine," Sarah's voice called back.

Christine swallowed and looked back at both men. "Okay...explain!"

Smith nodded and stepped away from the mirror. "Okay, we'll explain everything. But first you need to tell us something."

"What?" she asked.

Smith glanced at Avery. "What is it about Sarah? What's so special that people are trying to kill her over?"

"It's clear that you know," Avery added, before she could speak.

Christine thought about the question. She had already lied once about it, and she was a terrible liar; she knew that. But if she was going to talk, she didn't want to be the one to do it first. Yet, she had a feeling they were going to tell her a lot more than she was about to tell them. "Okay," she relented. "But then you tell me what the hell is going on."

Smith looked in her green eyes. "Agreed."

Christine took a deep breath. "She can see things," she said. "Sarah, I mean. She can see *inside* people."

Smith and Avery looked at each other again. "What do you mean?"

"I think she can see people's auras, like…their energy. And it tells her what kind of person they are inside."

The men stared at her for a long time. "Auras?" Smith asked.

"Yeah, you know, like a person's…reflection or essence or something," Christine explained.

"And what does she see?" Avery asked.

"She says she sees *colors*. And they mean different things."

"Colors," Smith repeated.

Christine nodded. "Colors. She said that children are white, and adults are yellow, orange, and red. Yellow is good, orange not so good, and red apparently means you're bad…evil or something."

"Is that all?" asked Avery.

She took another deep breath. "No. She also said that the color black…means someone is going to die."

Again, both men looked at each other curiously. After a long moment, Smith nodded and looked at Christine. "Okay, our turn," he said, leaning against the footboard of the bed behind him. "You may want to sit down for this."

"I'm fine," she said with a smirk, folding her arms in front of her.

"To begin with, my name is not Smith."

Christine raised her eyebrows. "You're not Smith?"

He shook his head.

"Are you at least Glen?"

"No." He shook his head again. "My real name is David Rand."

Christine did not say anything.

"And," he continued, "I'm here for Sarah."

"What?"

He frowned. "What I mean is, I'm here to help her.

To protect her."

"Well, I guess that's kind of obvious."

"No, that's not what I mean. I mean I'm here to protect her. From whoever is doing this."

"Yeah," she said sarcastically. "I understand that."

Rand sighed. "I'm not sure that you do." He considered his words carefully. "I'm not exactly *like* you."

Christine's expression became confused again. "And what does that mean?"

It was his turn to give her a sarcastic look. He pulled back his shirt and she looked down at his muscular stomach. "How many people do you know that heal like this?"

Christine's mouth dropped open as she finally understood what he was trying to say. "Oh…my…god!" she gasped. "You're an alien!"

Rand glanced at Avery and rolled his eyes. "No, I'm NOT an alien."

"Then what are you?" she said, shaking her head.

"Christine," Rand said. "When I say I'm here to protect Sarah, I mean I've been *sent* here to protect her. Someone is trying to kill her, and I'm here to make sure that doesn't happen."

Christine stood motionless, staring at Rand. "Sent? Sent by whom?"

Rand was surprised by her question. "By God."

27

One of the officers poked his head in the door to find Deputy Inspector Kim Darlington sifting through a large manila folder. As Deputy Inspector, Darlington was in charge of the 19th Precinct in New York and was frequently asked by the district attorney's office to run through cases when they found discrepancies that might weaken the case. It was their last chance to tie up loose ends and make the case as strong as possible before going in front of the judge. The one on her desk was one of those cases.

"Hey Kim," the officer said. "Got a call for you on line four."

"Who is it?" Darlington asked without looking up.

"It's Chaplain Wilcox."

Darlington looked up, considering whether to take the call. "Okay," she said, leaving the folder carefully in place. "I'll take it."

The officer nodded and ducked back out.

With an almost irritated look, Darlington picked up the phone and pressed the 4 button. "Hi Chaplain."

"Hello Kim, how are you?"

"Coming from all directions, just like usual." The chaplain had a way of getting people to put down their pens for him, partly because he was so well-liked, and partly because everyone was afraid of picking up bad karma. "What can I do for you?" she asked.

"I don't know if you've heard, but I've been sent down to D.C. to help after the bombing here."

Darlington glanced back to her folder. "I did hear something about that. How's it going?"

"Well," he replied, "it's a tough situation as you can

imagine."

"I sure can."

"The reason I'm calling," he continued, "is I was hoping to get your help with something."

"Sure, Padre," she mused and turned another page in the folder.

"If memory serves, I believe you have a friend at the FBI."

"That's right," Darlington replied. "In the Boston branch."

"Well Kim, I'm wondering if I might get your help in trying to get something expedited. I have some pictures I need to submit for analysis and was hoping we could get it turned around quickly."

"I can give it a try," Darlington answered. "What kind of pictures?"

The chaplain cleared his throat on the other end. "This may sound a little strange, but they're pictures of someone here I'd like to find out more about."

Darlington stopped perusing her folder and looked up, thinking. "I take it this is someone you can't ask, or no one there knows?"

"That is correct," the chaplain answered. "It's someone on the investigation team."

"Doesn't the investigation team require clearance?"

"Yes, they do," he replied "That's where it gets a little curious. He has clearance, but evidently it's a very high clearance."

"Hmm…" Darlington thought out loud. "So, this guy has some special clearance and no one knows who he is?"

"Exactly," the chaplain said. "I managed to snap some pictures of him on my phone, and I'm hoping your friend at the FBI can quickly run them through their system and see if they can get a visual match on him."

Darlington shrugged. "Like I said, I'll give it a shot. You want to email the pictures over to me?"

"Of course. I will do that right now. Thank you."

"My pleasure, Chaplain." She was just about to hang up when he interrupted.

"Oh Kim, one more thing," he said. "Have you seen Cheryl Roberts lately?"

"Mmm…I saw her a couple days ago. If I'm not mistaken, she had today off. Why?"

"Well," he said, "I've left a number of messages for her in the last couple days but haven't heard back."

Darlington frowned. "That's strange. She's pretty responsive. I'll look into it and see if anyone has talked to her."

"Wonderful, thank you Kim. I do appreciate your help."

"No problem, Padre," she said. "I'll give you a ring when I hear something back."

She hung up the phone and turned back to her case.

Darlington was still engrossed in the folder twenty minutes later when someone knocked on her door.

"Come in," she answered with a hint of exasperation.

"Deputy Inspector?" asked a large man as he opened the door.

"Yes."

Ramirez took a small step inside. "Hi, my name is Mike Ramirez. I'm part of the computer forensic team downtown. Am I bothering you?"

Darlington inhaled and leaned back in her chair. She shook her head and motioned for Ramirez to sit down, which he did.

"I'm trying to find officers Griffin and Buckley. I was told you might know where they are."

Darlington furrowed her brow. "You know I haven't seen them. I know they had to drive to Washington D.C. a couple days ago." Now curious, she leaned forward and looked out through her glass door. She could see both of their desks on the far side of the room, but both were empty. "Strange, they should be here. Did you ask the

officer at the front desk downstairs? Maybe they're sick."
Both sick at the same time? She didn't believe that as soon as it rolled off her tongue.

"Yes, I did. The woman downstairs didn't know anything either," Ramirez answered.

Darlington was getting an odd feeling. "Why are you looking for them?"

"They came to see me just before they left for D.C. It was about their case. I had some more information for them, but I can't get a hold of either one of them on their cell phones. I sent one text to Officer Griffin a few days ago that went through, but everything I've sent after that has bounced back." He leaned forward in his chair. "I took the liberty of looking at the system, and it looks like both of their cell phones may be turned off."

"Both of them?"

"It looks like it," Ramirez said. "I believe Officer Griffin was having a problem with his phone before they left, so I thought maybe that was the reason. But checking the carrier's system logs, it looks like his service was successfully ported to a new phone he purchased just north of D.C."

Darlington looked at him curiously. "How did you get access to the carrier's system logs?"

He gave her a quick wink. "I'd rather not say."

Darlington leaned forward and dialed a number on her phone. She left it on speakerphone. A voice quickly answered. "Personnel, 19th Precinct."

"Hi Tina, it's Kim upstairs," Darlington announced.

"Oh, hi Kim."

"Tina, is there any time or special hours submitted for Griffin or Buckley in the last few days?"

Tina paused for a moment. "Nooo…I haven't seen anything come over."

"They had to drive down to D.C. a few days ago to see someone at the State Department. Do you remember when they came back from that?"

"I don't." Tina went silent as she looked again. "Oh wait, I have a note here. Looks like we got a call from that State Department office saying our guys missed their appointment. Said they would have to reschedule."

Darlington looked across her desk at Ramirez. Something didn't feel right.

28

Oh boy. Christine thought to herself. *These guys have gone off the deep end!*

Rand watched Christine take a step backward. "You're not a believer," he said matter-of-factly.

"In God?" she said. "Oh sure I am, of course. Although, I haven't been to church in a while."

"But you don't believe me?" Rand asked.

She looked over her shoulder at Avery and stepped away toward the other wall so she could see them both. "Look, maybe you have some special genetic thing going on here, but I think that's quite a leap from, you know, *being sent by God.*"

"I see," Rand said. "Are you sure about Sarah's gift?"

"Her gift," Christine said, a little taken back. "Meaning what, the aura thing?" She shrugged. "I can only believe what she tells me, but she saved our lives by keeping us off an elevator that fell eight stories. And she knew what was about to happen in that McDonald's. She also tried to save my cat."

Rand lowered his head slightly but kept his eyes on her. "Christine, I think you need to prepare yourself for the possibility that what Sarah sees is something entirely different than what you think."

"What do you mean?" She watched Rand and Avery exchange looks again. They were doing that a lot.

"What Sarah sees," Rand said, "is not an aura or some energy field. What Sarah is able to see is a person's *soul.*"

Christine did not reply. She simply stood there, stunned and staring at Rand. Eventually, she blinked and looked at Avery who made it clear that she was the only one startled by what he said.

"What did you say?"

"It's not an aura," Rand repeated.

"You said it's their *soul?*" she asked slowly.

"That's right."

Christine continued to stare at him. She didn't know what to think, but she was coming around to the conclusion that even though these men came to her rescue, they were nutty, to put it mildly. She felt her brain shift into a different gear. *How do I get out of here?*

Rand watched her calmly. He expected this was going to be difficult for her. It sounded like she was not religious which didn't help matters. She was going to need some extra convincing.

"Can I," she started, "just chat with Sarah for a few moments?"

"Of course." Avery took a small step to the side and opened the door. "Sarah!" he called. "Can you please come here for a minute? Christine's eyes opened wide. That was not what she had in mind.

A moment later, small footsteps could be heard coming down the hall. When she reached the door, Avery opened it up wide, and when Sarah looked at everyone, she seemed less surprised to see Rand than Christine was. Instinctively, Sarah crossed the room and stood in front of her.

"You okay?" Christine asked and patted her shoulder.

"Mmm…hmm."

"Sarah," Rand began, "do you recognize me?"

Sarah looked up at Christine with her big eyes. "What does recog-nice mean?"

Christine smiled. "It means, do you remember him?"

Sarah nodded. "He came to the safe-" she wrinkled her nose. "What did you call it again?"

"The safe house."

"Oh yeah," said Sarah "He came there. And to McDonald's too."

Rand smiled. "Sarah. We wanted to talk to you, about

how you can see people in your special way."

Sarah titled her head, unsure. "My mommy said I wasn't supposed to talk about it to other people."

Rand nodded. "We understand. But we think this is a time when your mom would have wanted you to share with us."

Sarah silently looked up at Christine who put her second hand on Sarah's shoulder and nodded back.

"Okay," was all she said.

This time Rand looked at Christine. "Sarah, what do you see when you look at Christine?"

"A yellow shadow."

"Can you show us where?" he asked.

Sarah turned and looked at Christine. "It's all over, but mostly here," she said, circling her hand in front of Christine's chest.

"And what do you see when you look at Mr. Avery?" Rand asked.

Sarah looked over at Avery. "He's yellow too."

"And yellow is good?" Rand asked.

"Yes."

Rand spoke to Sarah again but was still looking at Christine. "And Sarah," he said. "What do you see when you look at me?"

Sarah's expression became nervous. She looked at Rand but quickly turned back to Christine.

Christine looked down at Sarah supportively. "It's okay Sarah, you can tell us."

Sarah slowly turned back to face Rand. "He doesn't have one at all."

29

The cabin abruptly bounced as the jet's wheels touched the runway, and the high pitch of the engine's reverse thrust shrieked loudly outside, slowing the aircraft.

As the plane slowed and began to taxi, Aaron Bazes remained slouched in his leather seat, looking out the window at the bright lights of Tel Aviv. The last several days had painted a grim picture, and he was now the unfortunate messenger. This was a trip home he was not looking forward to making.

The new Learjet 85 passed the terminal's main gates and proceeded to a smaller private section of the airport. When the doors opened, Bazes reluctantly stood and walked down the empty aisle to the front of the cabin where the attendant handed him his bag.

"Is there anything else I can get you, sir?" the attendant asked.

Bazes never heard him.

The private gate afforded him a distinctly better experience traveling in and out of the country. To begin with, it was spacious and plush and void of any security personnel whatsoever. In fact, the entire building was designed for and dedicated to just a handful of people, and Bazes was one of them. He passed only one person on his way to the driver waiting for him outside, and that one person was the sole customs agent who sat at the desk as more of a formality than anything else.

The agent bowed his head slightly as Bazes approached and stopped on the other side of his desk. He withdrew and swiped his Ambassador passport under the scanner. He then placed his hand on the small, brightly lit screen as it passed up and down, capturing a high resolution image of his hand print. With that, he quietly walked down a long, well-decorated and immaculate hallway into the chilly air outside.

The dark underground corridor was very old and lined in rough limestone with a finer limestone serving as the exterior finish. It was the same stone used to construct the Egyptian pyramids. And while the stonework were of similar age, the difference was that everyone had seen the pyramids, but only a handful of people on the entire planet knew this hallway and the chambers ahead had ever even existed.

Bazes' footsteps echoed as he walked calmly down the dimly lit corridor. At the end, it opened into a larger room. In the middle of the room was a giant, six-pointed star carved into the floor and emblazoned with gold. Bazes stopped before the circle and closed his eyes. After a short prayer, he stepped inside and smoothly slid down onto his hands and knees. Without interrupting the motion, he continued down until his lips touched the cold floor. He silently rose and rocked back onto his knees before falling forward and pressing his lips to the floor again. His twelfth time was as slow and deliberate as his first, symbolizing the original Twelve Tribes.

Bazes slowly raised his head and looked at the glass structure before him. Standing at nearly ten cubic feet and made of thick, clear glass, it was vacuum sealed and maintained at a perfect temperature of 55 degrees Fahrenheit and zero percent humidity. Before the structure, engraved in the stone floor and also lined in gold was a single sentence in Hebrew.

"...for my house will be called a house of prayer for all nations." (Isaiah 56:7)

Behind the glass stood a large, cube-shaped, wooden box and behind it a thick canvas fabric made of cotton, layered neatly atop dozens of long, wooden staves bundled on the floor. Beside the folded cloth was a chest made of ancient acacia wood with a bronze cover, and next to that, sat a heavier cover made of solid gold with two angelic statues at either end.

Bazes stared at the artifacts and finally closed his eyes once more, dropping down and touching his forehead to the golden lettering.

What stood before Bazes was one of the most sacred artifacts in all of human history, moved when necessary, but hidden and protected for thousands of years. Together the pieces made up the fabled *Tabernacle of Moses*. The sacred place where God chose to meet his people during their forty-year wandering in the desert. On the floor behind the glass was the legendary Atonement Cover on which Moses stood to communicate directly with God and which served as the lid to the Ark of the Covenant.

Bazes sat in a chair with his hands folded on an ancient wooden table before him. Around him were twelve men dressed in Techelet blue, hand woven Talliths with golden tassels along the arms. They were seated in a semicircular arc around Bazes, six on each side. Few people knew who these men were, yet they were secretly some of the most powerful men on the planet. Their faces were just barely recognizable in the dim candlelight, but it didn't matter; Bazes knew each voice and seat position by heart.

"We are happy to have you back," the man in front of him began.

"Thank you," Bazes replied in a low voice.

"What did you find?"

Bazes lowered his head gently, dreading what he was about to say. "It is him."

All twelve men looked at each other grimly.

"Are you certain?"

Bazes nodded. "I am certain."

"How do you know this?"

"Inscriptions were left in the cathedrals. They were not difficult to find. I believe they were left for us. A message, to mock us. I also had some traces analyzed and they all matched. The type, issuance, and grade are all the same."

"What did the inscriptions say?"

"*Prepare*," Bazes frowned.

"What about the written records?"

Bazes nodded. "It took some time and the records appeared to be altered, but the details and signatures are unmistakable."

"Does anyone else know?"

"I don't believe so," Bazes said shaking his head. "We are the first."

An old man to the speaker's right lamented, "What do you think he will do?"

"I do not know for certain. I only have fears."

The old man nodded. "Then what do you fear he will do?"

Bazes glanced around at some of the other men before looking forward again. "Something very terrible." *If they didn't like what he just told them, they were going to like what he said next even less.*

30

Rand opened the front door and quietly stepped out onto the front deck. Christine was sitting in one of the chairs, her hands propped up on her knees and covering her mouth.

She said she needed to be alone for a little while, so Rand was careful to keep his distance. He stopped several feet behind her. There were no sounds around them except for the breeze moving through the trees.

"As you can probably guess, I'm a little freaked out right now," she said without turning around.

Rand said nothing.

After another long silence, she lowered her face into her hands and shook her head. "Why would he do this to us?" She stood up and looked at Rand then turned and looked in through the kitchen window. She could see Avery and Sarah sitting across from each other in the small living room. Sarah was watching the board very carefully while Avery taught her how to play checkers. "What god would do this to *her*?"

Again he said nothing.

"What god would put her through this…horror? Why would he surround that perfect little girl with nothing but death and destruction? Why would he kill her mother right in front of her?" She shook her head. "What kind of god is *that*?"

Rand took a deep breath. "It can be hard to understand."

"Oh please!" she snapped. "Spare me the *God works in mysterious ways* dribble! I've seen my share of cruelty from the same god who supposedly loves his children!"

Rand looked at her curiously.

"That's right," she said. "I went to church, I know the scripture. He loved us so much that he put us here to prove ourselves, by worshiping him. What kind of free choice is that?" She looked at Rand accusingly. "Tell me, who creates a universe, an insanely complex planet, and then the human race and everything else, just so he can watch them spend their tiny lives worshipping him? I mean how much more ridiculous could an explanation be?"

"It's not that easy," Rand replied quietly.

"Not that easy?" she scoffed. "Not that easy but still easy enough to put an unimaginable gift into a beautiful little girl and torment her at every turn. What a wonderful test of our faith!"

Rand shrugged. "Well, that's one belief."

"Yeah, well I DON'T believe it!"

"I can see that."

"And then-" Christine said. "And then he picks someone like me. Of all the people in the world, he picks *me.*"

"I think he made a good choice."

"He couldn't have made a worse choice!" she said angrily. "Geez, you could throw a dart blindfolded and hit someone better." She turned and looked back out at the trees.

Rand frowned. "Why do you say that?"

"Because it's true!" she cried. "Sarah's not alive because of me, she's alive *in spite* of me. I'm not a fighter. I'm not tough. I can't protect her like you."

"She responds to you," Rand said. "She needs someone like you, someone not just to protect her body, but someone who can help protect her heart. To make sure she comes out of this okay."

It was then that Christine began to cry. She wiped the tears away as they ran down her cheeks. "You don't know what you're saying."

"Look at me, Christine," Rand said. "This is not some

joke, or some twisted irony, and God does not look down from a pearly throne deciding who to bless each day. Nor does he guide every step and every decision that we make. He gives us what he can and has faith in *us* just as we have faith in him."

"What does that mean?" she sniffed.

"What I'm saying is, this is not about the things people wish they had and then pray for, or about helping a friend who might be down on their luck. This is a *fight*! God created a place of hope in a sea of darkness and evil, and he is locked in a struggle for every second of every day. He fights endlessly for this world he created and the survival of his children living upon it, against forces that want nothing more than to destroy it all." He glared at her. "He chose *you* to help him."

Christine looked dumbstruck. "Why didn't he pick someone better?"

Rand's expression showed her he didn't understand her question.

"I told you; I used to believe," she said. "And I was devout. But he destroyed it all and left me to pick up the pieces. *God* showed me just how cruel he could be."

Rand watched as Christine began to walk away and then turned around to face him.

"I was sixteen." She closed her eyes for a moment and took a deep breath. "God, I was so young and so stupid." Her eyes were quickly welling up. "One night I asked my parents to drive me over to the house where my friend was babysitting so I could help her. But they couldn't because they were both sick. So I begged my dad to take me over. I kept begging him. And even though he felt terrible, he finally agreed to drive me."

Tears began running down Christine's face. "But I lied to him. We were babysitting, but we were doing it so some boys could come over to meet us. And my dad, as sick as he was, drove me all the way across town. Not knowing that I was lying to him the whole time." Her voice began to shudder. "I remember how hard he was coughing while he drove me. And on his way home... he was killed in a car accident!" Christine lost control and started sobbing.

Rand took a step closer but didn't speak..

Christine shook her head and backed up. The sobs kept her from speaking. She quickly pushed past him, ran down the wooden steps, and headed for the trees.

He watched her run to a giant pine tree and rest her head against the trunk, crying into it.

Christine slowly began to regain her emotions when she heard Rand's footsteps in the grass behind her. She sniffed and wiped her eyes before turning around.

"I killed my father," she said, her voice still trembling. "And the guilt has haunted me every day since. Every single day. I not only lost my father, but I *widowed* my mother. And you know what? Those boys never even showed up." Her voice began to quiver again, but she forced it back. She took a deep breath and looked up at the tree above her. "I must have cried for a whole year. The guilt was so bad I couldn't even go on a date without breaking down. Even in my late twenties, when I was finally in a relationship, I would cry constantly. And children," she said rolling her tear filled eyes. "Every time I saw a child, I saw my dad, sick but with a glint of pride in his eyes...for his daughter, the babysitter." She looked directly at Rand. "Now do you see what a terrible choice he made? Why would God do that to poor Sarah? Why would he give her someone like me?"

Rand thought about her question. "Sometimes we don't need to understand, we just need to believe."

She looked past him. "You know I've never told that to anyone. I can't believe I told you."

Rand was quiet for a long time before speaking. "You were supposed to."

"What?"

She gave him a puzzled look, and Rand cleared his throat. "Listen to me," he said. "Since I was born, I knew what I was here to do. From my earliest memories I knew who I was. I knew I would find Sarah, and I spent my whole life preparing for it, and training, every single day. Constantly doing another new exercise to get stronger. Nothing else mattered to me. And nothing else matters now." He took a step closer. "All that time I knew things. Not everything, but some. Who I was, who God was." He frowned at that. "Not what the churches preach today, but who he *really* is. I also knew what Sarah looked like and where I would find her."

Rand looked into Christine's eyes as she sniffed and wiped her nose.

"But there was something else that I knew, one piece of information I never understood. I never knew why I was supposed to know it. It never made any sense. Until right now."

She tilted her head, curiously.

"Christine. You did not kill your father."

She was suddenly startled, trying to understand if she heard him right. "What?!"

"You did not kill your father."

Her expression changed to bewilderment. "Wh-why are you saying-" She took a step back as Rand moved toward her. "What are you doing?"

He looked at her sternly and followed her as she backed up even farther. "Listen to me, Christine. Even without that accident, your father would have died less than five months later. He would have died of a *heart attack.*"

Christine gasped. She just stared at him, shocked and unable to breathe.

Rand did not stop. "Your father's name was Louis Richard Rose, wasn't it?" She didn't answer. "Wasn't it?" he repeated. "He was born in October of 1935." Christine began sobbing again. "He was a craftsman, and he loved you. He loved you, but there was nothing you could have done to save him. He was going home, with or without that accident."

Christine looked up at Rand. Tears were streaming down her face. "No, it was me, it was because of me!"

Rand grabbed her shoulders. "No, it wasn't. That accident was bad luck. God cannot control *everything*. It was just bad luck!"

Christine's wobbling legs gave out, and she fell just an inch before Rand grabbed her and held her up with his own arms. She finally let her head fall forward into his chest and continued to sob uncontrollably.

It took almost twenty minutes for Christine to cry it out. Exhausted, she leaned her head back and looked at him, her face covered in tears. "Are you…sure?"

Rand nodded. "I'm sure. It was not your fault, and none of that guilt belonged to you. I was meant to tell you this. You must believe me."

She closed her eyes and let her head fall softly back against his chest. "All that time…and all that guilt."

"It never belonged to you," he whispered.

31

Christine sat on the ground cross-legged on a thick layer of pine needles. Rand sat across from her with his back leaning against the tree. One leg was propped up in front of him while his other lay flat on the ground.

Christine spoke in a low voice. "So are you immortal?"

Rand smirked. "Uh, no."

"Then how did you…" she trailed off, pointing at his stomach.

"I heal quickly," he shrugged. "One of my assets."

"*One* of your assets? You have others?"

"I also age slower. One of the side effects of the healing."

She tried to keep from rolling her eyes. It was beginning to feel like for every answer Rand gave, he was creating three new questions. "So why can't Sarah see your soul? Or your shadow?" she asked with an understanding smile.

Rand inhaled deeply. "Because I don't have one."

"Excuse me?"

"I'm not like you, Christine. Not exactly. You are one of his *children*, and he loves his children more than anything. So much that he gave all of you the most precious thing he could, a soul." Rand looked around at the trees. Millions of green pine needles swayed and seemed to glitter from the soft breeze. "You don't know how lucky you all are."

"Are you saying you're not one of his children?" she asked.

He shook his head. "No, I'm a soldier. Sent here to help him fight."

"Fight who?"

Rand nodded back toward the cabin. "To protect Sarah. He gave her a gift, and I'm here to protect it."

"For how long?" Christine asked.

"Not much longer. Soon it will happen."

"What will happen?"

"My reason for being here," Rand replied. "All of the years of preparation. All of the training. There will soon come a point when she needs me the most."

Christine frowned, trying to understand. "And then what?"

At this question, a genuine smile spread across Rand's face. "Then I get to become one of you."

"One of us?"

"I will be awarded a soul," he said. "It's what all of us wish for."

"All of who?" she said.

"Those of us who are sent to fight, the *lochem*."

"Lochem*?*"

"God's warriors."

Christine was surprised again. "You mean there's more of you?"

"Not now, not today. But there have been before," Rand explained. "At different times we have been sent, to fight in your world, in the flesh."

"And this is one of those times," Christine finished.

"Yes."

Christine stared at him and finally nodded. She took a deep breath and looked around at the tall grass. The silence was deafening and peaceful at the same time. She had never realized how much noise she'd grown accustomed to while living in a city. The difference was incredible.

She looked at Rand with a hint of regret. "I guess you were pretty upset then, when we ran out of the house last night and took off in the car."

She was surprised when Rand smiled. "Well, it wasn't my preferred choice, but it did show me how well you think under pressure."

Christine rolled her eyes. "Uh yeah, most people refer to that as *panic*."

"No, it wasn't," Rand replied. "It may feel like you panicked, but you would be surprised how many people would have simply frozen. Mental paralysis in an emergency is what gets most people killed. But you were thinking. And you knew enough to realize that you didn't have any good options available to you, other than to flee. So you took it." The admiration was apparent in his voice. "You and Sarah are both alive because of it. Don't underestimate the abilities you have within yourself. You were selected for a reason. Embrace it."

Christine opened the front door and stepped through with Rand following closely behind. Sarah looked at Christine excitedly and ran to her.

"I won! I won!" she squealed.

Christine looked at the checker board where Avery was still sitting. He looked up from his chair, impressed. "She's sharp," he said, standing up. "Beat me fair and square. And that time I was trying."

Sarah squeezed Christine then looked up and noticed her red face. "Are you okay?"

Christine smiled down at Sarah and gave her a giant squeeze back. "I'm good honey." She glanced at Rand. "I'm really, really good."

Sarah was still looking up. "Can we go outside?"

Christine looked at Rand and Avery with raised eyebrows. "That okay?"

Avery opened a panel on the wall, not far from the door. There were over a dozen lights tied into the panel displaying the status of various sensors all surrounding the cabin. They were all green. He nodded. "Sure. But please stay close."

Sarah giggled with excitement and instantly pulled Christine back out the front door. Rand closed it quietly behind them. He looked at Avery who was watching the girls through the window.

"She gonna be okay?" Avery asked.

"I think so." Rand turned and looked through the window too. "She's a lot tougher than she thinks."

Outside Sarah and Christine stomped through the tall grass and approached an old bird bath, long forgotten and dry and covered in dark mold.

Sarah examined it curiously. "What's this?"

"It's called a bird bath," Christine explained. "You fill it with water so the birds come and drink out of it. This one is old and dirty though."

Sarah looked at her eagerly. "Could we clean it for them?"

"We'll see," Christine answered in her best noncommittal tone. She watched Sarah trace her finger along a small stone flower, one of the only clean areas on the small statue. She cleared her voice. "Um, Sarah?" she said.

Sarah looked up at her.

Christine took a deep breath. "Listen, I know things have been…hard. Especially what happened the other night at McDonald's." She frowned trying to find the right words. "Are you…okay?"

Sarah considered the question and then nodded her head, looking back down at the bird bath.

"I mean," Christine continued, "some bad things happened." This was not coming out the way she had hoped. "Do you want to, you know, talk about it?"

Sarah stared at her for a moment and then gave her an innocent shrug. "They were bad men. They were reds."

"Well, I don't know if all reds are supposed to die," Christine offered.

Sarah shook her head. "They were *really* red."

Christine cocked her head and thought to herself. *Did that mean all of the colors had different degrees or shades?* She suddenly realized that she didn't know what to say next. Fortunately Sarah spotted a tree over her shoulder, with branches close to the ground.

"Can we play on the tree?" she asked without actually waiting for a response. Instead she ran to the tree and grabbed the lowest limb, but she could not get any higher. "Can you lift me up?"

"Sure," Christine said, "but don't go too high."

Slowly and determinedly, Sarah climbed up several more branches and then stopped to peer out.

Something beeped and Christine looked around wondering what made the noise. She realized what the familiar sound was and felt around the pockets of her pants. Reaching into one of her front pockets, she pulled out her phone.

I thought I turned this off, she said to herself. She then realized that the power button must have somehow gotten depressed while she was sitting on the ground. Looking at the display she could see there was no cellular signal, but not surprisingly the phone still managed to receive a text message. She was a little startled when she saw who it was from.

Christine, where are you? Are you okay? Danny

She grinned. It was almost beginning to feel that the whole world was after them. Reading Danny's message set her mind a little at ease that everything, eventually, just might turn out okay. Still grinning she typed a response.

Yes. Am fine. Thx. Just not in the area now. Will call you soon.

She hit send and watched the screen confirm transmission. With a feeling of growing optimism, she turned the phone off and dropped it back into her pocket. Christine smiled back up at Sarah who was trying to entice

a small squirrel with a pine cone.
    It was a good day.

32

Zahn sat comfortably in his oversized seat aboard the Boeing 757, watching the television affixed to the wall in front of him. To his right sat Kia Sarat and behind him nearly two dozen more of his staff.

Zahn watched his boss, the secretary of state, give a speech on the latest bombings in D.C. and Philadelphia. The impassioned speech was filled with platitudes and empty promises, just as they always were. Zahn could not think of a more worthless politician and stopped listening after he heard the fifth promise for *justice*. However, even with his disgust, Zahn remained somewhat elated. Had it not been for his boss, all of this would have been significantly harder.

He switched channels to another program and listened to the anchors discuss the news that the Pope himself was planning to visit the United States in a couple days as a gesture of faith and solidarity. The man and woman on TV were tripping over themselves to agree on what an important gesture it was to the US citizenry.

He looked at his watch and pulled out a small phone he had purchased in Dubai. He powered it on and waited until he could turn on the GPS feature. After a few minutes, it finally reported them flying just south of Shanghai.

Zahn typed a short text message on the phone and sent it. He then turned to Sarat, who had intentionally cleared his throat after reading a message off his own phone.

"We've received communication from Rose. We're working on their exact location now," Sarat reported.

"Well, that wasn't too difficult." Zahn said, leaning his chair back a little.

"It was a good idea."

"It's time to reign them in. Send everyone in the area. I don't want another hole for them to slip through."

Sarat nodded.

Zahn looked down when the phone in his hand made a chirping sound, indicating the receipt of a new message. He opened the small window and read it.

Systems locked and loaded. Virus in place and verified. Bots waiting for command.

Zahn pursed his lips and nodded approvingly. He remembered finding Ron Tran. Finding someone who wanted to change the world was difficult enough, but finding someone who also had the skills to do it, and was a world class hacker, was far more difficult. So much so that it caused him to consider whether perhaps fate had somehow intervened.

Zahn was surprised at how smart Tran had turned out to be after their first meeting. A little young, but he had a firm grip on what made the world tick, who benefited, and how the elites would do almost anything to keep it that way.

Zahn typed a message back.

How many bots?

Tran's reply was short.

Almost 7,000,000.

Zahn smiled. He was not as tech savvy as he would have liked to be. Having to immerse himself deep within the political system in order to pull this off was hard enough, but Tran made up for it and then some.

In fact, knowing what was involved, Zahn was a little surprised Tran was able to actually deliver. Seven million compromised computers, more than he had promised, waiting for the command to do his bidding. He was impressed. Seven million, all standing at the ready to carry out what was going to be the largest 'head fake' in human history. It was enough to make Zahn grin from ear to ear.

Sarat watched Zahn's exchange with Tran with interest. Sarat had never liked Tran. He was a young kid, or *bache*, amongst an entire generation addicted to self-servitude. But he also knew that Tran was an integral part of the plan.

Sarat thought of how he and Tran could not have come from more different experiences. Tran was raised in a world of gluttonous technological wonder, while Sarat was raised in the deserts of Afghanistan trying to survive. He wondered how Tran would have turned out after being told since the day he was born, as Sarat and his friends were, that the Russians had killed their fathers. To be born and bred for hatred and revenge, and dream of the day they could strike deep into the heart of the very beast that had robbed them of ever knowing their own fathers.

In the end though, it was not just hatred that drove him. It was also desire. Desire to rise from his humble, even desperate beginnings, to greatness. He wanted to destroy the monster that had consumed the world and to become a king in the process.

Zahn ended the text exchange with a single word and closed the phone.

Begin.

Zahn turned his attention back to Sarat. "Continue."

"Argentina is ready."

"Excellent." *It was getting close*, he thought.

"Another thing," Sarat said. "Your boss sent you an email congratulating you on the progress in Dubai."

Zahn almost laughed. He wondered how many trips and "talks" he'd made representing the country in the last several years. The State Department was the perfect organization to use. They had tremendous clout in Washington, although he always found that rather laughable. They thought as highly of themselves as almost anyone else in government, and that was really saying something. In the end, Zahn likened the department to an old guard dog that couldn't see, couldn't hear, had no teeth, and just barely could find his food bowl.

Yes, the State Department was the perfect place from which to justify his many trips to the Mideast and forge the relationships he needed. In fact, he doubted that when it was all over they would even be able to put enough together to realize the sheer depth of that irony.

"Send him my standard, humble reply." It was virtually too late to stop anything now, but being thorough, right up until the last minute, was the smart thing to do.

The television caught their attention. They both turned to listen to another newscaster talk about the Pope's arrival to New York in two short days. The city was working to quickly put together a reception worthy of the leader of the worldwide Catholic Church.

The news channels spoke at length about the support the Pope's visit would provide, but Zahn and Sarat knew the real reason was to prevent a nationwide panic.

Uninterested, Sarat turned back to Zahn. "So, what are we doing when we get the girl?"

Zahn thought about the question. What was so special about that Baxter girl? She'd spotted him in front of Saint Patrick's Cathedral just moments after the bomb went off. Why was she staring at him? There were hundreds of people running in every direction; smoke and debris were everywhere, and she was staring at him. Did she know who he was, or was she just wondering why he was the only person not running? Did someone tell her? The mother admitted nothing before her death, but someone had to know. How else would the girl have known? He had to find out. Until now, his planning and execution had been perfect, without anyone suspecting a thing.

The easy solution from the beginning was to just kill the girl. He wanted to get rid of her quickly before she could tell anyone else, but now it had been too long. She must have told someone by now, which meant things could still unravel quickly. The frustration over not knowing how she saw him was gradually turning into anger. He *had* to know.

"Get her." He finally replied to Sarat.

Sarat's eyes opened showing his surprise. "You mean take her alive?"

"If at all possible. If not, kill her and the woman." Zahn's tone was matter of fact. He could not take the chance of being exposed. Not now. Not this close.

Sarat nodded without objection. What Zahn didn't know was that his man Sarat was beginning to have thoughts of his own regarding little Sarah Baxter.

At that moment, twenty-five thousand feet below Zahn and in downtown Shanghai, Ron Tran exited another internet café and walked south toward the Huangpu River. It had been four days since his visit to the café in Beijing where he had begun compromising machine after machine and adding them to his bot network. The process had gone viral and was now secretly inserting itself into nearly 50,000 computers per hour and accelerating.

The afternoon was warm and overcast with an unusually thick curtain of dark pollution. Sadly, every year China was experiencing more and more days declared unsafe by their government and was advising citizens to stay inside.

On that day, many people who needed to be outside, including Tran, wore a thin surgical mask over their nose and mouth as they quickly walked from building to building.

Tran could taste the smog through his white mask, and it made him nauseous. It was a shining example of how another government was in the process of killing its own people, as they struggled to maintain an iron grip on their power base.

Tran covered the last few blocks and crossed over the large street. He waited for a long line of cars to pass, then walked along the paved sidewalk running beside the river. He finally stopped at one spot near a restaurant where the water met the pier just a few feet away. Tran walked to the edge and looked down into the small swells lapping at the wooden pillars. The color of the water was a dull gray. He shook his head and looked around casually. A few people wandered by, but no one seemed to pay him any attention.

Tran reached into his pocket and pulled out the phone he had just used to exchange messages with Zahn. With one quick motion, he tossed it up and over the rail, watching it splash into the polluted river. He smirked to himself, realizing that his sudden act of polluting had just made him part of the problem.

What the hell, he thought. *Soon it won't even matter.*

33

As the spiritual leader of over one billion Catholics worldwide, Pope Pius XIV was arguably the most recognized and influential person on the planet. As the latest in a line of successors to Saint Peter, to whom Jesus gave the *keys of Heaven*, the Pope was also one of the most protected individuals on that planet.

The level of security required to ensure his protection at all times was an enormous challenge, one that fell on the shoulders of Dario Burk, the head of the Pontifical Swiss Guard, the sole military arm in charge of protecting the Pope since the 15th century. Their efforts to protect a leader who liked to maintain a level of human touch at every turn made their job far more difficult to deal with than any other security team, anywhere. And a sudden public appearance of the Pope in another country was Burk's worst kind of problem.

He hung up the phone with Carolina Flores, the Director of the Secret Service, and leaned back in his chair. This was going to be a nightmare.

Being surrounded by thousands of people, outdoors in an open area, was bad enough. But adding several other high ranking political figures, including the U.S. President, was like pouring fuel on a fire.

On top of it all was the crisis emerging from the church bombings and the mass hysteria spreading across the United States. God forbid should an attack happen in another country; the panic could go global. They had to get the Pope in front of this, but the danger was significant. The only possibility was to revert back to more conservative and, frankly, older tactics. No one within a twenty meter perimeter, no touching, and no one within two hundred meters who had not been patted down.

But even those precautions barely relieved his anxiety. Flores assured him there would be spotters and sharp shooters on almost every rooftop in a six block radius and every item larger than an apple would be physically examined by weapons inspection teams. Then there were the Popemobiles with their bullet-proof Plexiglas and reinforced, armored side panels. Frankly, to put him into anything less visible would just add to the fear and nervousness of the public.

Burk looked at the phone. It had been his twenty-eighth call to Flores in just two days. Everything he and his team could think of had been addressed as well as it could be, given the compressed timeline. But Burk knew it wasn't the things he could think of that worried him. It was the things he couldn't foresee that kept him up at night.

They had less than twenty-four hours before they were due to be in the air. He knew he would not be able to sleep through any of them.

34

Kim Darlington stood at the window in her office, looking slightly pale. Never before had she opened a case for a missing officer, let alone three. She felt sick to her stomach. Griffin and Buckley had now been missing for four days, and Cheryl Roberts for three. And so far, they had no leads.

She looked down at the dark street a few floors below, and watched the cars and people passing back and forth. *It had to have something to do with that social worker and the little girl they were protecting. But how?* They both disappeared shortly after the attack at the safe house, which meant they could be anywhere. There was no word from any of them. No phone records, no credit card activity, and no eye witnesses. In the end, she hated doing it, but nothing got people's attention like an abducted child.

Darlington turned from the window and stood over her desk. Her eyes had just wandered to her laptop screen which had her email program open, when she noticed a new email had arrived from her FBI friend in Boston. The one from which the chaplain had asked for help.

At that moment, something occurred to her. *Why hadn't she thought of that?* She quickly leaned down and scanned the email before picking up the phone. *The chaplain!*

The phone rang several times before Chaplain Wilcox answered. "Hello? This is Douglas speaking."

"Hi Chaplain, this is Kim Darlington."

"Oh, hi Kim," he replied. "I'm glad you called. I'm on my way back to the hotel and was getting ready to call you." He sighed on the other end of the phone. "I heard about the investigation. I'm very distraught. Do you have any more information?"

"I'm afraid not," Darlington said, pulling her handset cord with her as she stepped back to the window. "We've got over a hundred officers on it now though. We'll find them."

"Good." The chaplain's voice was low and didn't sound very confident. He had seen enough missing person's cases to know if they didn't have any leads after the first three days, the odds were not good. "What can I do?"

"Well, it's funny you should ask. I called for two reasons. First, when was the last time you talked to Cheryl?"

"Let's see." The chaplain stopped to consider. "I believe it was Tuesday evening. We met at the library. She wanted to talk about the bombing at Saint Patrick's."

Darlington frowned. "Why did she want to talk about Saint Patrick's?"

"She said she thought there may have been a connection with one of her cases, the one with the little girl."

Darlington froze. *The Baxter girl!* "What did she say?"

"Mmm…we didn't really get that far. She said they had a girl and her social worker in protective custody and someone was chasing them," Wilcox said. "We were supposed to talk again the next day."

Darlington sat down in her chair and rested an elbow on her desk. "How was her case connected to the explosion?"

"That I'm afraid I don't know," the chaplain replied. "And I don't think she knew either."

Darlington remained still, listening and thinking. She twirled a strand of her thick, curly hair and leaned back. *If Roberts thought the bombing was related, and she was working the Baxter case with Griffin and Buckley, then the bombing may very well be a link to their disappearance. But what was it? What had Roberts learned?*

Darlington frowned. She just didn't have enough yet. She took a deep breath and changed the subject. "Okay, well listen, I just got some information back from my friend in Boston. Are you ready?"

"Yes, of course."

Darlington looked back at her computer screen and the email. "She didn't have much, but what she did have may leave you with more questions than answers. The man's name is Aaron Bazes. He's from Israel and, you're right, he has one serious security clearance. In fact, he's got an ambassador level passport which means he pretty much comes and goes as he pleases."

"Wow," the chaplain replied through the phone's earpiece.

"That's not all. My friend says his passport has a special flag on it. She says that if it's scanned by anyone, it says 'not to be delayed or detained.'"

"Delayed or detained," Wilcox repeated. "I've never heard of that before."

"Neither have I."

"So what else did she find on him?" he asked.

"That's it."

"That's it? What do you mean?"

Darlington shook her head. "I mean that's it. That's all she could get. A name, picture, his country and clearance. She has a physical description, but you already know what he looks like."

"Wow," the chaplain said again. "That's not a lot. He's from Israel and can go wherever he wants." His voice disappeared for a moment while he mulled it over. "So, what was he doing poking around the bomb sites?"

"You got me," Darlington said.

"Hmm…" He realized that Kim was right. He did have more questions than answers. "Okay, I'll have to think on this a bit. I was hoping for more."

"Sorry Padre." Another light on her phone lit up, and she looked at the number. "I'm sorry Padre, I'm getting another call. I'll call you when I have more."

"Okay, no problem."

Darlington clicked over to the other line. "This is Kim."

"Hi Kim, I have a call coming in. From a Mike Ramirez."

Darlington recognized the name of the computer forensics expert that had come to see her. "Okay, put him through please." She waited for the line to transfer before answering. "Kim Darlington speaking."

"Hello Ms. Darlington, this is Mike Ramirez. We met a couple days ago when I came in."

"Yes, I remember."

Mike cleared his voice. "I wanted to call and tell you about something."

"Okay," Darlington said.

"So, I was telling you that I hadn't heard from Detectives Griffin or Buckley."

Darlington leaned forward on her desk. "Correct."

"Right, well I saw your announcement tonight on the news, about your investigation, and I think there's something odd here," Ramirez explained.

She raised an eyebrow. "What is that?"

"So," Ramirez continued, "the other day when I got back to my office, after speaking with you, I wrote a small program. I was thinking I could create an app that would periodically parse through the server logs and search against their phone numbers and, if it found anything, to email me."

Darlington perked up. "Did you find something?"

"I believe so," Ramirez answered. "I got an email not too long ago."

"What did it say?" asked Darlington, now eagerly leaning into the phone.

"It shows Detective Griffin's phone connected briefly to a cell tower, which means if it was turned off before, then it was just turned on."

Darlington suddenly stood up. "You're kidding."

"No, I'm not." Ramirez was staring at his screen on the other end of the phone. "I'm guessing it was turned on for about six or seven minutes before it was turned off again."

"Where? Can you tell where they are?!" Darlington almost yelled into the phone.

Ramirez was expecting this as her first question. "Well, I can tell you what tower they connected to, but unfortunately I can't pinpoint their location."

Darlington's heart was racing. "That's a start."

"Maybe," replied Ramirez.

"What do you mean maybe?"

"They were connected to the tower for several minutes, but the weird part is where the tower was located."

Darlington squinted her eyes. "Where *was* the tower located?"

Ramirez had checked his data three times. He had to be sure about this. "China."

"China?" She hoped she hadn't heard him right.

"China," he confirmed. "And it gets stranger. His phone was turned on, sent and received a text message, and then turned right back off."

35

Sarah sat patiently on Christine's lap as Christine brushed her wet hair. Avery was straightening their bed atop the large sofa while Rand stood near the kitchen window, looking outside into the forest. He turned and looked at Sarah with her blond hair combed straight down, then calmly returned his gaze to the window.

Avery patted the blankets and stood up.

"Sarah, would you be okay out here if I took a quick shower?" Christine asked, peering around the side of her tiny shoulder.

"Sure."

She set the brush down and began to stand up when Sarah whispered into Christine's ear. Christine looked at Avery then back to her.

"I don't know," she whispered back. "Ask him."

Still shy, Sarah looked at Avery who was watching her with interest. After appearing to contemplate something, she slowly walked across the room to him. Avery bent down slightly as she approached.

"Can we please play checkers again?" she asked.

Avery gave her a hard stare which turned into a soft grin. "Do you promise to take it easy on me?"

Sarah smiled. "Yes."

Avery straightened with a satisfied look and motioned to the small table in the kitchen. "Do you remember how to set it up?"

Sarah smiled and trotted over to a shelf and retrieved the game, then began laying it out on the table in front of Rand who was watching her with a grin. Christine had noticed that Rand's stone like expression softened when he watched Sarah.

Christine looked at Rand and Avery. "That okay?"

They both nodded. "I got the things you asked for and left them in the bathroom." Avery said.

Christine opened her other eye and then carefully handed the .40 caliber Springfield back to Rand. "How was that?"

"Good, but remember to keep your shoulders more forward."

"It's a lot to remember," she said with a frown.

Rand took the gun, smoothly replaced the magazine, and slid it back into his holster without looking.

"I think I'm just going to need a lot more practice."

"We don't have much time," he replied.

Christine gave him a hopeful look. "Maybe whoever was doing this is gone. Maybe he was one of the men that you killed."

He shook his head. "It hasn't happened yet."

"What, what hasn't happened?"

Rand squinted and peered out over the field. "I don't know exactly. But it's coming. And I must be there."

"And what if you're not?"

He turned and looked at Christine solemnly. "Then I fail. I fail her, and I fail *him*. I fail everyone."

Christine took a deep breath. She had wanted to say something for a while. "Listen, I have to admit I'm still struggling with this. I mean God and this constant battle of good and evil; it's a little hard to imagine."

Rand stared at her. "Do you believe in God?"

"Of course I do."

"Do you believe he cares for you?"

Christine nodded. "I do."

"And do you believe evil is real?"

"You mean like Satan and demons, that sort of thing?"

"If that helps."

She sighed and folded her arms. "Yeah, I guess I do."

"Then why is it such a leap? If you can believe that he created you, why are you unable to believe that he also fights for you?"

"I don't know," she said with a shrug. "I guess that's just not how I learned it."

"You learned wrong," Rand replied, reaching down to pick up his AR-15 assault rifle. He turned it over and checked the chamber.

"What's that supposed to mean, 'I learned wrong'?"

"The religious teachings that most people believe in today are far from the truth. The Bible was not intended to be a book of interpretation. Interpretation and time are the enemies of truth. What you have today is a version of the Bible that has been twisted so many times that it can now be used to vindicate almost anything. It's no longer the true word of God."

Christine tilted her head, her arms still folded. "Then what *is* the truth?" she asked.

He began turning away but then stopped abruptly and looked at her. "The truth? The truth is that your God fights for all of you, for all of his children, and he's *losing*!"

Christine stepped back. "Losing? I thought he was all powerful."

"He is. But evil is far stronger than anyone believes. They've successfully led you all down a road of sloth and apathy, a path you are all too eager to travel. Even your churches have strayed. They have compromised for little more than to guarantee their tithe, and now even they struggle to fill their seats. The number of God's children who still speak to him is diminishing." Rand looked away with a look of disgust on his face. "He fights for you, but who fights for him? I mean really fights!"

Christine frowned and looked out over the open field in front of them. Another thick wall of trees stood behind them and separated the pair from the cabin. "Maybe it's the suffering," she said. "Maybe it's the pain of watching terrible things happen in this world, like millions of innocent people being wiped out by horrible dictators, or thousands of children being molested and ruined for life. Or maybe it's the countless people wasting away, dying of cancer right in front of the ones who love them most." She looked back at him. "I think it can be easy for people to lose faith when they see things like that every day."

"That may be true," Rand replied, slinging the rifle over his shoulder. "Except for one thing."

Christine looked at him expectantly.

"Those are not God's decisions or choices. He's not the one making those things happen. It's them. God is the one trying to stop it. He has a plan, but he's losing the fight. He's losing the fight, because *he's losing his children.*"

Rand began walking back when Christine called after him. "Rand."

He turned back to face her.

"If he chose me," she said with a solemn expression, "then *I'll fight.*"

The sun finally dropped behind the mountains as Christine and Rand walked in through the front door to find Avery and Sarah making dinner in the small kitchen. Sarah stood beside him on a folding stool, reaching almost to his shoulder. She was looking inside a large pot and had dropped the dried pasta in just as Christine cleared her voice.

Sarah looked up and climbed down the stool to run over.

"What are you doing?" Christine asked with a smile.

"I'm helping Avery cook," she explained. "We're making pasta."

Avery smiled from his spot next to the stove. "She likes to cook too."

"Wow." She looked down as Sarah hugged her. "That's very impressive."

Sarah looked up at Christine and then over to Rand.

"Dinner is going to be ready in ten minutes," she said.

"Twenty *minutes*," corrected Avery.

"Dinner's going to be ready in twenty minutes!"

Christine laughed while Rand smiled. They watched Sarah run back into the kitchen.

"She's a great kid," Christine said.

"Indeed."

Over her shoulder, Christine realized the TV was still on in the other room. She walked over to it and grabbed the remote control, trying to turn it off, but accidentally hit the wrong button which changed the channel instead.

Two news anchors instantly filled the screen, talking about the first New York church bombing. But it was what Christine saw on the screen next, and more specifically what was pictured at the top, that caused her to freeze. Pictured on the screen were headshots of three people she knew!

"...Griffin, Michael Buckley, and Cheryl Roberts, all officers from downtown's 19th Precinct have been confirmed missing for three days. The statement was issued today by the precinct's Deputy Inspector Kim Darlington."

Christine gasped and turned around to face Rand as the anchor continued on the screen.

"The department reported that there are no leads as of yet, but confirmed the three officers were working together on a case involving a woman and child."

"Oh my god!" Christine took a step back and placed a hand on her chest after pictures of her and Sarah also appeared on the television screen.

"Police say the woman, Christine Rose, may have abducted the girl who was at the time under police custody..."

"No!" Christine cried. "No! You've got to be kidding! I'm WANTED?! What the hel-" She turned to look at Rand again and found that Avery was now standing next to him, peering at the screen too.

"...ask that if anyone has any information that they call the number below..."

Christine leaned forward and turned the sound down just as Sarah grabbed her hand.

"Those are the men who helped us at the hide house," she said.

Christine was staring at the screen, speechless.

"Aren't they?" Sarah asked expectantly.

Christine nodded. "Yes."

Sarah studied Christine and spoke softer. "Did something happen to them?"

Christine looked at Rand and Avery again and then finally down to Sarah. "Maybe."

"Did the red ones get them?"

Christine covered her mouth with her other hand as her eyes began to fill with tears.

"It's only begun." Rand said quietly.

Christine took a few steps and collapsed down onto the couch. Still holding her hand, Sarah silently climbed onto Christine's lap. She tried to wrap her other tiny arm around her.

"My god, what's happening?" Christine cried out through her tears.

Both men looked at her quietly, and Rand took a step forward. "It's okay; we're safe here for now."

Christine blinked and suddenly looked up at Rand with a frightened expression. "Oh my god! Danny!" She pointed to the screen. "Danny!"

"What?"

"Oh no! Oh no!" she said, feeling a sickening sensation spreading through her gut. "We're in trouble."

Rand and Avery looked at each other. "What do you mean?"

She abruptly stood up, still holding onto Sarah. "He texted me. HE TEXTED ME!"

Neither of the men were following. Christine took a deep breath and tried to slow down. "He *texted* me. Danny. Yesterday. I accidentally turned my phone on, and a text from Danny came through."

Rand and Avery's eyes widened. "What did you do?"

Her face filled with guilt. "I replied."

Rand raised his voice. "You did what?"

"I'm sorry," Christine cried. "I didn't know. I just told him that I was fine and would contact him later."

Rand instantly had his gun in his hand without Christine even having seen it drawn. He turned to Avery just as all the lights went out, and the cabin was plunged into darkness.

36

Avery's silhouette ran to the wall and opened the panel, revealing the security system and all of the sensors around the perimeter of the cabin. All the lights were red.

"We have company."

In the darkness, Rand reached under a bookshelf near the television, pulled out several magazines, and stuffed them into his pocket.

"Get them in the back," his voice said in the darkness. Avery had already grabbed both Sarah and Christine and was rushing them down the dark hallway.

Outside, over two dozen dark figures spread out in a perfect circle, were closing in on the cabin. Their progress was slow and methodical as they took small, quiet steps through the grass.

Murad Sarat led the team forward. Unfortunately, cutting the power and warning whoever was inside was unavoidable. They needed to sever all forms of communication, including what might be powering any transmissions. He held up his hand and gave the signal to lower their night vision goggles, a signal that was passed around the circle to everyone almost simultaneously.

Rand waited quietly. He needed them closer, a lot closer, or they would see him. He felt the familiar surge of warm blood course through him. He waited, eyes closed, listening to the soft steps through the grass.

Murad and his team slowed even more as they neared the structure. He was near the front and gave a 'stop' signal as he and another of his men approached the first step of the wooden porch. They both aimed their rifles and scanned the entire porch carefully. They couldn't hear anything moving inside, just the warm breeze behind them.

He unclenched his fist and gave the signal to move in just as Rand's feet left the roof, near the back of the cabin. He came down hard, crushing one of the dark figures below him into the ground. In a flash he was up, pulling the unconscious figure back onto his feet as a shield to block the gunfire that immediately erupted from the side.

Rand turned to his right and simultaneously fired his Springfield, dropping three men immediately. Without any hesitation, he wrapped his right hand around his dead shield and fired, killing two more attackers with two shots each to their neck and face, the only vital areas not protected by armor.

Even through the gunfire, Murad's men did not scatter or break position. Instead, they all flattened themselves against the outside walls of the house. The two nearest to the shots on each side instantly teamed up and inched themselves slowly toward the back, while Murad and the others held their position.

The four men quietly approached the back and spotted bodies on the ground, but all were motionless. Each two man team scanned up the exterior wall and along the roofline. Finding nothing, they turned back to the bodies. Still no movement.

The four men then turned their attention to the small back porch and closed in. The old door had been boarded up. What they hadn't examined closely enough, however, was that one of the bodies on the ground was not bleeding.

Murad heard several more shots and froze again. *What the hell was happening? He wasn't going to wait outside forever while someone picked them all off.* He quickly gave the signal and all of his men rushed into the house. He and two others stormed the front porch firing several shots into the front door as they barreled inside. On the sides of the house, three windows were smashed as the rest of Murad's team hurled themselves inside.

Rand heard the smashing windows from the rear of the house. He replaced his magazine and stepped over one of the bodies. He heard movement behind him and turned back toward the trees to see seven more muzzle flashes appear from the darkness. Dirt and wood exploded around him as the bullets tore through the ground and into the wood planking of the house. Already running, Rand fired several shots into the trees and bolted up the steps, smashing through the old boarded door.

He stumbled inside, past the door now hanging from one remaining hinge and around a corner just as hundreds of rounds destroyed the porch and door frame behind him. Rand unslung his rifle in one smooth motion and, in complete darkness, fired a volley down the long hallway heading forward to the living room. He ducked back out of the way and slammed his fist several times against a large, blank wall. A moment later, a thick, hidden door opened with Avery behind it. He grabbed Rand, yanked him inside, and pulled the door closed behind him. Once the thick door was closed, Avery slid a giant bolt lock back into place.

Through the dim light inside, Rand could see Christine and Sarah huddled in the middle of the empty room.

"There's too many," he whispered to Avery. "We can't get out."

Christine stared at him with a look of determination. "We have to do something!"

"Well, I'm fairly certain negotiating is out," Rand said, withdrawing another magazine from his pocket and slapping it into the bottom of the rifle. The movement was so fluid that Christine was not entirely sure what he had done.

"Is there another way out?" she asked, trying to keep her voice down.

"No."

"So we're screwed?" she yelled under her breath.

They could hear someone on the outside tapping their rifles along the wall, looking for the latch. A moment later it was joined by what sounded like two more rifles.

They all sat silently as the men outside found the hidden latch and began trying to pry it open.

"Oh god!" Christine whispered, as she watched the large bolt on the door begin to wiggle.

"They won't get in," Avery replied calmly. "This room is lined with two inches of solid steel."

Christine rolled her eyes. "Wonderful, but unless you have a bathroom and a hell of a lot of food, we eventually have to come out."

She pulled Sarah in tight and watched both men in frustration as they sat listening to the sounds outside. The giant bolt had stopped moving and now the sounds were spreading around the room while Murad's men examined all sides, looking for a sound of weakness in the wall and a way in. Then, all at once the tapping stopped, and some shuffling could be heard on the other side of the door.

Christine jumped when she heard three shots hit the other side of the wall with a loud *thunk thunk thunk*.

She looked worriedly at Rand. "They're going to shoot their way in!"

Rand looked at Avery. "Checkmate."

Avery nodded. "They're on all sides now."

Rand slowly stood up and looked down at Christine and Sarah. "Both of you lay down on your stomachs."

Oh my god! They going to try to shoot their way out! Christine thought to herself as she let Sarah pull away and slide down onto the floor. Nervously, Christine lowered herself down next to her, while Sarah watched both men curiously.

Rand nodded silently to Avery who nodded back. With that, Rand turned and pushed on a small area of the wall causing a door to pop open. He pulled the small door all the way back revealing a single, large button. He looked down at the girls and, without pausing, he smashed his palm against it.

Murad lined up several of his men and instructed them to fire at the door where he believed the lock to be located on the other side. He wanted them to fire into the same spot, from the same angle, and to use a hail of bullets to drive a hole through the door.

What he did not hear, however, was the strange sound coming from out in front of the house, as the old bird bath tipped over and fell to the ground. Nor did he realize, a second bird bath was located behind the house which fell over at the same time.

Below the ground and from where the broken statues had stood, something large and black rose up from below. The two objects were both M134 Miniguns, each electrically driven with six Gatling-style barrels that were capable of firing 4,000 rounds per minute. Both were connected to a large belt of ammo and sat atop an auto rotating platform.

Inside the small room, Rand and Avery fell to the floor and covered both Sarah and Christine with their bodies. Rand above Sarah, and Avery covering Christine.

In less than a second, a small, red light on each gun changed to green, and the miniguns opened fire directly at the cabin from both ends. Instantly, the powerful 7.62mm bullets ripped through and began shredding everything in the house like tissue paper. As the screaming barrels spun, both guns rotated back and forth within a thirty degree angle, covering the entire structure.

Rand brought his arms and legs in tight, protecting every inch of Sarah's small body. All around them, the bullets tore through Murad's men and slammed into the thick steel walls, causing large dents to appear on the inside. Some dents grew larger as bullets hit the same spot, but Rand and Avery kept their heads down and remained motionless.

In the front of the cabin, the support beams gave way and the roof collapsed onto the porch. The weight and impact pulled down even more of the roof, exposing what was left of the front living room and kitchen areas.

The noise inside their tiny room was deafening as the giant dents continued appearing on the walls inside, but no one moved. The men held them both tight until, after an agonizingly long two minutes, the guns ran through their ammo belts and spun to a stop with smoke rising from the black gun barrels.

The terrible noise ended as quickly as it began. Rand and Avery did not move immediately. Instead, they waited and then slowly looked up around them. The walls held.

"Stay down," Rand whispered as he got to his feet. He grabbed the AR-15 and checked the chamber. Behind him, Avery picked up a second rifle and knelt down on one knee in front of the girls. He held his gun ready and pointed at the door.

Rand slowly slid the bolt lock open, surprised that it still moved smoothly. He gently pushed the door open and peered through the open crack. After a moment, he turned to Avery. "I'll be right back."

Several minutes went by before three shots were heard in the distance, followed by silence. It was another ten minutes before Rand stepped over Murad's men and poked his head back in.

Avery stood as Rand stepped into the room and put his hand on Christine's back. "You can both get up. It's safe."

Christine and Sarah looked up and around the room, and then gradually got to their feet. "Okay," Christine quietly. "I wasn't expecting *that*."

"We have to go." Rand looked down. "Will you come with me, Sarah?"

Without any hesitation, Sarah walked into his arms and

he picked her up. She wrapped her arms around his thick neck. "I'm not scared with you," she said.

Rand smiled at her. "Good." He gave her a gentle pat on her head. "Now, I need you to close your eyes, okay?"

Rand looked at Christine. "You might want to do the same."

37

Their eyes were closed tight, and Christine tried not to think about what they might be stepping over as Rand and Avery led them out. After they stepped over the last obstacle, she could feel the chill of the evening on her face followed by the tall, soft grass brushing against her shins and knees.

After a long pause, Rand gave the okay and she and Sarah both opened their eyes and looked around. With a little moonlight through the clouds, they could just make out the shape of the dark and eerily shaped cabin they had left behind.

Rand lowered Sarah to the ground and unslung the Bushmaster rifle. He held it in both hands and scanned behind them, while Avery walked to a nearby tree and rolled a large boulder to the side. He reached down and silently pulled up a handle to a door hidden underneath the thick layer of pine needles, then reached further down and retrieved a large dark object. When he returned, Christine could see it was a giant duffle bag and, judging from Avery's posture, a heavy one.

They walked over a half mile to reach the car, kept in a small building painted a combination of earth tones, which Christine assumed was a mountain version of 'camouflage'.

The 1969 Dodge Charger R/T was considered by many one of the toughest cars ever made. Cranking out an astounding 425 horses, the 426 Hemi engine weighed nearly half a ton. Furthermore, unlike modern cars, the R/T was made of strong steel and could take a real beating if it had to, especially with some modifications.

Christine rested her head against the copper colored

vinyl in the back seat with Sarah asleep in her lap. An hour after they left, Rand killed the headlights and pulled off the empty road onto a smaller dirt one. He slowly rolled beneath the outskirts of a small forest, coming to rest under a thick canopy.

When he turned off the car, the sudden silence from the engine's absence was almost deafening.

Avery opened the passenger door and stepped out. "I'm going to scout." He grabbed the 12 gauge tactical shotgun from off the floor and carefully shut the door as quietly as possible. As he walked away, Christine heard him work the slide action of the shotgun to chamber a shell.

Rand remained in the front seat, keys still in the ignition, watching the darkness around them.

After several long minutes, Christine broke the silence with a whisper.

"Rand?"

He turned his head sideways, viewing her from the corner of his eye.

"Can I ask you a question?"

"Yes."

"Where did you grow up?"

He furrowed his brow. "Why do you ask?"

"I was just wondering what your life was like," she said softly. "Are your parents still alive?"

Rand took a deep breath and exhaled, turning his head forward again. "No. I was an orphan."

Christine's eyes saddened in the back seat.

"We're always orphans," he added.

"Always?"

He nodded. "It makes it easier to focus. Emotionally."

"Did you have parents?"

"Foster parents, yes." Rand could still see the image of his foster mother's gentle, round face in his mind. She was older, in her late fifties by the time he left. She was kind and gentle, as was the father, and their relationship was caring and...polite.

"Did they know?" asked Christine. "You know, about you?"

Rand almost chuckled. "Yes, they knew. Not many kids have scratches that begin to heal before they even get the band-aid out."

Christine watched him as his thoughts turned inward.

"And school was a distraction," he continued. "I did it primarily to blend in."

"Did you ever *tell them*, your parents?"

"I did. When I was a teenager." He still remembered it vividly. "They were devout Christians which helped. In the end, I think they were secretly relieved. It explained why all I ever asked for was more exercise equipment."

Christine nodded but couldn't quite bring herself to smile. "Did you ever have fun?"

"There were times of happiness, but probably not what you would consider fun. I'm not here to have fun."

Christine rolled her head to the side and looked out her small triangular window. She felt a pang in her heart when he said that. What a lonely life he must have had. After a while she looked back. "Can I ask you something else?"

As Rand turned his head sideways again, she could see some of his eyelashes highlighted by the moonlight reflecting off the hood.

"If we've really lost our way, like you said, why would you want to become one of us?"

He thought about the question. "I can see why he loves you so much. You are capable of so much, more than you even know. Your connection to the world around you is almost limitless. Just look at your artists and your musicians. So many of you can connect with the world in ways that we never will. You are so much more like him than you know." He paused. "There is nothing you cannot do, if you can just get beyond your weaknesses."

She stared at him quietly. "What kind of weaknesses?"

"You're drawn too much to pleasure. It's what they use against you."

"They?"

"Those from the darkness. The Evil."

She was quiet again, thinking about everything that had happened. "Do you think Danny and the other officers are okay?"

His gaze dropped. He couldn't lie to her. "No, Christine, I don't. I'm sorry."

In the back seat, she nodded and looked back out the window. Through the rearview mirror, Rand could see the tears glistening in her eyes.

"Rand?" she asked with a shaking voice.

"Yes?"

Christine spoke before the lump in her throat stopped her. "Is there a heaven?"

This time he turned and looked back at her. "Yes. There is a heaven."

She wiped the tears away and tried to grin.

"It's not what most people think, but it's a good place."

"What do you mean?"

This time he smiled at her. "Well, you don't fly around and eat whatever you want."

She saw his smile and couldn't help but chuckle. "I guess that's a bit much to ask, isn't it?"

As he turned to watch out the front window again, the smile slowly faded from his face.

Behind him, Christine nestled against the door trying not to wake up Sarah. They were both quiet for a long time before she broke the silence yet again.

"One more question?"

She asked a lot of questions. Rand turned back again. "You should really try to get some sleep."

"I will," she promised. "After this."

"Okay, what?"

"Avery." She turned her head back to the window, looking out and in the direction he had left. "He's one of you isn't he?"

Rand didn't answer immediately. "Yes."

"He was a soldier too?"

"Yes." Rand turned his head toward her again. "Each soldier helps the next. If he can."

"What was he here to do?" Christine asked.

Rand let the side of his head fall gently against the headrest. "It was during World War II. The Germans were trying to build a nuclear weapon, but they needed an important element, something called "heavy water". It's required to produce Plutonium. There was a fertilizer plant in Norway that produced heavy water, and the Germans eventually captured it. They extracted enough to ship back to Germany. On the way back, a single commando was able to fight through the German occupation, reach the boat, and sink it." He paused. "Avery was that man."

Christine was stunned. "What would have happened?"

"If he hadn't destroyed it?" Rand finished her question. "The Germans would have developed the first atomic bomb, in time to avoid Berlin being taken. They would have vaporized much of the British and American alliance and scared the Russians enough to withdraw temporarily. Germany's second and third atomic bombs would have achieved a surrender by enough countries to break the back of the Allies, and Hitler would have won."

"Oh my god."

"They thought they were going to win." Rand said and looked outside. "But God sent Avery."

38

Stuxnet was the scariest computer virus most of the world had never heard of. When it was first detected in 2010, it was mistaken for a common, run of the mill virus; it was not until experts started to dissect its computer code that it became deeply frightening.

The very first computer virus was little more than a friendly prank when, in 1982, a young 15-year-old kid played a trick on his friends by writing a tiny computer program that could pass between Apple II computers via floppy disk. It then displayed a funny message every fifty times the computer booted up.

Later that year, a graduate student at the University of Southern California by the name of Fred Cohen demonstrated his computer code, running on a giant UNIX mainframe, which allowed him to take over the entire system within 30 minutes.

However, it was not until 1986 that the first self-replicating virus was spotted in "the wild". It was a small piece of computer code written by two Pakistani brothers, whose purpose was to guilt users of a non-copyrighted program into contacting them to obtain the "vaccination" and to undoubtedly pay up.

Since then, viruses had quickly grown in both frequency and sophistication, giving birth to a multi-billion dollar industry dedicated solely to fighting computer viruses and "worms". Yet, the damage inflicted with most of these modern viruses was mild, usually ranging from deleting data to collecting personal information. But in 2010, Stuxnet changed everything.

Originally flagged as a common worm, engineers at a large anti-virus corporation spotted and categorized

Stuxnet's software characteristics as something called "malware". Their job was to study it and find a way to clean the worm so the corporation's anti-malware programs could defend against it.

Yet the study of this particular worm was unusual from the very beginning. One unique characteristic was *how* it propagated or traveled from machine to machine, which was primarily by detachable memory sticks called flash drives. Another oddity was the size of the program, which was much larger than usual.

The mystery deepened as the layers of the code were seemingly peeled back, and the worm appeared to grow more and more complex, using multiple programming languages including C and C++. The mystery deepened further still when the worm was found to take advantage of four different computer vulnerabilities, called zero-day attacks, while other viruses and worms used only one.

But when the encryption certificates were stolen from two separate and well known corporations, the investigating engineers knew Stuxnet was much more than a simple worm. It was too complicated and far too sophisticated to have been created by kids in high school or college students hyped up on Mountain Dew. The level of expertise and funding needed to create something like Stuxnet meant it had to have happened at the corporate or *state* level.

Yet, the largest mystery of all was how it *behaved*. Most viruses and worms were designed to infect and act upon as many computers and systems as possible. But Stuxnet was different. Stuxnet wanted to spread, but once it did, the program would essentially "look around" and determine what kind of computer it was on, then disable itself. This was extremely odd and told the engineers that Stuxnet was not looking for just any computer system; it was looking for a very specific computer system.

Rumors began to spread across the internet since the majority of Stuxnet infections were in the middle-eastern countries, such as Iraq and Iran. It did not take long for some experts to suggest the program was created to target one of those two countries.

Finally, when the worm gave up the last of its secrets, it became clear what it was after. Stuxnet was looking for a very unique computer environment, one that was used for refining nuclear material.

When Stuxnet found the system it was looking for, what it did was revolutionary. The process for refining uranium is extremely delicate and time consuming. What Stuxnet did was change the spin of the centrifuges just enough to render the material unusable, but it would do so while it told the computer's monitoring system the process was running smoothly. This meant that Stuxnet was able to sabotage the process without anyone noticing.

When this behavior became known, many intelligence specialists believed the creator of the worm was Israel. Not surprisingly, just a few months after the computer industry learned of Stuxnet, the country of Iran confirmed that it's enrichment facility had indeed been infected. Intelligence experts surmised the cyber-attack likely set Iran back one to two years in their enrichment efforts. And soon after, the creator of Stuxnet was actually found to be the United States.

In the end, Stuxnet changed history in one very remarkable way; up until then, cyber-attacks remained anchored in cyberspace, a virtual world made only of computer bytes and silicon chips. What made Stuxnet truly frightening, was that for the first time, a virus or worm within cyberspace, had been able to jump the virtual barrier and create real physical damage. In other words, it was the first virtual world weapon to cause real damage in the *physical world*.

Ron Tran sat in front of a large monitor in yet another computer gaming cafe. He was again surrounded by teenagers and young adults glued to their own screens, weaving in and out of dark rooms, shooting at someone who often sat in another part of the world, in front of their own screen.

Some of the "gamers" had even pushed themselves past the absolute limit by playing for almost 96 hours straight, fueled by nothing more than soda and junk food, only to pay the ultimate price by collapsing dead onto the floor. But the deaths did not deter the rest. Their addiction was total.

Just like before, it provided the perfect cover for Ron, since no one ever managed to look away from their own screens to observe what he was doing.

He now had almost ten million infected computers waiting for his command. Tran triple checked the details in his window before hitting the Enter key. This was it. There was no turning back after this. But he was ready and had been for over a year.

He purposefully hit the Enter key with his forefinger and watched the letters scroll slowly in the window, showing the command was being sent to all bots in a daisy chain. They were being loaded with all the computer network addresses of their intended targets. Phase One had begun, and when all of the bots had received their data, they would wait for the next command, or Phase Two.

Tran looked around at the crowded room of gamers. They were the personification of the world around him. Bright but completely under the spell of an electronic drug that turned them into cattle. It was complete sensory addiction.

These kids spent thousands and thousands of hours every year playing the latest games. When they finished or got bored with one, there was always another waiting for them. Tran thought about his last two years, spent in front of a monitor for a very different reason. He was collaborating with dozens of other secret hackers, all having no idea what each other looked like, yet working for a common goal. It had not been hard convincing them, since many shared his anti-government, anti-greed views, but he still kept them segregated and working on smaller pieces of code. Tran had divvied up the job to ensure none of the others knew what the final virus would do. Of course, some already had relationships with each other and probably talked, but they would need many pieces of the puzzle to really know what it would do. Frankly, some of them did not even care. They knew Tran's reputation and were excited to have a hand in changing a horribly corrupt system.

Tran logged out of his computer session and removed the DVD. He stood up and took one last look at the screen. *Stuxnet was nothing,* he thought. They had taken its original design and framework and created something truly incredible. In fact, they were about to show the entire world the original Stuxnet was child's play.

39

Zahn was furious. "No contact? How in the hell did we lose contact?! How many did you send?"

"Thirty," Sarat said quietly. "Led by Murad."

Zahn closed his eyes and put his hand over his face. Murad was one of the best they had. He was ruthless and a natural warrior. By comparison, Murad considered the Taliban and Al Qaeda to be nothing more than sloppy, religious zealots. If you wanted to affect real change, you did it from within. Murad was as committed as anyone, but worst of all, he was Kia's brother.

"How long has it been?" asked Zahn.

"Almost six hours."

There was only one conclusion to be drawn. The girl and the woman were not alone. They had help, a lot of help. Zahn let his anger go. He had to think about this. He didn't know who or how many others were involved, but the girl clearly had talked! Time was growing short, yet it was still possible for things to unravel, and quickly. He couldn't take any chances.

"Get me their last coordinates," Zahn said. He reached for the phone and picked it up. There was no one on the other end at this hour, so the phone automatically forwarded to one of his staff at home.

"It's me," he said when she picked up the other end. "I need to talk to Benecke at Homeland Security right now." Zahn hung up and looked back at Sarat.

"Do we go after them?" Sarat asked.

"No, god no," said Zahn. "They're most likely all dead." He saw Sarat visibly flinch, but it had to be said. "They could have *driven* all the way back by now!" He looked at his watch. "Christ, they could have done it without even breaking the speed limit! No, we need to find out where the girls are and where they're headed."

The phone beeped, and Zahn quickly picked it up. He waited a moment while the phone was transferred to Ron Benecke, the Director of Homeland Security.

"Hello?" answered Benecke on the other end. There was no doubt he had just been woken up.

"Benecke, it's Zahn."

"What is it?"

Zahn glanced at Sarat as he spoke. "I need one of your drones."

"Foreign or domestic?" Benecke asked.

"Domestic."

There was a short pause. "Do I want to know why?"

"No," Zahn replied. "And I need full access, including all archived data."

Benecke sighed. "Let me make some calls." He promptly hung up.

Zahn stood up and walked over to the window. He looked out over the sleeping city of Washington, D.C. Its golden lights sparkled across the low lying hills as far as the eye could see. "Get another team ready."

Unfortunately, using a drone for the strike was out of the question. It would draw immediate attention from nearly every arm of the government, and he couldn't distance himself from something like that. But using the drone's surveillance capability and picture quality, they could still find them.

40

Chaplain Wilcox walked through the empty lobby of the hotel and headed for the elevator. He had spent the entire day meeting with families, holding group prayer and counseling sessions, and he didn't want to look at his watch to see what time it was.

He smiled and waved to the young clerk at the check-in counter before heading down the carpeted hallway toward the elevators. Once inside, he sighed, pressed his floor number, fell softly against the elevator wall, and watched each floor light up at an agonizingly slow pace.

Finally, the doors sounded a *ding* and opened, revealing the green patterned carpet running down the long hallway to the far end. Wilcox stepped out and walked two-thirds of the way down the hall to his room. He found his card, slid it in and out of the slot, and waited for the small light to turn green.

The chaplain opened the door to find the lights were off, so he felt for the wall switch and flipped it on. Still nothing.

Is the power out? he wondered. The chaplain quickly caught the door behind him before it closed. He peered out at the bright lights in the hallway and wondered what was wrong, when he suddenly felt the tip of a gun barrel press into his soft back.

The chaplain gasped and froze where he stood. Someone behind him reached out and pushed the door handle out of his grip, letting the door close shut and plunging the room into darkness.

Wilcox stood shaking, now unable to see anything at all.

"Are you alone?" a man's voice whispered into his ear.

The chaplain nodded his head nervously.

"Move forward." The man prodded him away from the door, and the chaplain slowly walked forward in the darkness, trying to remember where the coffee table and small couch were located. After several steps, he abruptly ran into the arm of the couch.

"Sit down," the voice said.

The chaplain felt around the cushioned arm and lowered himself down. His eyes were beginning to adjust, and he could see a silhouette standing in front of him. Without warning, a bright flashlight came on and blinded him momentarily until it was set down onto the coffee table, pointing toward the ceiling. The chaplain was stunned to see the man's face. It was Aaron Bazes.

"What are you doing here?" the chaplain stuttered.

Bazes stared down at him. "Why have you been investigating me?"

The chaplain was petrified. "I uh…just saw you at some of the sites. I didn't…I was just curious…"

Bazes watched him fumble and then reached behind himself, causing the chaplain to stop when he spotted the semi-automatic pistol.

The chaplain closed his eyes hard, trying to remain calm, then looked back up at Bazes. "Listen, I'm just here to help. I saw you at the church and remembered seeing you in New York…" He trailed off as Bazes continued glaring at him.

Bazes lowered his gun. "You're lucky you did."

"Lucky?"

"Otherwise, I wouldn't be here right now." Bazes' expression relaxed.

"What do you mean?"

Without a word, Bazes motioned to the chaplain's right. Wilcox turned and peered into the darkness. "OH LORD!" he cried. Wilcox jumped off the couch and backed away quickly, staring at a dark figure sitting motionless in the chair in front of the window. After a few moments, he looked back at Bazes and then back at the large man in the chair. "What's happened?!"

Bazes calmly looked at the chaplain and then back to the chair. "He was waiting for you when I got here."

"What?"

Bazes reached behind himself and re-holstered his gun. "He was already here. And he didn't seem very friendly."

The chaplain felt like his head was spinning. He kept looking back and forth trying to understand. "What? Why? Who is he?"

"I don't know," Bazes replied.

The chaplain took a worried step forward. He could barely make out the man's features. Dark hair and dark skinned. His head was tilted onto the back of the chair with his mouth slightly open. "Is...he dead?"

"No. But he's going to need some medical attention when he wakes up."

Wilcox took the hint. "He was here to hurt me?"

"That's my guess since he broke all of your light bulbs," Bazes said sarcastically. He picked up the flashlight and shined it directly on the man. He was dressed in black clothes with what appeared to be a gun tucked under his thin jacket. "Then again, maybe he's just a light bulb salesman. Either way, neither one of us should probably be here when he wakes up."

The two men exited the hotel through the front doors, with Bazes walking slightly behind the chaplain. They continued down the long driveway where Bazes nodded toward a small park across the busy street. They crossed and headed through the trees, far out of sight from the hotel, and toward a small round fountain. A small, gray statue of George Washington stood next to it.

"The bench closest to the fountain," Bazes instructed.

The chaplain walked to the bench. It was shorter than usual, but he managed to lower himself down onto it with a quiet grunt.

Bazes wasted no time. "Who else is trying to find out about me?"

The chaplain could see him clearly now. He guessed him to be in his late forties with a shaved head and slender, yet muscular frame. He looked military but definitely not a front line soldier. "No one else, just me." He shook his head.

Bazes looked around. They were alone and the fountain was loud enough. "What do you want?"

The chaplain held his hands out innocently. "As I said, I was curious who you were. I saw you both in New York and then again here, looking through the rubble."

"A lot of people were looking through the rubble."

The chaplain shook his head again. "Not the way you were."

"And what did you see?" asked Bazes.

"I don't really know. You looked like you were poking around in some pretty specific places. Like around the altars."

Bazes stared at him quietly. "And what did you find out?"

"You mean from the FBI?"

"Yes."

The chaplain shrugged. "Not very much. You seem to have the shortest file of anyone I've seen. All I know is your name, where you're from, and that you have a security clearance higher than any of us have ever seen before."

"What else?"

"Nothing. That's it. Just your name and country. Both being Israeli. Actually your name is Hebrew if I'm not mistaken."

Bazes continued to study him. "I find it hard to believe that you were just curious."

This time the chaplain was quiet for a moment. He finally sighed and continued. "Well, I suppose I was a little suspicious." He glanced at the fountain. "This whole thing…these attacks…they're more than a little weird."

The expression on Bazes' face became curious. "What do you mean?"

The chaplain rested a hand on the bench. "I just think there are some things about these attacks that don't make a lot of sense."

"Such as?" Bazes pressed.

"This is a strange interrogation." Wilcox rocked back on the bench and took a deep breath. "In a younger life, I used to be a theologian, or a research scholar." He looked at Bazes. "I'm going to assume you already knew that." Bazes' lack of reaction told the chaplain he was right. "These bombings look a lot more like an attack on faith than terrorist attacks."

"Terror attacks *are* an attack on faith," Bazes replied dryly.

"That's true," the chaplain conceded. "They can be considered that, yes. But when I say faith, I don't just mean Christianity, I mean all faiths. I originally thought this might be some kind of resurfacing of the ancient Crusades by some fanatical group, as Saint Patrick's was a Catholic cathedral. However, the Washington National was different. It is dedicated to *all* faiths. And when you consider the bombs were not set off to yield the highest casualties, it makes me wonder what denomination or sect might be next." Bazes was listening to him intently. "Even leaving some important things out, like the real meaning of jihad, something here still feels awfully strange." He tried to manage a small smile. "And you putting a gun in my back doesn't help."

Bazes continued watching him carefully. He sensed Wilcox to be a much more intelligent and knowledgeable man than he let on with his grandfather-like image. "What else?" Bazes asked.

"I think that's enough," frowned the chaplain. "At least until you tell me who you really are."

Bazes tilted his head slightly. "Do you *have* more

information?"

"I might."

Bazes shook his head and looked away. He was frustrated. What he was about to do was forbidden, on every level. But time was running out and the stakes were too high. Besides, he certainly wasn't about to the kill the man.

Bazes scanned the area around them again and kept his gun easily accessible. "Okay," he said. "What do you want to know?"

The chaplain sighed. "Son, I'm an old man. I've had a long life, raised a couple boys, and got to marry a miracle of a woman." He dropped his head and looked at the dark grass in front of him. "Unfortunately, my wife was called home many years ago, and I've been alone for a long time." The chaplain cleared his voice and looked back at Bazes. "In my life, I've seen darn near everything: the good, the bad, and the very, very ugly. At my age, there is only one thing that any man wants…"

Bazes raised an eyebrow.

"The *truth*," added Wilcox. "I'm near the end of my road now, and all I care about is the truth."

Bazes let a small grin creep across his lips. This was no ordinary chaplain. He nodded his head. "Okay. The truth you will get. But then you must help me."

"Agreed."

Now it was Bazes' turn to take a deep breath. He was suddenly nervous. "You're right, my name is Hebrew, and it's one of the oldest. It's an Israelite name. I belong to one of the oldest and purest Israelite bloodlines in existence, going to back to Levi."

The chaplain's mouth opened in surprise. "You're a Levite?"

Bazes nodded. "Of the Twelve Tribes, the Levites were tasked by Moses with the highest responsibility and the highest honor of all. To protect the word and the *truth*, of God. That not only means the word of God but everything related to it. We have dedicated our lives, and given those lives, without hesitation for over 3,000 years to ensure the truth of God is never lost." He paused. "But now…now I believe we face the greatest threat to that task in the history of humanity."

Across from him, Wilcox sat speechless.

"I agree the attacks on the churches were not acts of terrorism, at least not as we know it. I believe they were carried out by a group of people, led by one specific and evil man, who intend the greatest harm to God's children that we have ever known."

41

Christine woke up when the car's engine started and roared to life. She blinked and opened her eyes, squinting into the bright morning light. Rand pulled the car forward, rounded several trees and slowly rolled back down the dirt road the way they came.

Sarah stirred on her lap as the bumps shook them gently from side to side. She looked up at Christine and smiled.

"Good morning, Sunshine," Christine whispered and stroked her hair.

Sarah blinked and glanced at Rand and Avery in the front seats. She lay her head back down and snuggled in closer to Christine with her arms tucked in tight.

Christine watched her. She was so beautiful and so innocent. The thought of someone trying to hurt Sarah caused a feeling of rage deep inside of her, and it was growing. She no longer cared about herself; all she wanted to do was keep Sarah safe. *And she would fight to the very end to do it.*

Rand pulled the Dodge back out onto the road and continued south, while the girls in the back watched the rising sun through the opposite side window.

Avery tucked the shotgun down next to his door and reached into the back seat next to them. He pulled a second bag out of the larger duffle bag and unzipped it, handing each girl an energy bar and bottle of water.

He smiled. "I know it's not exactly a continental breakfast."

The girls took them appreciatively. After Avery turned back around, Christine opened a wrapper and handed the bar to Sarah with a wink. She grabbed it with her small hands and winked back.

"Is that what a grandpa is like?" Sarah whispered.

Christine almost laughed. Aside from his white hair and some wrinkles, Avery was almost as far as you could get from a traditional grandfather. But just as quickly, Christine suddenly felt a sadness in her heart, wondering what had happened to Sarah's grandfathers. How much disappointment did this girl have to endure?

They merged onto a larger two-lane road and joined a steady line of traffic. Both men scanned the thick, tree lined highway and watched as much of the sky as they were able to see from the front seats.

Christine leaned forward. "Where are we going?"

"We're vulnerable and can't hide under trees forever," Rand said, still scanning. "They know where we were, so they're likely trying to find us from overhead satellite or aircraft." He looked up again through his side window. "Our best option is to hide somewhere they can't easily track us."

"Where is that?"

"In plain sight."

Christine had just sat back and put her arm around Sarah's shoulders when she heard a loud chime. She lifted her hips, reached into her pocket and was startled when she pulled her cell phone out.

"Oh my god!" she cried. "My phone is on again!" She looked back and forth between Rand and Avery. "I didn't turn it on this time, I swear!"

Rand's eyes stared at her in the rearview mirror. "Your phone has been compromised. Get rid of it!"

Christine looked around. "Now?"

"NOW!" they both said in unison.

Christine immediately grabbed the metal handle on her door and cranked it counter-clockwise, rolling down her window. The loud, cold air rushed in as she took one last look at her phone, and threw it out.

Rand accelerated and passed the car in front of them. He wished the trees were not cut so far back away from the road. They could use some cover.

They rode silently for several miles. Sarah, now sat on the driver's side behind Rand with her legs on top of the large bag. She watched quietly as the cars and signs went by. After a few minutes, she slid back over to Christine and whispered in her ear, "Do you know how to play I-spy?"

The traffic became increasingly dense as they merged onto highway 206, but when a string of brake lights could be seen ahead, Rand and Avery grew concerned.

Soon the cars slowed to a crawl as some kind of obstruction could be seen ahead in the distance. It was a road block with three police cars creating a barrier across both lanes, letting just one car through at a time. Several state troopers took turns surrounding the cars as they came to a stop.

Trooper Williams watched the other team let a car through before he sighed and waved the next car in his lane ahead, up to where he was standing. As the car stopped next to him, the driver lowered her window and he leaned in.

"Hello, ma'am," he said, looking through her car. "You traveling alone today?"

The elderly woman nodded. "Yes. What's wrong, are you looking for someone?"

"Yes ma'am." Williams smiled. "Sorry for the inconvenience." He straightened up and waved her forward between the parked police cars, to the open highway beyond.

Williams glanced again at the other officers while he waved a copper colored Dodge forward. The driver, an older man, wore sunglasses and looked up at the officer as he brought the car to a stop.

"Morning, sir," Williams said. He looked into the car

and glanced at the passenger, a younger woman with long, dark red hair. She was wearing large sunglasses, but something looked familiar about her. He looked over the top of the car at his partner who looked back with a raised eyebrow.

"Where are you headed, sir?" Williams asked the driver.

"Into town," Avery replied. "Why, what's going on?"

"Just a routine stop," the trooper said. He looked at the girl again. "And who are you traveling with?"

"This is my granddaughter," Avery responded. "This isn't a routine stop. I come through here all the time."

"Well, we're just looking for someone who may have stolen a car." Williams straightened and nonchalantly took a piece of paper out of his back pocket. He held it above the roof of the car and quietly unfolded it to reveal pictures of Christine and Sarah.

"Why would you stop everyone if you're looking for a specific car?" asked Avery.

Williams didn't hear him. Instead, he was showing the picture to his partner over their heads. His partner, on the other side of the car, slowly motioned downward to the back seat. Williams glanced through the back window and saw a large bag on the seat and what looked like a lump on the floor covered by a blanket.

"What's in the bag, sir?"

Avery remained calm. "Just some odds and ends."

"What kind of odds and ends?" asked Williams.

"Some car parts that I need to have repaired. I'm a collector."

"Hmm," said the trooper. "And what's that lump on the floor?"

"More car parts."

"I see." Williams turned his body to block the view of his hand reaching back and unclipping the safety strap on his holster. "Sir, would you mind stepping out of the car?"

Avery frowned. "I'm sorry, I'm afraid it's difficult for me to stand up easily."

"Well, I'm sure-" Williams began but stopped abruptly. He peered curiously back over the roof of the car. He couldn't see his partner. "Rog?" Williams got no response, so he leaned down and looked through the car to the other side. Still nothing.

Williams' heart started to beat faster. He stepped back and ran into something. He never found out what it was, as his body stiffened and a painful jolt of 500,000 volts ran through his system. Before he could scream, Rand grabbed him from the side and smashed his fist into the trooper's lower jaw, triggering the cranial nerve and instantly knocking him out. At the same moment that Williams' knees gave out, Avery thrust his left arm out the window at a 90 degree angle and grabbed the front of his uniform. He pushed him up and then pulled him against the car to keep his body upright.

The car horn behind them began blaring when the driver witnessed Rand's attack on the trooper, which caused the troopers in the other lane to turn their attention to the honking car. The driver inside was waving at something. It was all the distraction Rand needed.

By the time the other three troopers had turned away from the honking car and back to Williams, who appeared to be leaning on the car, Rand had already covered the distance. He quickly pushed the stun gun into the stomach of the first trooper, an older, overweight man who screamed and fell onto his knees. As the trooper collapsed to his knees, Rand yanked the trooper's yellow Taser gun from its holster and fired over the top of the car, hitting a taller officer and sinking both electrodes into his neck and shoulder. The second trooper's lips immediately curled down, exposing his teeth, and his body jerked backwards, already beginning to convulse on the way to the ground.

The third trooper watched wide-eyed in a moment of shock as the other two fell , but he was young and reacted much faster than the others. He reached for his gun and already had it out of the holster when Rand's boot found its mark. His eyes instantly rolled into his head, and he fell forward into his older partner, taking them both to the ground. With a single strike, Rand knocked the larger man out and spun with the momentum, launching himself over the hood. The tall and lanky trooper was still shaking violently. The image of Rand standing over him was the last thing he would remember when he woke up again.

Rand returned to the Dodge and withdrew his pistol, shooting out two tires on each patrol car. Avery lowered trooper Williams' body down to the pavement. They both turned and looked at the line of cars behind them. Not a single vehicle made a sound; instead, the shocked drivers simply stared at them with open mouths.

Rand knelt down and examined the gun in Williams' holster. Satisfied, he pulled the magazine out and took two more from the trooper's belt. It was not the same model of magazine, but it was the same caliber bullet. He stood up and pushed them into his back pocket.

Rand looked inside the car. "Everyone okay?"

Avery smiled, looking over his shoulder at Christine and the small lump on the floor behind her. He opened his mouth to reply when they heard an ominous sound, the distant, thumping blades of a helicopter. They turned and saw the shape of an Apache AH-64D attack helicopter approaching in the distance. The roadblock was not intended to stop them; it was merely meant to slow them down.

Rand immediately reached behind Avery and pulled the large bag closer. He reached in and retrieved an AR-10 and several magazines, two of which had thick bands of red tape around them. He stuffed the magazines into his remaining pockets and wrapped the rifle's sling around his shoulder. He then ran around the back of the car and stopped at Christine's window. "You'd better get in back and stay down."

Christine was instantly out of her seat, scrambling over

the top and into the back. She settled down onto the floor and lay on top of Sarah.

"Are you okay, honey?" she whispered.

Sarah peered out from under the thick fabric. "Yes!"

Rand stepped forward and planted himself on the edge of the hood. "Go!"

Less than a mile away, the helicopter slowed to a hover, just forty feet above the empty highway. Behind it, Rand could see a second chopper; it was a Blackhawk. Six ropes trailed to the ground, and dark clad soldiers quickly descended. They reached the ground and squatted low, assessing their position before fanning out. The Blackhawk quickly turned and retreated while the Apache continued hovering in place.

Avery zigzagged the Dodge through the police barricade and stopped, facing the empty road ahead. The attack helicopter tilted forward and began accelerating in their direction.

Avery revved the engine and looked at Rand through the windshield. "This car can't take anything that thing has!" he yelled. He floored it, and the Dodge Charger instantly leapt forward.

They both accelerated towards each other, quickly covering the distance. Inside the cockpit, the pilot's integrated helmet display slaved the 30mm gun to his line of sight. As they grew closer, the pilot's display zeroed in on the car, and the giant barrel located just beneath the aircraft's nose, adjusted accordingly.

At the same time, Rand peered through his high-powered, red dot scope and tried to adjust for the shaking of the car.

The pilot targeted the car and wrapped his index finger around the stick's trigger. Suddenly, three bullets hit the cockpit glass in front of his face. They didn't penetrate, but it startled the pilot enough to disengage and dive for cover. The aircraft dropped close to the ground, and the pilot pulled up just as the Dodge sped under him.

The pilot's mouth tightened in anger as he continued further away and swung around in a wide arc. The large cracks in the window were now too large to use the 30mm Chain Gun accurately, but the Hellfire's could target by themselves. He just needed enough room.

Avery slowed the car less than a thousand feet from the soldiers running toward them. Unless they were carrying something really big, the extra thick steel and glass on the car could take whatever they had. He turned the car and stopped in a broadside position. Rand jumped down from the hood and ran forward towards the Apache which was finishing its turn. As the helicopter straightened its approach, he replaced his magazine, inserting one with red tape. Inside it was armor piercing rounds.

He quickly lay down on the gravel and pressed the stock of the rifle securely into his shoulder. The large distance the pilot took to circle back meant he was preparing to fire an air-to-ground missile, and that meant a Hellfire. And if the aircraft were fully loaded, it would be fired from the pilot's right side rails and arm itself within the first fifteen feet of flight.

Christine suddenly screamed, as bullets began pelting the side of the Dodge. Dents appeared on the inside, and two rounds hit the window and froze inside the special laminated glass, cracking it.

Avery looked at the dents and yelled out the other window to Rand. "We're okay!"

Rand's heart slowed. He closed one eye and watched carefully for the one sign he would have when the missile fired. Then he saw it. For only a split second, the fire and smoke from behind the missile could be seen *igniting*. At the same instant, Rand began shooting, and kept shooting, pulling the trigger as quickly as he could.

The Hellfire armed itself but traveled only thirty-six feet before it was struck head on by a hot loaded, armor piercing bullet, then was hit again at forty-four feet. It detonated immediately, and the helicopter was too close to avoid the explosion. All of the armaments were ripped from the sub-wing pylons, with one of the rails tearing a hole through the right wing. Two large chunks of metal shrapnel punched larger holes in the aircraft's side body armor, severing one of the main hydraulic lines, and a third piece of shrapnel removed almost two feet of rotor blade.

The pilot felt the loss of control immediately, as the helicopter began a horizontal wobble of which he was rapidly losing control. Within a few seconds, the secondary hydraulic line took over for the primary. Control was restored, but the wobble from the now unbalanced blade was increasing and had the potential to shake the helicopter apart. The pilot had to beat it to the ground before that happened, which meant a very hard landing.

Rand was back on his feet as several more slugs hit the far side of the Charger. He reached the passenger door where Avery had both hands on the steering wheel and the engine running.

Rand peeked around the curve of the front windshield, looking for the soldiers who had dropped from the Blackhawk, but quickly ducked back when a bullet ricocheted off the hood.

"Get past them and then get the car out of sight," he said to Avery, scanning the sky above them. He knew they could easily be seen from a number of aircraft, perhaps even a drone which could fly high enough to remain completely invisible. No matter where they went, they were undoubtedly being watched from a live video stream.

Behind them came a terrible noise as the Apache helicopter smashed hard into the ground, breaking itself in two. Rand looked at it over his shoulder and turned back to Avery. "Find a safe place, and I'll meet you on the other side."

Avery nodded but said nothing. He dropped the transmission into drive and punched the accelerator, causing the rear tires to kick up a wall of dirt before speeding away.

Farther down the road, one of the six soldiers shooting at the car paused and raised his eye from his scope. He watched the tiny figure of a man run into the trees. He'd never seen anyone move that fast before.

42

"Hold on!' Avery yelled over the roaring engine. The car bounced off-road and over the brush as he circled away from the men shooting and then rounded back in their direction. "We're going to have to drive right through them! And we're going to take a lot of fire. So stay down!"

Christine settled her arms on both sides of Sarah, keeping most of her weight off her tiny frame. Nothing was going to get Sarah that didn't go through her first.

Downrange, the black clad men watched the Dodge turn back in their direction. They lifted their rifles up and waited. Just moments before, they had all watched the attack helicopter come smashing down to the ground. Fortunately, the fuel was contained, and there was no explosion, leaving it to be enveloped in a giant cloud of dirt and debris. *How the hell did they bring that down?*

Avery was now heading in their direction at full speed. His eyes scanning the area ahead, trying to judge the best angle that would receive the minimal damage. He finally decided there was no best angle, and instead stayed on the road and kept the pedal hard against the floor, opening the engine into a thundering scream. Bullets began peppering the front windshield and gradually moved to the right-hand side door as Avery pushed quickly past their positions. Once the car was past, the soldiers halted their firing. They had to save their ammo. There still someone in the trees.

The soldiers moved together in a slight arc, rounding and coming in toward the area of trees where they saw Rand disappear.

The third man in line motioned with hand signals, telling the men to move in slowly. They were Delta Force, some of the best in the military, and they had hunted plenty of human targets before. They were also extraordinarily good at it and not the least bit rushed.

The man they had seen was not a runner, he was a fighter. The natural human reaction was to find the first decent shelter and dig in, which meant he was likely less than a hundred yards from where he entered the forest. He was also unfamiliar with the immediate area. This increased anxiety and the sense that a person being pursued had less time than they actually did, which meant rash decisions.

The head of the squad was a man named Fish. He was strong, methodical, and savored the act of hunting another man down. He halted the team and then motioned for the two men on the outside to spread out and widen the circle. They would enter about a hundred yards further down, then form a circle and slowly tighten the noose.

It took several minutes, but once in position and almost like clockwork, all six members began closing in slowly and silently. As the noose continued to close, Fish could taste the slaughter.

They were more correct than they knew; Rand had not gone far. He sat waiting to see if any of them entered the thick wall of trees behind him. After a long wait, he could finally hear one of them approaching, but what Rand didn't know was that the other five were already *in* as well.

One of Fish's men, a short, stocky ranger with his face painted in black stripes, moved in, making almost no sound. He moved his rifle in step with his head, sweeping side to side at a 45 degree angle, occasionally stopping to listen. Hearing nothing, he continued on.

He was now just twenty feet from Rand. They were also right about Rand's general vicinity, but what the Delta members were not expecting was where he would be waiting for them. Rand was not twenty feet in front of the man. He was twenty feet *above* him.

Almost all soldiers were trained to look up in a pursuit, but under stress very few actually did. The fact was, ascending a tree took far more time and energy than was practical, and it was a veritable trap, leaving the person very little room for movement. No one in their right mind would paint themselves in that kind of corner. Only a person who could climb effortlessly, or knew how a trained soldier thinks under pressure, would do it. Rand was both.

43

Natirar Park was a 411-acre park dedicated to the preservation of the farming and agricultural history of New York State's Somerset County. Named after the Raritan River which ran through it, the park included trails and many farming and residential buildings from the late 18th century. The park was also a popular field trip destination for many of the surrounding elementary schools, and the early spring trips had begun the preceding week.

Two large buses and a few dozen cars filled most of the large, shaded parking lot, and children and parents walked back and forth to the main building where the tour was about to begin.

Avery let the engine idle quietly and drove around to the far end of the lot to avoid attracting attention. He found a large maple tree to park under and shifted the car into park before turning off the engine. Both Christine and Sarah emerged slowly from the floor behind him. They looked over his shoulder at the crowd gathering in the distance.

"Is this a school?" asked Sarah, eyeing all the children.

Avery shook his head. "No, Sarah, it's a park. Do you like parks?"

Sarah nodded and continued watching.

"What do we do now?" asked Christine.

"We need another car." Avery eyed the large canopy of trees overhead. "They can see where we are, and no doubt where we just pulled into." He turned and eyed Christine. "How's your dexterity?"

"Huh?"

Christine watched the crowd, and followed one of the mothers who held the hands of two little boys as they stood in line waiting to buy tickets. She had followed the woman from the parking lot, noting the large, baggy purse she carried. It looked to Christine like the woman had simply tossed her car keys into her purse which she hoped meant they were sitting on top of everything else in the bag.

Christine edged closer, trying to look casual. The woman was less than two feet away and had her purse slung over her right shoulder as she struggled to pull a small cooler chest behind her and the boys.

Not far away, Avery and Sarah both waited under a shady tree, watching. As Christine nervously tried to get even closer to the woman, Sarah noticed a park ranger emerge from the large building. He was overweight with a balding head of thin hair, and he walked excitedly toward the children who were waiting.

The man suddenly clapped his hands and said in a loud voice, "Hi kids!". Most of the children just looked at him. "I said HI KIDS! Who's here for the big tour?" This time several children answered and raised their hands.

At the ticket booth, the woman in front of Christine stepped up to the small window and bought her tickets. She pulled her keys out and put them on the wooden counter to retrieve her wallet.

"Mom," one of her small boys whined, "it's gonna start!" He pulled at his brother's hand.

"Hold on, hold on," she snapped and fumbled with her tickets and wallet.

"Okay," called out the park ranger nearby. "I need some tickets!" He knelt down as the children surrounded him, holding out their paper tickets. The man smiled broadly at the children and patted the head of one of the boys. "And what's your name?"

The mother at the counter was pulled forward by both

of her boys now. She frantically stuffed everything into her purse with a quick glance backward; then she trotted forward to catch up.

Christine walked as fast as she could away from the group without looking back. She gripped the woman's keys tightly in her hand. The sign on the ticket booth showed the tour to be a little over an hour long, and if those three were part of a larger group, it could buy them a little more time before the woman noticed her car was missing.

She reached Avery and Sarah and motioned for them to get moving. But Sarah didn't move.

"Sarah!" Christine whispered loudly. "Come on!"

Sarah turned slowly to Christine who was holding out a hand for her. "That man over there," she said, looking back at the park ranger who was still kneeling down and was now resting his hand on another boy's shoulder.

"What about him?"

Sarah looked back at her and Avery. "He's a bad man."

Christine's heart skipped. She looked back at the ranger. He continued to play with the children. "*How* bad?"

Sarah had a look of forlorn on her face. "Very bad. He's really, really red."

Christine watched him closely. Knowing something was wrong, she could see it now. It was very subtle, but he was being a little too friendly with the children. She noticed he kept his hand on the boy's shoulders just a little too long. Christine felt her stomach turn.

Avery saw it too, but they had no time. "We can't do anything about it. We have to go."

She forced herself to turn away, pulling Sarah gently along with her. Sarah kept watching the man over her shoulder until they reached the parking lot.

The car was a recent model Honda sedan, not too old

but not too new either, which Avery explained would blend in well. They transferred the large bag as the girls climbed into the back seat and fastened their seat belts. They quietly pulled out of the parking lot and headed south again, but immediately pulled off at the next exit, following two other cars. Avery then followed an older road away from the highway where he reached a row of large trees and parked. He turned the car off and placed his shotgun on his lap.

"Now what are we waiting for?" asked Sarah.

Avery scanned the area around them. "Rand."

Fish was growing concerned. His team was tightening the circle, and they were going to be upon each other at any moment. They should have engaged the target by now, or at least found more tracks. What Fish didn't know yet was that two of his men were missing. He slowly continued forward with his finger hovering just above the trigger.

He also didn't know that Rand was gone. Fish was not his priority, Sarah was. Rand merely needed an exit and made one. While Fish and his team were crawling through the thicket, Rand was running south at full steam.

Avery heard a noise and had his gun trained on Rand by the time he emerged from a group of tall, wild ferns. He ducked down and peered in the back seat again.

"Everyone alright?"

They both nodded. Rand opened the front door and got in.

"We don't have much time with this car," Avery said, and slowly pulled out from under the trees. He drifted back toward the highway and joined in behind another car.

Christine leaned forward in the back seat. "We're heading back to New York aren't we?"

Rand turned around to face them. "Yes. With

overhead surveillance, it's too easy for them to see us now. We have another safe place to go but we need to lose them first or they'll track us the entire way."

"And how do we lose them in New York?"

Rand shrugged. "We find a large crowd."

44

Dario Burk burst into the small, private cabin aboard the Airbus A320, where Pope Pius sat surrounded by several of his cardinals. The Pope looked up at him as he approached.

"Forgive me, Your Holiness," he said with a bow, "but we must abandon our plans immediately."

The Pope was a slight man, humble, but very sharp. He looked up at Burk from under his white eyebrows, unsurprised.

Burk continued. "We have received a credible threat to your presence in New York."

"How credible is it?" asked the Pope in a quieted voice.

"Very credible." Burk's expression was respectful but intense. "From Israeli intelligence."

The Pope looked at his aide sitting across from him and then to the other cardinals. He turned and peered out the window to his left. The sun was beginning its ascent over the Atlantic Ocean. The bright sunlight was glistening off the deep, blue water far below.

There were always threats, and the Israelis were known for the best intelligence in the world, but even they were not perfect. *Was this another false alarm or was it real?* The Pope leaned back in his seat. *Did it even matter?* The world was frozen in a grip of terror from the attacks. Participation in their Catholic churches had plummeted around the world as the public feared the attacks would spread, and their church could be next.

The Pope took a deep breath. He was the leader of the Roman Catholic Church. He was the one that hundreds of millions looked to for spiritual guidance in a difficult world. And what was more difficult than this? If there was one thing that everyone needed, beyond the cars, the televisions, the expensive vacations, beyond all materialism, was safety. Safety from all that was dark and evil in the world. What would happen when they no longer felt safe in the house of God? And what message would it send if he were to turn around and run because someone thought he was in danger? *Wasn't everyone in danger now?*

The Pope slowly shook his head. "I'm sorry," he said to Burk. "We cannot."

Burk's eyes widened in surprise. He was refusing? Burk stood motionless. His priority was the safety of the Pope above all else. All else.

"Pardon me, Your Holiness?"

The Pope smiled warmly. "My son, you have sworn to protect me," he said. "I understand this. But *you* must understand that I have sworn to something much greater, and to someone much more important."

Burk had no reply. He stood looking respectfully at him. In a single sentence, the rug had been pulled out from under him. He sighed, and quietly turned around. Before reaching the door, he quickly turned back. "May I at least assume the threat is valid and take all appropriate precautions?"

The Pope nodded. "Of course."

Burk left the room and closed the door gently behind him. *Please let this be another false alarm.*

Zahn picked up the phone and held it to his ear.

"Zahn," came Benecke's voice, "we've lost them."

"You lost them?" Zahn was incredulous.

"Only for the moment," replied Benecke. "We think they switched cars, and we're trying to verify, but we're 90% sure. If we're right, then it looks like they're headed for the city." He was quiet for a moment. "Do you want to tell me what they did?"

"They're involved in a plan to assassinate one of our

diplomats."

"Isn't that under the jurisdiction of the CIA?" Benecke asked calmly. "Because I spoke with Mr. Ha at the CIA and he knows nothing about this."

"No," Zahn raised his voice. "This is State Department jurisdiction!"

Zahn wanted them, and he wanted them without interference from any other agency. They would all know soon enough, but if someone else picked up the girl and she talked…he couldn't afford any cracks, not this close.

Benecke sighed. "I don't suppose you have anything resembling a warrant?"

"When was the last time any of us used a *warrant*?" Zahn answered sarcastically. "Besides, they fired on, and brought down, one of our helicopters!"

"I don't believe all of the details have been confirmed yet."

"Just tell me when you're sure of their location. My team will be ready." He ended the call.

On the other end, Benecke hung up the phone and shook his head. Zahn was not someone to be screwed with, everyone knew that. *But where on earth did he get all of that power?*

Zahn pounded the desk with his fist. He hadn't spent years carefully forming alliances with other department heads and politicians to allow some new boy scout to start asking questions now. He thought about what Benecke had said. If they *were* headed back to the city, it must be for a reason. What were they planning? He leaned back in his chair. If they were able to bring down a helicopter all by themselves, then he had a pretty good idea.

45

Hundreds of thousands of people surrounded the Cathedral of Saint John the Divine, the largest cathedral in New York City covering an area of over 121,000 square feet and towering over 232 feet tall. It was here that both the President and Vice President were set to appear with the Pope, along with several other dignitaries from around the world. The Pope's speech would be short, but he hoped it would show the world that his message was for *all faiths* and on all continents.

Dario Burk stood next to Carolina Flores, the head of the Secret Service. The crowd was enormous and spread nearly half a mile in every direction. What they wanted, what they needed, was to see and hear their Pope.

He looked up and scanned the nearby buildings. Every rooftop was either manned or watched by the Secret Service, FBI, or New York Police Department, including swat teams from all three. Overhead, dozens of helicopters watched from the air, while on the ground thousands of police officers milled through the crowds, watching for anything out of the ordinary. As if there was such a thing as ordinary in a crowd this large.

There would be absolutely no physical contact of any kind with the Pope. He would appear on the large platform constructed outside the cathedral, wave, and speak to the world. He would end with a long prayer and be quickly swept away as soon as he was out of sight. The Swiss Guard had every member of their team present, and they would surround the Pope as a veritable wall, both on his way to the platform and away from it.

The only time the Pope would not be completely covered by security was when he was safely inside the cathedral, relaxing before his appearance, and that was only when he was far away from windows. Burk and his team were taking absolutely no chances.

Fish and his team had found their missing members. They were alive, but just barely, and had been airlifted to the nearest hospital. Just minutes after the evacuation chopper had left, another Blackhawk landed to retrieve them.

Once Fish and the rest of his team were aboard, the pilot lifted into the air and dipped the craft forward, heading East. Intelligence had confirmed the targets were headed toward Manhattan Island, and Fish now wanted them more than ever.

Avery pulled away from the toll booth leading into the Holland Tunnel and watched through his rearview mirror. Rand did the same out of his side mirror while he pulled his rifle back out from under his legs.

They listened to the car's radio as the newscaster spoke about the thick traffic headed into New York to see the President and the Pope. Once out of the tunnel, they turned south on highway 9A, away from the giant crowd amassing near Central Park.

Suddenly, the small radio on the dashboard came to life. It was the radio Rand had taken from one of the attackers. He turned it up as a loud voice came through the speaker.

"Alpha Bravo Team pursuing East. Over."

"Confirmed Alpha Bravo," came a reply. "Vehicle is a silver sedan."

Rand and Avery looked at each other. The leader of the attack group had just made a mistake. Surely he was aware one of the radios was missing. And if he were, he had forgotten to change to the backup frequency before using it to broadcast again.

Rand looked at Avery. "Head north instead."

Avery frowned. "You realize with that size of a crowd it will be packed with police."

"I know. But judging from that message, they can probably see us, and with everyone gathering north, it will make it even harder to hide anywhere *but* there. Besides, the majority of security is likely to be concentrated closer to the Pope and the President." He watched a car speed past. "We can skirt the outside of the crowd and continue north on foot until we can get back out of the city."

Rand looked at the assault rifle laying across his lap. They certainly wouldn't be able to bring the rifles, which meant concealed handguns only. Not what he was hoping for as it meant they would have to move very quickly. They wouldn't be a position to fight back.

He turned and looked at Sarah in the back seat. She was sitting up straight, looking out the left rear window at the Hudson River. "Sarah, we're going to need you to stay very close to us okay?"

Sarah nodded calmly. "I know."

He then looked at Christine who smiled back at him over Sarah's response.

The crowd was bigger than anything Christine had ever seen. Columbus Avenue, which eventually turned into Morningside Drive near the church, was simply a *wall* of people. They were packed in much tighter than she expected. Incredulous, she walked behind Rand and Avery, holding Sarah's hand tightly.

"My god," she whispered as they entered the very outskirts of the crowd. They walked their next block; the crowd quickly grew dense, prompting Christine to reach out and hold the back of Rand's jacket.

He felt her behind him and glanced back. He slowed and took Sarah's other hand as Avery forced his way through the crowd, where everyone was pushing to get any kind of view.   As they continued walking, Christine watched some people trying to scamper up onto the small roof of a bus stop. Rand and Avery continuously scanned the crowd as they pushed forward.

Between them, Sarah looked back and forth with wide eyes. She had never seen so many people in one place, nor had she seen so many *shadows*. It was incredible.

Christine watched her expression. "What does it look like, Sarah?"

She shook her head in disbelief. "Colors, everywhere!"

Ahead of them, Avery turned a corner and continued down a side street, when Sarah tripped and lost both Christine's and Rand's hands.

An older Asian woman behind them reached down to help Sarah up. As she stood, the woman's gaze fell onto Christine who was reaching back for Sarah. Something looked familiar about them. The woman continued watching them and suddenly remembered, they were the two she had seen on the news program.

"Hey!" she said, with a trailing voice. "HEY!"

Almost in slow motion, several of the others in the crowd looked at the woman and then followed her gaze to both girls.

"It's them!" The woman began pointing. "It's them! The two on the news!"

The faces of the others, staring at Christine and Sarah, flashed a look of recognition as they studied the pair closer.

"I think you're right." hollered a man standing behind her. He pointed along with the woman. "It's them!"

Christine turned to see several people staring at them now. As more people turned around, more eyes widened, and the same phrase was repeated, louder. *"It's them!"*

Christine grabbed Sarah's hand tighter and rushed after Rand who was now pushing through the mass of people with Avery.

More and more people turned to follow the noise

which finally reached three policemen on a nearby street corner. The officers looked up and peered over the crowd to see people shouting, and something or someone surging forward through everyone.

Rand stopped and put a hand on Avery. He could see three uniformed officers approaching. He turned and looked over Christine's head at the crowd behind them, and found two more officers trying to get through from the rear. He spotted a small storefront less than twenty feet away and grabbed Christine and Sarah, pushing them forward toward the building. It was a small dentist's office which appeared to be closed.

Rand kept the girls back and kicked in one of the tall narrow windows. Instantly, an alarm began shrieking from inside as Rand jumped through and reached back out for Sarah. He then ran toward the back of the dark office with Christine and Avery right behind him.

Less than a minute later, the officers reached the front and flattened themselves against the gray wall on both sides of the broken window. With guns drawn, one officer quickly leaned out and peered through the broken pane then ducked back. He immediately did it again, taking a longer look. He pulled back again and looked at the other officers, shaking his head. One by one, they began jumping in through the window and over the broken glass.

Rand reached the back of the office and opened the back door, which led into a long, white maintenance hallway, connecting a string of neighboring offices. He spotted the large exit sign at the end of the hall, hanging above a large metal door. With Sarah still in his arms, he glanced over his shoulder to make sure Christine and Avery were still behind him and ran the length of the hallway.

The door at the end of the complex opened out near the street, which like the others, were crowded with even more people. Some of them were standing just a few steps away and turned, curious when they noticed the door behind them opening.

Rand peered outside and scanned the crowd.

Sarah, suddenly squeezed his neck and began screaming when she saw several shadows change color in front of them. "BLACK! BLACK! BLACK!"

In the moment Sarah screamed, Rand recognized someone across the street who spotted them and immediately raised his rifle to his shoulder. It was one of the men from the Delta Force team.

Rand instantly turned to shield Sarah and grabbed the door handle, pulling it back in as quickly as he could. As it was closing, one large man slammed against the wall, lifeless, just before the door clicked shut. Immediately, large dents appeared on the inside of the door, as it became a giant shield.

Still carrying Sarah, Rand turned and looked back down the hall. He knew there was no escape without putting her at risk. She had to survive, yet any moment the officers would reach the back of the office and find the hallway they were in.

Several blocks away, Burk rushed back inside the cathedral. He, along with everyone else, heard the warning over their tiny earpieces. *Gunshots fired nearby!*

Burk entered through the west end of the church and ran past a large group of security agents who were running the other way. He passed the altar and the church's famous stained glass windows and sprinted for the large sacristy. When he burst into the room, Burk found the Pope kneeling in his gold and silver striped vestment. Outside in the distance, he could hear the Vice President's speech abruptly end as he was rushed off the large stage. Burk was certain the Secret Service already had the President in his limousine and headed away from the church.

The Pope looked up at Burk as the three Swiss Guards

already in the room stepped in behind him.

"We're evacuating," Burk said firmly.

The Pope nodded at Burk and stood up. He could hear that something was wrong. The crowd outside was beginning to yell out questions. He could also hear shouting within the church as the various security teams scrambled to get all of the dignitaries out.

Burk looked over the Pope's shoulder at the three guardsmen. "Benziger and Gavin are getting the others and securing a path to the car. We'll escort him in standard two by two positions. Once we-" Burk was suddenly interrupted when four men walked into the room with AK-47 assault rifles shouldered.

Irritated, Burk turned and began to wave them away, insisting they were already moving the Pope, when he noticed the make of their guns. He jumped in shock when the men raised their rifles and fired on the three Swiss Guardsmen next to the Pope. Burk's hand was already in motion, reaching for his sidearm when he was shot in the arm and the gun tumbled to the floor. The impact caused him to stumble backward and fall over one of the large chairs. He quickly scrambled to reach his dropped weapon with his left hand, but was shot twice more in his other shoulder.

Burk cried out and fell back onto the thick carpet. Without the use of either arm, he couldn't reach, or even prop himself up. With his head on the floor, he quickly looked around the room and used his legs to push himself away, but he froze when Zahn stepped forward and pointed a gun at the Pope.

"Stop!" Zahn warned.

Burk stopped, but his mind was racing. He had to keep the Pope alive at all costs. He had to do *something*, even if that meant changing tactics. "Don't shoot," he cried. "You want him alive."

Zahn watched Burk, lying on the floor with his chest heaving. He turned to Sarat standing next to him and motioned toward the door. Immediately, Sarat ran to the door and looked outside. Seeing no one, he closed and locked it, then returned to Zahn's side with his gun raised again.

Taking a few steps toward Burk, Zahn stood over him, watching as he tried still to maneuver with two arms that didn't work. "Mr. Dario Burk." Zahn said with a smirk. "The famed head of the Swiss Guard." He dropped his chin in a sympathetic gesture. "No doubt your brain is now frantically working through scenarios to keep your dear Pope alive. However, in a few minutes you'll come to the uncomfortable and ironic conclusion that 'throwing him to the wolves' is your best and only option." Zahn displayed a sick grin and watched Burk's eyes, waiting as he desperately tried to think of any other way. After a short pause, Zahn continued. "And judging from the look of despair in your eyes, I can see that you've just reached that point."

Screams could be heard now from the crowd outside as people began to panic. Zahn cocked his ear. "That doesn't sound good," he said sarcastically. "In fact, that sounds a lot like *pandemonium*. I know English is not your first language, but I suspect you know what that means." Burk was still scanning the room looking for anything, any tool, any helpful item at all, but it was futile. He could barely move.

Zahn tried to relax. His plan had been long in coming, and he didn't have much time, but he wanted to savor every second he could. "I imagine now you're probably wondering *how* and *why*." He raised his eyebrows at Burk. "Yes?" He shrugged when Burk didn't answer. "The *how* was easy. Easier than you think." He turned to the Pope, now speaking to them both. "You can thank terrorism. After all, it was the 9/11 attack on our Twin Towers that gave the United States the new enemy it so desperately needed. It gave us both an enemy and a perfect distraction for the entire world. Put enough fear into the people, and governments can do anything, least of which is to justify and expand its military empire. And that constant fear of terrorism allowed us to do just that." Zahn looked to the Pope then back to Burk on the floor. "Unfortunately, politicians are rather stupid, and there were terrible consequences they didn't bother to think about. Do you know what I am referring to?" he asked, chiding him. "Why the laws, of course. Laws that called for all departments to act in tighter concert. What could go wrong?" A fiendish smile returned to his face. "Now, you lay there on the floor slowly bleeding to death and asking yourself how in the world we ever got past your security. The reason, is *because we were the security.*"

Sergeant Fish watched silently as Rand and Avery lay face down on the sidewalk, both bound in handcuffs. His team members stood behind him. The hysteria was still growing with more of the crowd beginning to panic and run, while the police officers tried to keep the stampede away from them and their prisoners. Fish smiled when he saw one older officer look around and then quickly kick Rand in the face with his boot. He promptly stepped back as blood began to appear on the cement under Rand's mouth.

Fish scanned the area, looking for the woman and girl, but there was no sign of them. He knew it wouldn't be long before the officers began to realize that neither of their prisoners on the ground could have been the one who shot into the crowd behind the building. They had to move fast, prompting Fish to step forward and show his military ID. "We have orders to investigate."

"We've got it contained," an officer growled.

Fish shrugged. "We can see that. But we still need to have a look and report back. Orders."

"Whatever." He motioned to the broken window. "We already searched the place."

Fish nodded and walked past him, examining the window pane momentarily before stepping inside what appeared to be the office waiting room. The rest of his team followed, and one by one they searched all the rooms and ended at a back door leading into a maintenance hallway. Fish looked up and down the hallway, noticing the dented circles in the far door. There were several other doors in the hallway too, all connecting to other offices or store fronts in the complex. They walked up and down the hall, trying all of the door handles, starting with the doors nearest the end. They used a standard entry technique with one man forcing the door open while two more swept in behind him with guns raised.

The first two doors led to a lawyer's office and a CPA firm. The two teams moved silently, through the various rooms and around desks, looking, but found nothing. They were undeterred. The two men had to have done something with the girls before they were taken. But what?

The next few doors led to similar businesses or empty spaces, but they found nothing. Fish knew that soon the police would be looking for *them*, wanting to ask more questions. He found the last door was unlocked and opened into the back of a small convenience store. The soldiers entered quietly and could hear a commotion up front which sounded like looting. There was yelling and screaming between multiple voices. Fish held up his hand for the team to stay back as he swept the back room with the barrel of his gun.

He opened a large, metal refrigerator door and stepped inside. After a few minutes, he stepped back out and shut it again quietly. On the other side of the room were columns of boxes, stacked almost to the ceiling, most of which were empty. There appeared to be little room between them for anyone to hide. He began to turn back to the door when he noticed several tall, thin CO_2 tanks stacked neatly in the corner. He studied them closely.

With the noise increasing from the front of the store, Fish slowly stepped forward toward the tanks. Without letting go of his rifle, he wrapped his left arm around one of the tanks and pulled it forward. He then bent down and looked through the gap and into the green eyes of Christine.

The sound outside was becoming chaotic as people badly wanted out from the middle of a frightened crowd. Hundreds of security personnel tried to keep the movement orderly, but their barricades were simply getting overturned or destroyed.

Zahn leaned on the back of an upholstered chair looking at the Pope, who stared back at him. The man did not seem the least bit afraid. Zahn was impressed.

Behind him, Zahn's men watched the Pope with disdain. Perhaps he would be more afraid if he knew, beneath the makeup these men were wearing, they were Islamists right down to their bones.

Zahn turned back to Burk on the floor, who was still fidgeting with two bad arms. The man just wouldn't give up. "Are you wondering *why* yet?"

Burk did not answer. He simply stared back with a look of defiance.

"Of course you are. Let's just say…this is payment for services rendered. A debt, if you will."

"Listen to me," Burk said with a strained voice. "Just keep him alive and unharmed. If you keep him unharmed, they will give you anything you ask. Anything!"

Zahn looked back to the Pope and then raised his eyebrows at Burk. "Oh, I know."

46

The death of the Pope was absolutely devastating. It was as if the entire world cried out at once. Millions of people simply burst into tears or fell to their knees, shocked at the news. Hospitals were packed with people who had collapsed or fainted, and from almost every developed country in the world came reports of people who had fallen dead right where they stood.

Brazil and Mexico, the two most populous catholic countries, suffered a nationwide freeze when almost no one showed up for work. Instead, the churches were overwhelmed with mourners. Italy fared even worse where in Rome the utter shock resulted in an eerie silence of nearly three million people. In Vatican City, the long held tradition of closing the papal apartment and destroying the Fisherman's ring following a pope's death seemed to be forgotten.

His death was horrific enough, but murder was beyond all comprehension. And while the devastation was unimaginable, the retribution was immense. Millions of Catholics immediately blamed the entire Middle East, including anyone with relations to them, even those who simply shared their skin color.

Worst still, no one had any idea who had done it. It had happened during the hysteria in New York, where Pope Pius and the entire Swiss Guard team responsible for protecting him were slaughtered. Every possible security department within the United States was scrambling for clues or information. It had happened quickly and in the church's sacristy, the chamber reserved for formal preparation. But during the mania, no one had seen anyone enter or exit the room. Never had the world demanded answers so forcefully and with such little information available.

Zahn took a drink of his scotch and leaned back into his chair. He flipped between news stations thoroughly reveling in the absolute chaos that was unfolding. It was even more delightful than he'd dreamed. After years of planning, it had gone off without a hitch. Without a single hitch. Doing something like this without a serious problem was virtually impossible, and it left him feeling as though he was *destined* for it.

He thought back over the two decades it had taken him to bring all of it to fruition. Years spent at the Department of Defense, the National Security Agency, and finally the State Department, all critical in arranging and achieving the greatest attack on the "church" ever imagined. So great was the impact, that talk spread around the world of the ancient Crusades and whether a war between Christianity and Islam had reignited.

The television screen showed scene after scene from around the globe of people sobbing, unable to believe it. And in the end, it was all due to one man, a man who had just changed the world forever.

Finally, Zahn smiled when he thought of the bonus, the second prize that clearly proved his destiny. *He had the girl too.* In fact, he had both her and the woman aboard the very plane he sat on. He wondered if it could get any better.

Kia Sarat approached with a serious face.

"Well?" Zahn asked.

"Iman put them both out," Sarat replied.

"And it will last the whole way?"

"He is sure it will."

"Good." Zahn sat thinking for a few moments and then finally nodded. He then looked up at Sarat and raised his glass. "Care for a drink to celebrate?"

Sarat did not appreciate the humor. Zahn knew he did

not drink. Alcohol was a poison and nothing more. He disregarded the comment and decided to let Zahn boast. After all, it was a great accomplishment. Something no one else could have done.

"We will be out of US airspace in two hours," Sarat said.

Zahn took a sip of his scotch. *Two hours.* And then he would never see the United States again. He felt no emotional loss at all. It was just a country, and by the time they figured everything out, it would be too late.

"Tell the pilots they're on radio silence. They're not to respond to anyone, for any reason!"

"They will respond to no one."

Their new home was Argentina. A beautiful country, ruled by a blatantly corrupt government, which was just what he wanted. He sure as hell didn't want to be in the northern hemisphere. "Are we sure we have everyone?"

"Everyone is aboard," Sarat replied. "Soon, we'll be home free."

Zahn smiled and took another sip. *Home free.* That phrase had always seemed a little ironic to him.

Rand thought about his decision and prayed. He simply didn't have a choice; he couldn't risk Sarah's life. And it was clear something had changed. Whoever wanted Sarah was no longer trying to kill her; they wanted to capture her. Ever since the elevator bomb, they had not shot or attacked until after Rand had. He prayed again and hoped, more importantly, that she and Christine had escaped.

He had no idea where Avery was, somewhere close most likely. Rand hoped he was still alive, as he himself lay on the floor barely able to breath. His entire body was black and blue, a keepsake from the guards after they learned where and why he was arrested.

Something bad had happened. What it was, he didn't

know, but it was clear they blamed him for it. Rand tried to open either one of his eyes but couldn't. He tried to remain as still as possible. Every part of his body screamed in pain, and he could feel bones broken, but what frightened him the most were the injuries inside. Each breath felt like a knife slicing through his abdomen, and it felt like it was getting worse.

Lying on the cold stone floor, he couldn't see it, but he could feel it begin. It was subtle at first, but steadily growing stronger. His hands were beginning to tremble.

47

Benecke walked into the large office and stood before Carolina Flores who was on the phone. She was tall with straight hair and motioned him to a seat in front of her desk. After a few minutes, she hung up and shook her head.

"Hello Ron," she said with a sigh. "Things are going downhill fast. The riots are spreading, and Italy is losing control."

Benecke knew what she was referring to. The first riots to take to the streets were in Italy, not far from Vatican City. They spread quickly through the other European countries, then across to Mexico and Brazil. If the number of rioters multiplied as quickly as they did in Italy, the other governments would have little hope of stopping them.

He looked at her for a long moment, trying to think about the best way to tell her. His drive over to CIA headquarters in Langley was full of questions, and given their friendship, she was the first person he needed to talk to, and fast.

She watched Benecke curiously as he took a deep breath. "What is it?"

"I need to tell you something," he said quietly. "And then we need to get everyone together."

Flores leaned forward. "Okay. And who is everyone?"

Benecke frowned. "The Joint Chiefs…and probably the President."

Less than an hour later, Flores and Benecke climbed out of the President's Marine One helicopter and descended the steps onto the green grass of the White

House back lawn. The high pitch of engines faded as they ducked under the slowing rotors and were ushered toward the large glass doors, where more of Flores' agents stood waiting for them.

They were escorted downstairs to the Cabinet Room where the others were waiting. The Chief of Staff met them at the door and waved them in. Flores and Benecke looked around the table and nodded to the others, all of whom they knew well.

As they sat down and scooted forward, they were informed the President and Vice President were on their way down.

Flores and Benecke nodded to Marc Ha, the CIA Director, on the other side of the table, then to the other seven men at the table, comprising the President's Joint Chiefs of Staff. Sam Foley, the Secretary of Defense, with his balding hair and hawkish eyes, was sitting next to Ha and nodded back, peering out from under thick grey eyebrows.

Less than a minute later, the President entered the room followed by the Vice President. President Lee was tall and lean and had the distinction of choosing the country's first female Vice President. Glena Ward, who followed him in and sat down at the table next to him, was no puppet or figurehead for the VP position. She was as tough as anyone in the room.

The President leaned forward and put his elbows on the dark mahogany table. "Okay, let's hear it."

Benecke glanced at Flores, the only person who knew what he was about to say, and then back to the President. "I'll make it short sir," he said. "We have evidence that we believe identifies the Pope's murderer."

Lee raised his eyebrows in surprise. "Really? Who is it?" With all that was going wrong at the moment, he was excited at the prospect of removing at least some of the pressure he was under from the other countries. The case was not going quickly enough for anyone.

Benecke didn't reply immediately. "Mr. President, I think it's better if I share the evidence."

The President looked puzzled but gestured to continue.

Benecke reached into his pocket and pulled out a small digital audio player. "As you know, four of the Swiss Guard were killed in the same room with the Pope." He paused and looked around the table. "It appears that one of them managed to start a recording on his phone before he died."

Everyone gave a surprised look as Benecke put a recorder gently on the table in front of him. "The recording is almost four minutes long and ends with the final slaying of Pope Pius." Benecke waited a moment for questions, and hearing none, he reached forward and pressed the play button. The recording started abruptly, and a deep voice could be heard clearly in mid-sentence.

"-you lay there on the floor slowly bleeding to death, and asking yourself how in the world we ever got past your security. The reason is because we were the security."

There was a long pause and everyone instinctively looked at Benecke's device on the table.

"Are you wondering why yet? Of course you are. Let's just say...this is payment for services rendered. A debt, if you will."

"Listen to me. Just keep him alive and unharmed. If you keep him unharmed, they will give you anything you ask. Anything!"

"Oh, I know."

Everyone in the room jumped when they heard two successive gunshots, and a few seconds later two more.

"Paid in full."

Benecke pressed the button again, stopping the recording. He looked at the President whose face, like everyone else's, looked ashen. No one moved; they simply could not believe what they had just heard.

"Is that," Lee began, with a whisper, *"Bill Zahn's voice?!"*

Benecke nodded. "Yes, it is."

The room was silent again. After a long wait, Ward spoke up. "Are you *sure*?"

"We analyzed the audio multiple times and each time the characteristics were a perfect match."

"There's no possible chance it's someone else?" Ha asked from across the table.

Benecke shook his head. "Very little."

"How little?" President Lee said, raising his voice.

"As in practically none, sir."

"My god." Lee closed his eyes and leaned his face into his hands. "Where…is Zahn now?"

"His plane took off almost two hours ago on a flight south. He will reach international waters in a little over thirty minutes."

"Why in god's name…" Lee's voice trailed off. He looked up and back at Benecke and Flores. "Tell me you're right about this. Tell me there is no way in hell you're wrong."

"We're right, sir."

Ward cleared her voice and spoke up with a more objective tone. "This may be a dumb question, but exactly how much do we know about Zahn? I mean, *really* know."

Benecke placed a thick folder on the table and pulled out some papers. "He's held three other government positions of significance over the last twenty-two years of service. The first was in the DOD for nine years as a nuclear and weapons inspector, then in the NSA for six years running their data encryption department, and the rest of his time in the State Department, as a political liaison and second in command."

Ward shook her head. The man was plugged in. "So, you're saying that Zahn, a high ranking member of the government, murdered the Pope. Why in the world would he do that?"

"I cannot even begin to imagine," the President said shaking his head.

The Chief of the Army spoke up. "This just doesn't make any sense. We've got to have something wrong here." They all turned back to Benecke.

He cleared his throat and went back to his folder. This time he pulled out several copies of paper and passed them around. Everyone picked theirs up and studied it. They were pictures, small pictures, that were arranged to fill the single page, and in each picture was a small group of men at different angles and different locations. "These are photos from the Cathedral of Saint John. As you all know, installing security cameras where none are present is common procedure for this level of protection. The four men you see in these images are the same men that we believe carried out the assassination If you look closely at the tallest of them, it's Zahn."

Simultaneously everyone stared harder at their picture. "Jesus," whispered Foley.

"Okay, he was there," Ha said. "How do we know they were the ones that did it?"

Benecke looked around the room. "Do you notice anything strange about these pictures?"

Everyone continued to peer at them. Ha looked up. "I recognize the man to Zahn's left in pictures four and five."

"That is Kia Sarat," Flores spoke up. "He is Zahn's right hand man and has been working with and for him for years. He checks out."

"What about the other two?" asked the President.

Flores took a deep breath. "Their ID's initially checked out, but now that we've had some time to do some digging, we're finding discrepancies."

"Discrepancies?" barked the head of the Army. General Hall was a bear of a man. Both tall and muscular, he looked like he could still get into the ring with someone half his age.

Flores spoke up. "One of the men we thought was named Ahmad, but we now believe he is Ferran Kamal, the nephew of an Islamic terrorist by the name of Malik. The fourth man, Iman, we believe also has a radical background."

The Chairman of the Joint Chiefs rolled his eyes. "And these guys just walked right by you?"

"We don't have time," Flores shot back with a look of irritation, "to do an exhaustive background check on every single person!"

Landeen, the Chairman, did not back down. "Well, why the hell NOT?! What the hell good is your check if we can't tell whether they're friend or foe until the damn attack is over?"

Flores was not intimidated. "Because they weren't passing through security! They were security!"

Everyone at the table froze. "What was that?" asked Vice President Ward.

Flores turned to address her. "What I'm saying is, these were not normal clearance checks. Those are for people not on the security team. But Zahn and his men *were* part of the security team. Almost all major departments were." She motioned to the recorder. "Zahn said it himself."

"Why the hell was the State Department part of the security team? They have no military authority," Foley said.

"Technically, they didn't have to sir," Benecke answered. "The passage of the Patriot Act was intended to improve communication by breaking down walls between government departments. The State Department does have some international authority, but the Patriot Act, in an effort to force the departments to exchange information more freely, essentially equalized them as part of a larger cooperative system. Security has been flattened, which means having Zahn and his team there was completely acceptable. This is why Ms. Flores' teams in the Secret Service had no reason to further investigate them."

Foley shook his head. "Christ! You're telling me that these bastards got through because of a giant loophole in the law?"

"Yes, sir."

Foley rolled his eyes and looked back to the President.

"Several of my team saw them there," Flores continued. "But they never saw them again, even when my men were getting everyone out."

"And there is also the oddity in the pictures," reminded Benecke. Everyone remembered his question and looked back at their sheets of paper.

Ha finally looked up. "I don't see it. What stands out?"

"They are the only ones in the pictures wearing long coats." The realization struck them all at once. It was clearly out of place and they could see it. "Those coats are not just hot; they're also long enough to hide AK-47s beneath them. And the AKs are another item. They're old, but they're extremely reliable. And Islamic freedom fighters have tens of thousands of them."

President Lee leaned back in his chair. "Is that it?"

Benecke glanced again at Flores. "No, sir. We've gotten information on a few diplomatic missions that Zahn had made for the State Department. It looks as though some of those meetings may have never taken place."

"What?" Ward said. "He never went there?"

"Not exactly, ma'am," Benecke replied. "He was certainly there, as we can tell from the plane's navigation and GPS history, but it looks like he may not have actually been talking to the people we thought he was talking to."

Ha leaned forward. "You told me yesterday Zahn wanted a drone. And that you later gave him access to an Apache and a Blackhawk."

Benecke nodded.

"So what was that for and who was aboard?" Ha pressed.

Benecke frowned. This was the part he was truly dreading. The reluctant admission that he had inadvertently helped Zahn.

"He said he was after some individuals involved in an assassination attempt."

"Dear god," the President moaned.

Ha continued. "And who did you put onboard that Blackhawk helicopter?"

Benecke lowered his head. "A Delta team."

The President stood up and walked to the window. He stared straight out across the lawn at the trees beyond. "Do you have any idea," he said, "what everyone is going to think when they find out *we* killed the Pope? That the United States Government killed their Pope?" He shook his head. "God almighty. This is going to start a war."

The room remained silent as everyone contemplated what the President said. Lee almost chuckled out of sheer exasperation when he turned around. "Well, I guess we're damn lucky we have the biggest military on the planet, because we are sure as hell gonna need it now."

Benecke looked around the room and then at the President. He raised his hand gingerly. The President looked at him with raised eyebrows.

"Sir," Benecke started. "We have a little time to figure out what our explanation is. Not much but a little. Might I suggest, whatever that is, it will look far worse if Zahn escapes as well?"

The President squinted his eyes. "What do you mean?"

"I mean that, whatever our story is, I think it would be very bad if Zahn were still alive to dispute it, let alone offer details we don't want known."

Silence filled the room until Landeen broke it. "I agree."

"So do I," added Ha. The President looked at the others in the room who nodded their agreement.

"So, we take him out while we still can."

"Yes, sir."

He turned to Will Douglas, the Air Force Chief. "Where's the nearest base, Will?"

Douglas, the tallest and youngest of the chiefs, responded immediately. "MacDill, sir. Near Tampa Florida. We have F-16s on the ground that should be able to reach them before they leave US air space."

The President absently reached up and rubbed an eye. Things were moving damn fast. But Benecke was as sharp as they came. He was still new to the post, and while not much for playing politics, he hadn't been wrong yet. Then again, was it possible he wanted to put it all on Zahn because he'd helped the man? Doubtful. He was a straight shooter, and Lee was sure he was right. Zahn did this, and now they had to clean up the mess as quickly as possible. *How he was going to explain this to the world, he had no idea.*

The President gave Douglas a solemn nod. "Bring 'em down."

48

The early spring was affecting Florida just as much as the rest of the East Coast, and the temperature was almost 90 degrees when the two pilots sprinted across the hot tarmac at MacDill in their flight suits. Barely out of breath, each reached the ladder for their plane and walked in a tight circle underneath, quickly checking the weapon racks and pneumatic pressures. Satisfied, they grabbed their steel ladders and climbed into their cockpit. They had very little time, but the preflight check was something every pilot did religiously, even those with a crew.

Once inside, they finished connecting their harnesses and zipped their G-suits up the rest of the way. Their crew chiefs quickly appeared over them atop the ladder and forcefully strapped them in. The chiefs then grabbed and attached the G-suit hoses to their left console before slapping their pilot on the head and climbing down to remove the ladders.

Inside, the pilots finished adjusting their switches and trim adjustments before putting their helmets on and attaching their oxygen hoses to the harnesses. They brought their main power online only seconds apart as every movement had long since become simple muscle memory.

Finally, after starting their main engines and with clearance from the tower, both planes immediately pulled forward and headed for the runway with the second pilot falling in behind the first. All told, both planes were airborne in less than six minutes.

The Boeing 757 was the preferred aircraft for heads of

state, including the office of the State Department. With a twin jet design, the plane carried two crew members and up to 280 passengers in the single aisle fuselage. The 757 was also capable of almost 4,000 nautical miles, depending on variant, which gave it an impressive range.

This 757 was traveling due south at 530 miles per hour when the F-16 fighters appeared and fell in directly behind it. The lead pilot verified the 757's call letters near the tail and gradually faded back to within a quarter mile.

The pilot spoke into his microphone. "MacDill, this is Falcon's Talon, do you copy?"

"Copy Talon," came the reply.

"Aircraft sighted," he said, "identification is November-Six-One-Seven-Alfa-Juliet."

"That is affirmative, Talon. Repeat, identification is affirmative."

The pilot nodded and switched frequencies. He shifted in his seat then stretched out his hand and relaxed it again around the stick. "Aircraft November-Six-One-Seven-Alfa-Juliet, this is Colonel Ainsworth of the United States Air Force. You are instructed to change course and return to MacDill Air Force Base immediately. I repeat, you are instructed to change course. Confirm."

Ainsworth waited for a response. After thirty seconds he hailed again. "I repeat, Aircraft November-Six-One-Seven-Alfa-Juliet, this is Colonel Ainsworth of the United States Air Force. You are instructed to change course. You are to confirm immediately."

Still in the conference room, Will Douglas looked up at the President, the phone still pressed against his ear. "Mr. President, Zahn's aircraft is not responding."

Lee shook his head. "Try it again."

Douglas nodded and relayed the command. After two long minutes of silence, he turned back to the President. "Still no response, sir."

Dammit. Thought the President. *What the hell is he*

doing? Did Zahn think this was some kind of game? *Or does he think I won't do it?* The President paced back to the window and stared out.

"Mr. President, we have eight minutes before they reach international waters," Landeen said. "If we wait, we'll have some questions to answer."

The President glanced over his shoulder and then back through the window. He was fully aware of the questions he would receive from other countries when they saw an explosion in international waters. "How many people are on that plane?"

Benecke spoke up. "The ground crew estimated twenty to thirty people when it departed Stewart, sir."

"Are they all Zahn's team?" the President asked. When no one replied, he turned and looked back at them. "I said, are they all *combatants*?"

"Yes, sir, we believe so," replied Benecke.

Lee shook his head again. Zahn didn't know he was being recorded in that room, which meant he wasn't expecting to be identified, at least not this early. He probably directed his pilots not to respond to any other aircraft to avoid accidental detection. Was he even aware there were two Fighting Falcons behind him? Or did Zahn think he could play him just like he played everyone else?

Ainsworth watched the large aircraft in front of him carefully. When the reply came back over his headset, he nodded and loosened his grip slightly.

"Copy that, MacDill."

He tried to relax as he locked the computer onto the target and waited for the missile under his wings to activate. He then re-gripped the stick and flipped the small cover off the top with his right thumb. He waited two seconds before firmly pressing the red button.

Below Ainsworth, the AIM-9E heat-seeking Sidewinder launched from his F-16. The ten-foot, 188-pound missile reached nearly Mach 1.5 before it slammed into the tail of the 757 and exploded in a giant ball of fire. The entire tail and part of the rear fuselage separated from the plane as the explosion ripped into the left wing, lighting half of the aircraft's fuel on fire and causing it to instantly engulf most of the cabin. The giant plane began to twist as both parts separated in midair and spun away from each other. The intense fire spread through the cabin and traveled through the fuel lines to the other side, causing part of the right wing to explode seconds later.

Both Ainsworth and his wingman watched the 757 disintegrate in the wind and fall away into thousands of pieces of burning metal.

49

It was widely controversial, and even considered a political and economic failure by some. The 1994 North American Free Trade Agreement was signed by the United States, Mexico, and Canada in an effort to improve economic free trade between the countries. Hotly debated, both at the time of signing and even years later, neither the economic benefits nor drawbacks of such an agreement were ever proven. In addition, many diplomatic and political holes remained, which simply underscored the agreement's deep faults.

One such hole was a secret relationship between Mexico and the United States providing a channel for "special" and "regulated" trade across the border of the two countries, and all with little or no oversight. Special cargo planes were flown almost on a daily basis and delivered goods to either country based on the sole discretion of government officials. The cargo planes were originally supposed to be packed with products such as medicine, clothing, and food, but, not surprisingly, all too often they were instead filled with drugs or guns. It was another loophole in the corrupted world of modern government.

What was different about this loophole, however, was that the program, called the Cross Border Assistance Program or CBAP, was pioneered by a man named William Zahn who at the time worked at the Department of Defense. While the CBAP was eventually considered by everyone to be a failure and a waste of 840,000 gallons of fuel every year, it would prove to be Zahn's best laid plan.

The ATR-42 twin prop regional airliner was old but

extremely reliable, requiring much less maintenance than jet engine aircraft. It was noticeably slower than more modern cargo planes, but on that day, reliability and safety were paramount. Furthermore, with the program considered a failure, very few people noticed when the ATR-42 flew past its usual destination and quietly continued on toward Argentina.

The blackness disappeared as the hood was pulled off, and Christine was blinded by the room's small light. Her head was still foggy, and she tried to focus through blurry vision on the person in front of her. Her head felt heavy, and she rolled it from side to side, trying to discern where she was.

"Where am I?" she mumbled. Her ears felt hypersensitive, as if she could hear her own breathing. The blurry figure in front of her didn't answer, and she tried harder to focus her vision. "What happened?"

Zahn watched her look around in a daze. She had been kept under the whole trip, which meant the readjustment would take a little longer than usual.

The picture began to clear, and Christine blinked hard to make sure she wasn't hallucinating. The person in front of her appeared to be sitting in a large upholstered chair, and the room behind him looked like…a living room. Christine looked down apprehensively when she realized her hands wouldn't move. It felt like she was on a hard chair, and her arms were nowhere to be found. She wondered if she were tied.

"Where am I?" she asked again.

"It doesn't matter," Zahn said. His voice sounded loud in her head, like someone left a radio on too high.

She shook her head sluggishly, feeling as though she was rolling it back and forth. "What happened?"

"I kept you asleep. It'll take several minutes to wear off."

For some reason, she accepted that and wondered if her head was nodding without her permission. Her mind was becoming clearer, but she had trouble thinking beyond any single thought.

"Where's...Sarah?" she asked.

"She's fine," was all Zahn offered.

Christine blinked several times which seemed to help. The man in front of her started to become clearer. He looked like he was in his fifties or sixties with salt and pepper colored hair.

"What's your name?" Zahn asked, testing her coherence.

"Christine. Christine Rose."

"Where are you from?"

"Mmm...New York," she answered, struggling to remember what had happened. She remembered Rand and Avery in a crowd, pushing people away, and a store with large windows. She seemed to remember Rand smashing them. And the hallway, a white hallway with a door at the end. And gun shots.

She could now see the man in front of her. She didn't recognize him. "Who are you?" She looked around the room again, this time noticing a large couch along a wall covered in paneling. On the other side of the room was a large door. "Where's Sarah?" she asked again.

"I told you, she's fine."

"Fine how?" Christine pressed. Her vision was now clear enough to see his grin.

"You should be worried about yourself," he said with his arms folded across his chest.

What happened? She wondered again to herself. She could remember the doorway and the gunfire, then hiding. She remembered Rand and Avery moving some large tanks around her. She felt a sudden surge of panic as she remembered being caught!

Zahn watched her expression. "Ah, now you're awake," he grinned. "Good."

Christine squinted through the last of the fog and stared at Zahn. He looked familiar to her, but she couldn't remember from where. He was clean shaven and dressed comfortably. She looked down and found that she was indeed sitting on a small wooden chair with her hands bound behind her.

"Why am I tied up?"

Zahn shrugged. "We won't need that forever."

Christine took a deep breath. Even through the rope, she could feel the blood slowly returning to her muscles. She leveled her gaze back at Zahn. "Who are you and *where* is Sarah?"

"You're persistent." He leaned forward slightly. "I told you Sarah is fine. As for who I am, right now, I'm the one in charge of how long you live."

"You're the one, aren't you?"

Zahn could see her lip turn up into a snarl.

"You're the one that's been chasing her. Chasing us. Aren't you?"

"Yes," he replied. "I lost several good men trying to get her."

"What do you want Sarah for?"

"You tell me." He leaned toward her a bit more and stood up.

Christine looked confused. "What?"

"Tell me. Tell me what it is about your little friend. How did she do it?"

Christine looked incredulous. "You don't know?"

"What I know," said Zahn, stepping toward her, "is that she saw me."

Christine watched him from the chair.

"She *saw* me!" he said again. "How did she do that?"

Christine shook her head, still confused. *What on earth was he talking about? She saw him? What did that even mean?* She started to mumble something when it finally hit her. Sarah had seen him somewhere. Somewhere before. *My god, was that why he'd been after her? Is that why he was trying to kill her?*

"She saw you?" Christine asked.

"You know she did. She must have told you." His eyes flared. "Now tell me how!"

She'd seen him. Christine thought to herself. She'd seen him and yet he didn't know how. How much did he really know then?

"So, you've been chasing us this whole time without even knowing why?" Christine found herself almost wanting to laugh. All of this time, he didn't know what Sarah could do. He didn't know she could not only see him, but she could see *everybody*.

Zahn stared at her with a look of amusement. The woman sitting in front of him was tied up and had no idea where she was. She was helpless and yet she was angry. She did not match the profile he had on her.

Zahn looked at his watch. He still had time. "You cannot possibly know what you are in the middle of. Christ, you weren't even alive yet," he said with disdain. "You're all so blissfully unaware of what happens in your world, what happens in the shadows. A world so free of real fear that all you can manage to do is fight with each other."

He stared at Christine with his crystal blue eyes. "You could never imagine where I came from, or why. You're just like them, so simple and ignorant, and yet, *I'm* the one who had to pay. I was the one who had to suffer, abandoned and forgotten."

She watched as Zahn walked over to a nearby wall. He looked at an old black and white photograph hanging in front of him, but she couldn't quite make out the image.

"Have you ever killed anyone?" he said, still looking at the picture. "Of course you haven't. You're just another sheep. I made my first kill in 1914. And you know what? I did it for people like you. I even spent forty years trying to redeem myself, forty long years, for something I had failed to be worthy of." He raised his voice and scowled.

"I spent all those years helping people, carrying the word forward, trying to rightfully earn it. But the others hadn't. The others hadn't, but I was somehow unworthy. So I continued, I did everything I could possibly think of. I gave, and I gave, and you know what I got? NOTHING!"

Christine jumped in her chair.

"And what was most pathetic…was I still thought it just wasn't enough!" Zahn turned back to Christine angrily. "But I was wrong. I *was* worthy and the truth, no matter how much I wanted to deny it, was that I was simply abandoned!"

Zahn snapped out of his trance, and a dark smile began to spread across his face. "I look pretty good for a hundred and seventy years old, wouldn't you say? Of course, I was supposed to be made whole, but when that didn't happen, I noticed something else. I continued getting *stronger*." His sick smile deepened. "I don't know why, but over time I healed faster and faster. In fact, it's odd," he said running his hand through his hair, "I've begun to grow wrinkles and this grey hair, yet I'm stronger than I've ever been."

He realized he was losing focus and turned back to Christine, raising an eyebrow. There was something strange about her expression. "Only three people have I ever revealed myself to," Zahn said. "Unfortunately for you, each time was just before they died. And frankly," he shrugged, "none of them ever understood what I was telling them anyway." He studied her closer. She was watching him, but there was something unusual in her eyes. Her face didn't show the slightest hint of confusion. Fear, yes, even a little desperation, but not confusion. She couldn't possibly have understood what he had just confessed.

He reached for a small remote control near the chair and turned on a monitor behind him. Christine gasped when she saw Sarah appear on the screen. The monitor showed her in a large, empty room, tied to an oversized chair, but there was nothing else in the room, nothing at all. She was completely alone.

Christine's eyes began to well up when she Sarah crying, tears running down her tiny cheeks. The fear she must have been feeling sent a jolt of pain through Christine's heart.

"No!" Christine whimpered. "She's just a child. For the love of god, leave her alone."

"TELL ME!" Zahn suddenly shouted. "Tell me *how!*"

When she didn't answer, he sighed. "Maybe it's me, but I get the impression you're not going to tell me."

Christine glared back at him resolute, her tears beginning to fall.

Zahn shook his head. This was certainly not the woman he was expecting.

Christine inhaled deeply and tried to push back the tears. "You know what I think?" she said in an icy tone. "I think you're *afraid* of her. I think you're actually frightened by that little girl!"

50

The "Dead Hand" system was a Cold War era nuclear control system used by the Soviet Union. Its design was to automatically launch the Soviet intercontinental ballistic missiles if a nuclear strike were detected by seismic, radioactivity, light, or overpressure sensors. Called a "Second Strike" capability, it ensured the Soviets could retaliate against a nuclear attack even if the Soviet Union had already been destroyed.

In other words, it allowed an automated nuclear attack without any human intervention whatsoever. It was also considered highly dangerous by every other country, and even by some inside Russia.

In the 1990's, several Russian military officers confirmed the existence of the Dead Hand system but would not confirm as to whether it was still in use. Many suspected it was.

Ron Tran sat on the famed Yalong Bay Beach, just outside of China's southernmost province Hainan. He dug his feet into the warm, white sand and looked past his laptop screen, out across the emerald blue water. He turned and peered down to the southern end of the crescent shaped beach with its dozens of giant hotels, frowning at the construction cranes in the background.

He wanted to spend his last days in China at one of its most beautiful locations. He had always remembered Yalong fondly from his childhood, when his parents would bring him during their summer holiday. It seemed so long ago, before they both died, and it looked a lot different now. Tran shook himself out of his daydream and reminded himself that Argentina had beaches too.

He turned back to his computer screen and watched one of the American news channels over the internet. The coverage on the Pope's death was everywhere, covered in every country around the world. The Pope was dead, and *that* was his signal.

The Pope's death was the trigger for initiating Phase Two of their attack. Nicknamed Stux2 after its more simplified predecessor, Tran's new version was truly impressive on a technical level. On an emotional level, it was terrifying.

Tran opened several windows on his laptop and prepared to send the final command. There was no one on the planet who knew what was coming, except Zahn.

Stux2 improved not just on the speed and ability to traverse and infect networks, but it benefited from a second, simultaneous attack that Tran liked to think of as the "mother of all head fakes".

With well over ten million drones or "bots" standing by, Tran would use them to launch a massive viral attack against the country least expecting it, China itself. The virus would attack all of China's public facing systems and servers from the outside. All public and government systems would be targets, and knowing how poorly government computer networks were maintained, many, if not all, would be brought to a veritable standstill within hours. After spending too much time attempting to stop the attack, they would eventually have to concede that cutting off access was their only option. But they would soon realize that was not easy, especially using computer systems that simply would not respond. In a short time, panic would spread as they became more desperate to stop an attack that would appear to be originating from everywhere in the world at once.

It was that panic that Stux2 would take advantage of. Most worms used one or two vulnerabilities to gain access to servers and networks which had not been properly patched. However, as Stux2 traveled, it would periodically create copies of lists and databases with *all* current known vulnerabilities. And since few computer systems were ever fully patched, it would allow Stux2 to move quickly through virtually any network, identifying its computer environment and looking for China's Command and Control System for the country's nuclear arsenal. It was here that Stux2 would go to work.

China was arguably more careful than Russia and never considered implementing a Dead Hand system, but China's computer systems were far more shoddy. At its very core, what Stux2 was designed to do was to "reprogram" China's control system *into* a Dead Hand system.

Tran expected the reprogramming to take only hours, which meant also reprogramming the system's manual safeguards. But when it was done, it would do the unthinkable…it would then simulate a nuclear launch against China from both Russia and the United States, and the Chinese Command and Control system would no longer be able to tell the difference.

In the end, China's systems would believe it *was* under attack, and automatically launch its entire nuclear arsenal against its attackers.

The United States' original Stuxnet worm was the first to leap the barrier from the virtual world to the real world. Stux2 would use that leap to launch a full-scale, global, nuclear war.

Tran stared at his screen for a long time. The world had become so terribly dirty and corrupted. He regretted having to do it, but he had realized long ago this was the only way to cleanse the system, all of the systems. Mankind had to start over.

He looked at his screen again and pressed the Enter key, which sent the command for the attack to begin in six hours. By then he would be on a plane and far over the Pacific Ocean.

51

Robert Correia wanted revenge. He wasn't supposed to, but he did.

Born and raised in the Bronx, he'd spent almost as many hours in church as he had in school. It was because of his mother, a devout Catholic. She was a believer through and through and would often tell her children when their actions went against God's will, so it was no surprise her four children grew up as close to the church as she had. They were true to their faith, and none of them had married outside the church. As far as his mother was concerned, their hearts and souls were pureblood.

But Correia stared through the bars with a pain like he had never felt. His Pope was gone, murdered in broad daylight. And worse, his mother was also dead. So distraught by the news, his elderly mother had fainted and collapsed. Two hours later, she was dead.

Correia was seething. His mother, his life, and his faith were all shattered because of the man lying on the floor on the other side of those bars. Correia was a deputy sheriff at Rikers Island, and at 2 a.m., he was standing silently before the cell of the man who destroyed it all.

He watched the dark shape on the floor and could hear a faint gurgling sound as the man tried desperately to breathe. The world was simply not meant for men this evil. He didn't deserve to be here. Correia gripped the metal baseball bat in his hand, looking left and right down the dark corridor. Everyone was asleep, and the two other deputies had conveniently decided to go downstairs in search of something.

Correia had already unlocked the door from a distance and now reached out and grabbed one of the thick bars, pulling the door outward. He looked up and down the corridor again and quietly stepped forward into the dark cell. The man at his feet had been beaten as close to death as anyone he had ever seen. In fact, no one could believe he was still alive, so it wouldn't come as a surprise if he unexpectedly died during the night.

The hate welled up inside Correia as he raised the bat up over his head. There would be no turning of this cheek.

"Don't you dare," came a voice from behind him. It was followed by the sound of the safety being released on a semi-automatic hand gun.

Correia froze.

"Put it down."

The deputy slowly lowered the bat down over his head, quickly trying to think of an explanation. "I...uh," he stammered. "I was just...angry. I wasn't really going to do anything."

"Lay it down and back up out of the cell."

Correia complied. As he exited the cell, he was thrown forcefully against the bars without warning and felt his nose break. "AHHH!" He groaned and stepped back but was slammed into the bars a second time, even harder.

The face of Bazes appeared from a shadow behind him, followed by the older chaplain. Bazes whispered into the deputy's ear. "If I see you move one inch, I'll make sure you never walk again."

"I can't believe he's still alive," the chaplain said as they eased Rand down onto a table in the infirmary.

Bazes simply nodded his head. He'd never seen anything like it. He reached up and turned down the brightness of the overhead lamp.

Below them, Rand managed to open one eye. "Who are you?" he whispered through swollen lips.

"That's a long story," Bazes smiled. "But we're here to help." The chaplain nodded from over his shoulder.

Rand slowly rolled his eye back and forth. "Where am I?"

"You're at Rikers Island," Bazes answered. He looked down at Rand's arms and noticed they were still shaking. Bazes put his hands on one arm trying to calm him but realized the tremors ran throughout his body. "I think you're having a prolonged seizure."

"It's not a seizure," Rand said quietly. "What time is it?"

The chaplain looked at his wristwatch. "It's two twenty-five a.m."

"What day?"

The chaplain looked curiously at Bazes. "It's Monday, the 8th."

Bazes looked into Rand's eyes. "Listen, I don't know who you are, but I have some idea. And I think you and I are looking for the same person."

"What happened in here?" Rand grimaced in pain when he tried to move.

Bazes looked at the chaplain. "They think you killed the Pope."

Rand let his head fall back onto the table and stared straight up at the ceiling. "The Pope is dead?"

"Yes, and I think the man we're both after is the one who did it," Bazes said. "And I don't think he's finished."

Rand's brow furrowed. "What do you mean?"

"I think he's planning something else, something worse. But I don't know exactly what."

Rand closed his eye. The trembling was getting stronger. There wasn't much time. He opened both eyes and looked back at Bazes. "Where's Avery?"

Avery was also lying motionless on his cell floor, but he was in worse shape. Due to his age, they hadn't beaten him as badly, but no longer having the ability to heal like Rand, his injuries were terminal.

Bazes and Wilcox helped Rand down onto his knee

beside him. He couldn't hear Avery's breathing, and when he checked his pulse he could barely feel it. He was slipping fast. Rand put his shaking hand gently on the back of Avery's head. Then he ran it over the top and down over his eyelids.

"Go home," Rand said softly, squeezing his shoulder. "You've earned it."

As he tried to stand up, Avery's hand suddenly moved and reached out for him. Rand quickly grabbed it. His lips were moving and Rand knelt down, trying to hear.

Avery whispered something, but it was still too faint. His strength was gone, but Bazes and Wilcox helped Rand down even further, so his ear was just inches from Avery's mouth.

"Tell Sarah," Avery whispered, "to be strong."

With that, Avery let out his last breath, his body relaxed and rolled back onto the cold floor.

Rand stared at him for a long time. Avery had given him so much, trained him, taught him and prepared him. Rand's jaw tightened as he took a deep breath and pushed himself up. With his teeth clenched tightly, he rose enough to get a shaking leg under his weight. Both Bazes and the chaplain reached out, but Rand stopped them.

"No!" he growled, rising up into a kneeling position and then sliding his second leg beneath him. Finally, with everything he had, he pushed himself up and onto his feet.

He turned and looked at the two men. "Can you get me out of here?"

"Yes."

"I need a plane, and I could use some help."

Bazes looked at the chaplain, then back at Rand. "I have resources."

52

"Well, if you're not going to speak, I suppose we'll need to help incentivize you."

Christine glared at him as Zahn walked to a nearby table and picked up an old style phone. She could still see Sarah crying on the monitor.

Zahn lifted the handset and pushed a single button. Kia Sarat's voice answered on the other end. "Our guest has decided she doesn't want to talk," Zahn explained. "Why don't you pay the little girl a visit. And feel free to be…creative."

Zahn hung up and watched with a smile as Christine's eyes grew larger upon seeing Sarat enter Sarah's room on the monitor. He retrieved a small blindfold from his pocket when Christine blurted out, "Okay Okay! I'll tell you! Just don't hurt her."

Zahn rolled his eyes and picked the phone back up. *God, they were all so predictable.* He rang the extension again, and Sarat stopped short of putting the blindfold over Sarah's eyes. He put it back in his pocket and left the room to pick up the call.

"Wait a minute," Zahn told him. "Someone's had a change of heart." He hung up the phone again and turned to Christine. "You were saying?"

"She can see things," Christine said reluctantly.

"What kind of things?"

"Souls. She can see people's souls."

Zahn wasn't just surprised; he was stunned. His mouth dropped open and he turned and stared at the monitor again, as if seeing Sarah for the first time. His expression was quickly replaced by one of fascination. "You're sure?"

"Yes."

That was how she did it. That's how she saw him! Never in his wildest dreams. He stared at the monitor for a long time and eventually began to chuckle. His chuckle then turned into a laugh. "My god, that's what this is about!" He kept laughing. "Why did I not think of that? I never-" He stopped and turned back around. "Oh, Ms. Rose, you are quite the idiot. You don't even know enough to realize you've given me the greatest gift of all."

Now it was Christine's turn to be surprised.

"You haven't the slightest clue what's happening here," Zahn said, regaining his composure. "I knew you had help protecting her, but I never thought it was this. This is truly the icing on the cake." His dark grin grew wider. "He doesn't know, does he?" Zahn cried with excitement in his eyes. "He doesn't know who I am! He's after one of his own, and he has no idea!"

Christine was stunned. *One of his own? He was like Rand?* But how could he be so old? It was impossible to live that long. Her mind raced, trying to put the pieces together. Rand said there would be a point where he must be there for Sarah. That was his mission. But what happened if he wasn't?

Christine gasped. "Oh my god, you failed!" she shouted at him. "You failed your mission!"

Zahn was taken aback, and his eyes quickly flared.

That was it! Sarah had seen him somewhere. She'd spotted him. And if he failed his mission way back then...then *he never earned his soul.* Which meant that if Sarah saw him, he would have looked like Rand, SOULLESS!

In a single moment, everything became clear to Christine. Sarah spotted Zahn, and he knew it, he just didn't know how! He simply couldn't figure out how she did it, until Christine actually told him. And that meant she was right; he *was* afraid of her!

Christine flashed back to her decision sitting in the back of the Charger, that she would fight to protect Sarah with every breath she had. And she realized her fight for Sarah wasn't then; it was now.

This time, it was she who smiled. Zahn stared at her curiously.

"You *are* afraid of her, aren't you?" Christine accused him. Her smile grew. "You've been afraid of her the whole time."

"Don't be ridiculous!"

Christine continued to press. "That's why you always sent someone else to do your dirty work. If you're truly like Rand, or even stronger as you say, you could have simply come yourself and been done with it. But you didn't." She sneered at him. "You were afraid of her. You were afraid of a child."

"Shut up!" Zahn snapped. "I had other responsibilities. You can't imagine what it took to make this happen. Do you think it happened overnight? Can you even fathom how many people I had to involve, most of whom never even knew. You have no idea!"

Christine glared back shaking her head. "How in the world does someone like you become so sick?!"

"HE ABANDONED ME!" Zahn suddenly flew into a rage. He stood over Christine with his nostrils flaring and eyes that were now black. "I tried to be everything I thought he wanted from me! I followed the path. I protected others. I even *saved* others, but he didn't care. He never cared!" Zahn caught himself. He tried to calm down and looked at a different picture on the wall. This time it was an old photo of a group of soldiers. "I even went to war for him. One of *your* wars. But I still fought for him." Zahn's focus drifted off again. "I'd stolen a British identity so I could fight on the front lines, and once there, I could switch identities with no effort at all. Just grab another card from a dead soldier. It let me use my skills without being noticed. And that's when it happened."

Zahn's gaze seemed to push deeper into the old photo.

"That's when everything changed."

While he stared into the picture, Christine silently traced the ropes with her hands down and around the bottom of her chair. But she could not find how they were tied.

"That's when the killing began," Zahn said. His voice slowed. "I did it for the good of god, for the side of the righteous. It was my chance to fight for him again, to prove myself again. So I killed the enemy, over and over and over, relentlessly. And I was good at it. After all, fighting is what I was made for, what all of us were made for. But instead of proving my faith, something else happened." He stopped briefly again, still staring at the wall. "Do you have any idea what it's like to kill hundreds of people, thousands? It's almost indescribable: sick, twisted, dark…but *powerful!*" Zahn closed his eyes. "Immensely so. There is something incredible that happens when you watch the life fade and disappear from another person's eyes." He opened his own eyes again. "Ironic isn't it? For years I fought for him, and in the end, it not only drove me to kill, it taught me to love it."

His voice grew cold. Christine wasn't sure if he was still talking to her. "I didn't realize it then, but after all those lifeless bodies, after I'd finally lost count, something broke. The world gradually became darker and darker, and I eventually began to understand the truth. And the truth is that he doesn't really care about any of us. We're just pawns to him, in a giant game, to use as he pleases and to throw away when he's done."

Christine kept her eyes on him and quietly tried to trace the ropes again.

"And when I realized that, when I realized he'd already lost interest in me decades ago, I finally felt it. I felt the freedom of truth, freedom from the belief we Lochem are born with, that he loves and fights for us all." Zahn shook his head. "It's not true, any of it. It is the ultimate lie. The ultimate lie about who we are and why we are here.

You want to know what our purpose is? To be sheep, just sheep, all helplessly controlled until he is done with us." His gaze remained locked onto the wall, almost in a trance. "But he made a mistake. He left someone here who refused to be one of his sheep, who refused to live and die by his whim. He abandoned the wrong person, a person who knows nothing except how to fight."

"And one day I saw the light. It was as if, after all those years, my destiny had finally found me. As the life left yet another person I had killed, and he slowly fell from my grasp, my revelation crystalized. With that kill, and every kill before it, I was doing what I should have done all along, rejecting him. *I was sending his precious children back to him*. The ultimate insult, and the ultimate power."

Christine froze when Zahn suddenly turned to her with a strange, twisted look on his face. "It was then my destiny became perfectly clear. Send them all home. SEND THEM ALL!"

Sarah sat shivering in the cold metal chair. Her tiny face was covered with glistening lines, tracks left by countless tears. She was so scared. She didn't know where she was or what had happened to everyone. When she woke up, there was no one to help her and no one to protect her. The only person she'd seen was the red man who would come into her room and stare at her for long periods of time.

The empty, grey room was completely featureless, except for the small camera and tripod at the far end. A single light bulb overhead was the only other item in the room with her. She tried to twist around to see the door but couldn't. She was so hungry.

Sarah didn't know she was being watched from a distance. She quietly squirmed in her chair trying to relieve some of the pain in her legs. She thought of Christine and felt the tears begin to fill her eyes again.

It was then that something stirred inside of her. She felt it in the deepest recesses of her little heart, something warm and comforting. She could feel the tears slow and some of the fear subside as the feeling grew stronger and stronger. *Rand was coming.*

Even in the evening, Bogota Colombia was hot and humid, much more than Ron Tran was expecting when he exited the plane. China had humidity, but not like this. The sweat began almost immediately as he walked across the tarmac toward the terminal.

All of his belongings fit into four large suitcases and a backpack which bounced lightly against his back. The computer in his bag looked like any other, and frankly any agent that asked him to boot it up would never have known what he was looking at anyway. Nevertheless, Tran never let it out of his sight.

He breathed a sigh of relief to find the terminal building air-conditioned, and he stopped to catch his breath. Looking around, he could instantly see the difference in security that a third world country had to offer. He spotted just two security agents, both eating dinner and engrossed in a conversation with each other. The rest of the travelers walked by them without attracting a second glance. Drug trafficking was the number one concern in Colombia, but not when it came to arriving flights. After all, who would bother bringing drugs *into* the country?

Tran checked his watch and subtracted some hours in his head. He browsed the video screen and found the gate number for his connecting flight to Buenos Aires. He had over two hours to wait. Tran spotted several televisions mounted from the ceiling in a larger waiting room and walked over. He could see what he was looking for before he even got close.

Only two of the seven screens displayed live video feeds from China. The rest were covering the rioting in

South America which was still escalating over the loss of the Pope. The two locations of the China feeds were different, but the images of the crowds were very similar. Unable to read the Spanish captions at the bottom, Tran watched silently as the effects of his super virus took hold. Behind the reporters were huge lines outside government buildings with hundreds, even thousands, of Chinese yelling and frantically pushing forward.

Tran's attack was in full force with millions of computers around the globe attacking every government controlled server or system they could find. Most were outward facing systems such as government controlled banks, social service departments, public utilities, and even airports. With millions of people unable to travel or access their bank accounts, fear quickly spread and a run on the banks ensued. Thousands more gathered around the country's limited social program buildings, demanding their assistance checks in cash instead of deposits into their bank accounts. To make matters worse, many of those working within the areas hit worst by the enormous crowds had left work when the panic began, leaving critical services such as gas and electrical plants mostly unmanned, and the ripple effect quickly began to spread through the country's economy.

Politicians and other public officials desperately tried to calm the crowds, which only seemed to deepen the fears of the citizenry. The panic was spreading rapidly, and the Chinese government was trying to identify the sources of the attacks and find a way to stop them. But the sources were far too numerous and distributed. The attacks were coming from virtually every country in the world with the highest concentrations originating from both the United States and Russia.

Yet, what no one was watching was the internal systems and networks where Stux2 had silently begun spreading the moment it detected the global attack on the outside. While both the government and the public continued to panic, Stux2 moved from server to server at lightning speed, finding vulnerabilities and compromising them, then checking for the unique technical characteristics of China's Command and Control System.

Tran continued watching the monitors as the chaos unfolded. The attack had begun barely eight hours prior, and the country was already in turmoil. He thought about what things would be like in another twenty-four hours, or forty-eight. They were all sheep.

Tran covered his mouth and shook his head, trying to show just the right amount of concern in case someone was watching him. He displayed a worried look and searched for a public phone. He found one and stood in front of it, pretending to dial and then speak to someone for several minutes. Finally, he nodded and hung up the dead receiver. He looked around again; no one was watching. Satisfied, Tran walked to a small café and sat down. He guessed it would take twenty-four more hours for Stux2 to find what it was looking for. When it did, it would quickly disable the overrides and safety switches by informing the system that all switches had *already* been turned off, and the nuclear authorization codes already entered. Finally, after it had found and programmed all 240 of the remote warheads, it would take full control of China's nuclear arsenal.

If people were afraid now, they would be absolutely petrified when they saw the exhaust trails of China's missiles overhead. By that time, *everyone* in the airport would be crowded around those televisions. And he would be gone.

55

The XB-70 Valkyrie had the honor of being labeled one of the most *exotic* airplanes on the planet. First conceived in the 1950s for the Strategic Air Command, it was a bomber prototype capable of traveling at a mind numbing Mach 3. But in the end, only two were built due to funding limitations, and they ultimately served only as research aircraft. Their hulls, still unique to this day, were made of stainless steel and titanium and their design allowed the Valkyrie to drop its wingtips by sixty-five degrees, radically improving stability during supersonic flight. They were also the fastest way to get two people all the way to Chile in time for another flight.

In contrast, the C17 was much slower and served as the primary means of transporting one of the world's toughest and deadliest Special Forces teams, the U.S. Army's 82nd Airborne Paratroopers.

While many Special Forces teams were well-known to the public, paratroopers were more obscure and trained in conditions that many could not even fathom. Put through every stressful environment and every mission challenge conceivable, paratroopers were the result of numerous secret military programs, all with the same goal: to create a truly and utterly fearless fighting force.

One such program, and the Army's most controversial, was termed COHORT, short for Cohesive Operational Readiness and Training. First documented by James Pulley in 1988, the COHORT program was designed to regain a fighting ability not seen since the United States' Civil War, where a soldier's ability to fight and resist was in the realm of legend. Nowhere in history was that ability found to be stronger, and after studying it for over a century, the Army finally knew why. Resistance ultimately came down to a single underlying factor…the strength of the *group*, and the COHORT program was America's modern equivalent. Yet, while official records showed mixed results in other brigades, the results in the 82nd Airborne were very different.

Captain Daniel Clausen stood at the back of the giant Boeing C17 transport plane, packed with exactly half his company. Men filled both "sticks" of the fuselage, with their ninety-pound packs wedged between their knees. The second plane with the other half of Clausen's team followed directly behind the first, both racing just 800 feet above the ground to avoid radar.

Clausen's COHORT company was as tight as any in the Army. No one had rotated in or out of the company since it formed, which meant his men had spent nearly every waking minute together for years.

Clausen eyed the two strangers at the front of his plane with disdain. He didn't know who they were or why they were aboard, and he had no intention of finding out. As far as he was concerned, they were on their own.

Near the front, Bazes watched Rand slide back and forth as both aircraft flew along the nap of the earth. Thundering along at 180 mph, they constantly dipped in and out of canyons like a giant roller coaster, sending Rand back and forth against the cold metal wall. He did look a little better than when they left, but Bazes could still see Rand grimacing with every sudden jolt of the plane. This flight was much worse on Rand than the supersonic Valkyries. Their rides to South America on the Valkyries was a dream compared to the C17.

Bazes turned to look at the rest of the paratroopers. They sat quietly with their heads and helmets bobbing along with the movement of the plane, patiently waiting. The paratrooper maxim was "anywhere in eighteen hours" but Clausen's company had been in the middle of high altitude maneuvers in the Chilean Alps. This put them just over 400 miles, or two hours, from Argentina and the identified target.

The White House had managed to get a forensic team on the ground immediately after shooting Zahn's 757 down, only to find far fewer remains than they expected. But Benecke already had his team working around the clock and found Zahn's old aircraft before their ruse was complete. Just thirty minutes before landing in Buenos Aires, Benecke found the old ATR-42 airplane. He watched from a satellite feed as Zahn's team exited the plane and was whisked away by several Argentinian military trucks.

Clausen's paratrooper company was immediately called upon, but they were instructed to sit tight until Bazes and Rand arrived. Fortunately, it gave the men more than enough time to restock their supplies and ammo.

The giant plane dropped again, causing Rand to lurch forward. Bazes instinctively reached out just as Rand caught himself. They were less than an hour from the drop, and he was having serious doubts about Rand.

56

Zahn stared at Christine and grinned. "So, how do you like the place?" he asked looking around the room.

Christine followed his gaze but remained silent and defiant.

"Do you know what this place is? It's a tad outdated as you can see." He picked up a magazine from a corner table. It was seven years old. "This, my dear, is a genuine Nazi bunker." He enjoyed watching her try to suppress her surprise. "You may not know, after World War II ended, many high ranking Nazis managed to escape Europe and relocate to Argentina where President Peron offered them sanctuary. Discretely, of course. But you see, the Nazis, while demented, were not stupid. They knew many people would never forget and would never stop looking for them, people like Simon Weisenthal who found many of them. So the Nazis, never much for accountability, built this bunker as a place to hide if and when that time came."

Zahn dropped the magazine back onto the table. "It was built to house dozens of people for years without any communication to or from the outside world. Alas, I had to make some modifications. And since all of those good Nazis are now dead, I found it an ideal place to watch my *finale.*"

Zahn watched Christine with a tilt of his head. "Still not talking?" He shrugged and walked toward her, suddenly grabbing the back of her chair and picking her up with it. Christine slumped forward, almost falling out of the chair, and was caught only by the ropes that bound her. She hung forward as Zahn demonstrated his incredible strength and carried her across the room with one hand.

When he reached the far side, he opened the large, metal door and carried her into a hallway, then turned right into another brightly lit and much larger room. With a jarring impact, he dropped Christine back onto the chair and its four legs, causing her to rock momentarily from side to side. She gritted her teeth hard but made no sound.

In front of her was a wall of monitors with several desks before them. On each of the desks were large computers and even larger screens showing a myriad of video camera angles around both the complex and what appeared to be the darkened jungle outside.

However, it was the wall of monitors where Christine could not help but look. On each of the four-dozen monitors were live news videos from all around the world, covering scenes which Christine could only describe as chaotic. Huge crowds of people from Spain to the United States to South Africa, all rioting and destroying cars and buildings. Reporters cowered behind large objects and continued to film from a distance. One monitor caught Christine's attention as a giant department store window was smashed into hundreds of pieces and people surged inside, grabbing any merchandise within reach.

She was shocked. She shook her head in disbelief as she watched the carnage on a global scale. After several moments, she noticed a different set of channels broadcasting from the streets somewhere in China. The people looked different, but the panic in the crowds was the same.

"Behold," Zahn said, spreading his arms out wide. "My vengeance!"

Christine blinked hard. "What, what did you do?" Her eyes caught sight of giant pictures of the Pope held high over the crowds, and she gasped. "The Pope! What happened?" No sooner had she finished the sentence than she stared at Zahn in horror. "You did this? You...you *killed* the Pope?!"

Zahn turned and looked at the same monitor. "I sent him back to god! If I could have put a bow on him, I would have." He quickly stepped forward and pointed at another monitor. "And there is the nexus of it all, Saint Patrick's Cathedral."

"What?"

Zahn turned back to Christine. His eerie expression had returned. "It's where it all began, so very long ago. It was only fitting that the end of the world begin where this all started, where young Ryan Kelly was trampled to death, and where I was denied my destiny. Irony at its best."

"Ryan Kelly?"

"He was my mission," Zahn said almost in a whisper. "The young boy who I was supposed to protect. A boy with a gift of intellect the world had not seen in a hundred years. Killed right before my eyes. At the very steps of where Saint Patrick's was being built."

Christine couldn't believe her ears. She was in total shock. "So you killed the Pope?"

"Oh, you've missed so much," smirked Zahn. "The Pope was merely a favor. A gift to those who have given so much to help make this happen. I owed them that much. And while they are fierce, my Middle Eastern friends are not exactly the sharpest tools in the shed. They haven't given much thought to what comes next. To them, the Pope was their mission, the end goal. To me, he was merely a stepping stone." He paused. "I was the wrong person to abandon, wouldn't you say?"

Christine was beginning to shake. "What are you going to do?"

Zahn took a slow, deep breath. Oh, how he was enjoying this. He had waited so long. It was all decades in the making. Now, all of the anticipation, all of the anxiety, the frustration, the excitement, it was all bubbling out…and it was intoxicating.

"Observe China," he said, pointing back to the Chinese news feeds. "Surely, you don't think they're rioting because of the Pope. They're not Christian; well, at least most of them aren't. No, China is under attack. After years of Chinese hackers attacking other countries, they now get a taste of their own medicine." Zahn watched a huge crowd of people screaming and throwing rocks and bottles in downtown Beijing. "I've always found it fascinating that with so many different human emotions available to them, you people will inevitably act the same way under various types of extreme stress. You panic. Which, I can see, is precisely what *you* are starting to do."

Christine closed her eyes and tried to control her shaking. She could feel the fear and hopelessness edging inward. There had to be something she could do. There was always something.

Zahn could barely contain his gloating as he continued watching the carnage on the screen. Oddly, he had no particular ill will toward the Chinese as a people; in fact, in some ways he admired them. But, unfortunately, they were the country that served his purpose best. "The Chinese," Zahn continued, "have been in such a hurry to catch up with the modern world that they've progressed too fast. Too fast to establish sufficient protocols and manual safeguards to protect themselves against the very technology that will destroy them."

Zahn knew, due to their explosive growth over the last few decades, China's nuclear arsenal and their Command and Control systems were more modern than those of the other super powers. This meant, in China, technology was more relied upon to maintain and control certain safeguards with their nuclear missiles. It was, therefore, more vulnerable to Stux2, which had already found and circumvented safeguards for 22 nuclear warheads.

"In just a matter of hours, the most insidious computer attack known to man will overcome and change the programming behind China's nuclear system and make it fully reactionary. Our virus will assume control of their early detection and warning system and convince it that a full-scale nuclear attack is occurring. And when China launches their missiles in an automatic response, the United States and Russia, who have very clear protocols after verifying real missiles are airborne, will retaliate in kind. Then comes Germany, France, Israel and India. And in case you haven't picked up on the irony, most of the world's nuclear warheads are both located and targeted within the Earth's northern hemisphere, which is why we're in the southern hemisphere. And no," he smirked, "I don't expect to survive, but I do intend to live long enough to enjoy watching the end of it all. Unlike those in the North, down here we won't simply go *poof!*"

Christine's mouth hung open. She was speechless. *It couldn't be, it just couldn't be true.* No one could do that. No one *would* do that. But the longer she stared at him, the more she began to believe it. "My god," she said, "you are completely insane."

"Insane?" Zahn scoffed. "Mengele was insane. I'm unforgiving. God left me here. I never got to go home. So now, as my revenge, I'm going to send *billions* home."

57

At the ten-minute warning, the bright lights went out in the C17 and were replaced by the plane's low, red, combat lights. The Jumpmaster standing near Clausen cupped his hands to his mouth and yelled as loud as he could over the deafening engines. "TEN MINUTES!" He held up both hands and flashed all ten fingers.

The paratroopers near the front nodded and turned to the men directly behind them, repeating both the message and hand signal. One by one, the message was passed down the line with a nod from each paratrooper.

Both planes thundered forward, continuing to hug the ground through every fold of the terrain below them.

Zahn turned when one of his men stepped into the room. He was dressed in black fatigues with his face painted to match. Zahn looked past Christine at him. "What is it?"

The man glanced briefly at the monitors behind Zahn and then replied. "Something just showed up on radar and disappeared again. Something big."

The look on Zahn's face changed instantly. "How big?"

"Very big. Probably four engines."

Zahn narrowed his eyes. That meant a transport plane, probably a C17. And if they saw one, that meant there were probably two. "Paratroopers," he said. They were coming in with a company of paratroopers, which was one of his most likely scenarios. *But how did they find him so quickly?*

"How far away?" Zahn asked.

"About eight minutes."

Zahn looked at his watch and thought for a moment. "Get your men ready. They'll drop about twelve to fourteen kilometers out and in the dark it should take them three or four hours to hike in through this terrain. They'll want to strike about 4:30 a.m. so the sun is rising by the time it's finished. These men are some of the best in the world, and they're going to come in hard."

The man nodded and left the room, leaving Zahn staring at the empty doorway. They must have somehow tracked down his old NAFTA transport plane. He shook his head and pushed it out of his mind. It didn't really matter how; he had known this was one of the possibilities. It just happened faster than he thought. Either way, this would be their only chance. The Stux 2.0 attack was well underway. There wouldn't be enough time for a second attack; this was it.

Paratroopers were very tough, and Zahn had a big surprise for them. What he hadn't noticed was Christine furtively loosening the rope's knot located below her chair.

The large red and green jump lights lit up next to the plane's large, metal door as it opened into the howling wind outside. The door continued turning outward and locked into place, becoming a shield for the paratroopers when jumping into 180-mph winds.

The Jumpmaster moved next to the door and yelled again. "Inboard personnel stand up!" Instantly the line of men closest to him stood. "Outboard personnel stand up!" The rest of the men on the far side of fuselage stood. "Check equipment!"

All of the paratroopers checked the front of their equipment and the back of the equipment of the man before them.

Near the front of the plane, Clausen watched Bazes struggle to help keep Rand on his feet and run through the checks they had been shown. Rand gritted his teeth and gripped the overhead strap tight.

"Hook up!" yelled the Jumpmaster. All of the paratroopers reached up and hooked their static lines to the overhead cable, then pushed the cotter pin through with the other hand to secure it.

Bazes did the same at the front and then reached for Rand's line but couldn't find it. He tried to keep himself steady with one hand and checked around Rand's leg for the strap.

"Oh, for Christ's sake!" growled Clausen watching them. Keeping a hand pushed against the ceiling, he quickly crossed over to them and pushed both of their hands out of the way. He reached around the right side of Rand's leg and immediately brought his hand forward with the strap.

"Three minutes!" yelled the Jumpmaster.

Clausen immediately reached up and attached Rand's clip to the cable, closing it with the cotter pin. He then checked Rand's gear, both front and back, to make sure it was secure. Like the rest of the paratroopers, these two men were jumping with full rucksacks too.

When Clausen finished checking Bazes, he leaned in close and yelled in his ear, "You go last!"

Bazes nodded his head.

"We're all out of here in 35 seconds! Understood?"

Bazes and Rand both gave a thumbs up.

Zahn picked up the phone again and held the receiver to his ear, waiting. After a few moments, he spoke. "Get the MANPAD's ready and get them as close as you can to the path and direction of the object your radar spotted. Don't forget those planes are flying low and fast which means they're going to fly past you and your men in the blink of an eye. As soon as you hear them, fire the missiles immediately. If you wait for a visual, it will be too late.

And save half for the second plane."

Zahn hung up and stood calmly thinking. His first surprise was going to deal the paratroopers a terrible blow.

It was not unlike the blow that Zahn was too distracted to see coming from behind him, when an untied Christine raised her chair up and smashed it over his head with everything she had.

58

Bazes noticed that the shaking in Rand's arms and legs was getting worse. He leaned in and yelled to him, "How are you?"

Rand winced. "Never better."

Bazes smiled back. That was as far from the truth as it could be. Still, Rand was stronger than when they left, and Bazes was not entirely sure how, but he wasn't about to start asking questions. "Are you going to be able to make this?" he yelled.

Rand opened his mouth to reply when they were interrupted by Clausen. He was standing in the open doorway, facing out, and yelling at the top of his lungs. "Let's take it to the barn, men!"

Next to him, the Jumpmaster smiled and called out, "Stand in the door!" The line of men shuffled calmly and quickly to the door.

Clausen peered out in the howling darkness and gave one last look over his shoulder. "Let's go get these bastards!"

With that, the Jumpmaster yelled "Go!" and Clausen was gone. Immediately behind him, the paratroopers surged forward, pushing out the door as fast as the Jumpmaster could repeat his command.

Nearly half of the men had disappeared into the darkness when an explosion suddenly rocked the airplane. It was immediately followed by a second explosion which ripped a giant hole in the tail and demolished its fins and rudder. The hole became enormous as a chunk of the fuselage dislodged and fell away.

The plane's yaw and pitch were instantly lost without a working hydraulic system, and the nose of the plane pitched up wildly.

The unexpected jolt caused the remaining paratroopers to lose their balance, and the heavy weight of their packs pulled them back toward the damaged tail. The overhead cable came apart at the ceiling, and over a dozen of the men tumbled backward out of control, right out the rear of the plane. Without their static lines, their chutes did not deploy and they fell straight down, hitting the ground at full force.

Those still inside, including Rand and Bazes, grasped for something to hold onto as the plane's nose quickly changed direction and began to turn into a dive.

The rest of the paratroopers were already pushing forward in a desperate attempt to exit the doorway, and the Jumpmaster began grabbing each man and throwing him out as fast as he could. Under normal circumstances, they would have fifteen seconds before they hit the ground. Now, the urgency was to get out while they still had time and the control to deploy their chutes, and that window was closing quickly.

Rand and Bazes struggled to get their clips off of the second overhead cable. Other paratroopers took the faster way out, and instead they unclipped, wrapped their lines in their hands and threw themselves out the back. Better to make it out with enough altitude and try to manually deploy their chutes than to make it out when it was simply too low to matter.

Rand unclipped his line and turned to Bazes who was struggling. His line was stuck, blocked by a protruding bulkhead support beam that had dislodged in the explosion. Over Bazes' head, the cable was taut against the beam, pinching his large metal clip. Rand tried to pry it out, but the clip did not move. He pried his own shaking fingers between the clip and cable and tried to twist it, but it still wouldn't budge.

The nose of the plane dropped further, heading into a terminal dive.

With only seconds left, Bazes grabbed Rand's shaking hand and pulled it away. Bazes pushed him hard backwards, yelling over the screeching and shaking of the plane. "GET OUT!"

Christine swung the chair hard a second time, but Zahn twisted and grabbed it in mid-air. His eyes flared as he yanked it from her hands. He threw the chair across the room, glaring at her as he touched the side of his head and pulled it back to reveal a palm full of blood.

She did not cower as he would have expected. Instead, even without a weapon, she stood her ground. In fact, she looked like she was about to attack again. "You're quite the fighter," he said, taking a step closer.

Christine glanced past him at the monitor showing Sarah sitting all alone. She snarled at Zahn. "I'm not afraid of you!"

"Oh, yes you are," smiled Zahn. "And you should be."

Christine gritted her teeth. "I'm not going to let you do this, and I'm not going to let you hurt her!"

Zahn looked at her with a fleeting glimpse of admiration, and then it was gone. In one sudden movement, too fast for her to even see, he struck Christine hard in the face, sending her several feet back and into the stone wall. Her body crumpled to the floor like a rag doll.

Sarat stood high up the mountain dressed in his black fatigues. He watched through his binoculars as the distant fireballs rose high above the jungle canopy, the smoke and flames slowly curling under to form bright, yellow mushroom clouds. Both transport planes had taken direct hits by the surface-to-air missiles and crashed into the ground in less than a minute.

Just minutes later, Sarat could see the bouncing headlights of his three Humvee's heading back uphill through the thick terrain. He had told them to get out quickly. The place for engagement was not there. It was higher up where they had the advantage.

The question he was wondering now was, *how many survived?*

The lights were blinding. She painfully rolled onto her side and tried to shield her eyes from the overhead lights. Her face felt like it was on fire. Christine worked her hand down and touched her jaw. The swelling felt immense which meant it was likely even worse.

She groaned and peered through her tight eyelids, watching the grey concrete floor slowly come into view. The outside edges in her vision were still fuzzy when she saw a set of boots walk across the floor toward her. She remembered they were Zahn's just before he swung a boot and kicked her hard in the face again.

Blackness.

Clausen had lost nearly half his men. Most were either unable to get off the C17s before they exploded or never had enough altitude for their chutes to open. It was the greatest single loss of paratroopers ever.

But those who did survive reached the ground and still had the area secured within minutes. The enemy withdrew immediately which allowed them to search for all survivors, but those who were still alive were in no condition to fight.

Clausen left four men to protect the survivors while the rest prepared to advance. They were losing time and had a long way to go. His men instinctively slung the heavy packs on their backs and checked gas masks on their left side. After the remaining checks, they pulled their night vision goggles down over their eyes and leveled their M4 assault rifles forward. Payback would be unmerciful.

Clausen and his men moved steadily and silently, managing to cover the distance in record time. At two kilometers out, they stopped and scanned the open field in front of them with their Bi-Ocular FLIR goggles. Using infrared, the paratroopers could see any object with a heat signature for almost a quarter mile, which meant anything with a respiratory system. The field ahead was black, showing only a few white shapes of tiny animals scurrying away. When Zahn's men did appear, the paratroopers would see them as clear as day.

But what Clausen didn't know was that Zahn's men were expecting them, and their fatigues were invisible to the paratrooper's FLIR goggles. Each pair of black fatigues was designed with a mylar-aluminum prototype liner that created a perfect and complete seal around the wearer. Along with a flexible hood and special face mask, Zahn's men gave no external heat signature at all, allowing them to appear as black to infrared as the bushes they lay in.

Sarah jumped when she heard the gunfire outside. Her small lips quivered and she cringed at the loud, constant bursts which quickly grew louder and longer. She heard yelling outside and several minutes later the door opened behind her and closed again.

She heard footsteps cross the room behind her and knew immediately who it was. As he stepped in front of her, she looked up into the dark and deadly face of Kia Sarat.

"You're coming with me," he said and bent down to untie the rope around her tiny legs.

"W-where are we going?" she asked quietly.

"A long way from here," he answered, raising his voice over the shooting outside. "Where you can show me, and some others, what it is that makes you so special."

"W-what about Christine?"

Sarat paused with the rope in his hand and looked at her. He continued without a word, unraveling the line from her body. He had just stood up and grasped her arm in his giant hand when the door was suddenly ripped off its hinges from the outside.

Sarat instantly reached for his gun, but it was too late, Rand was already in the room pointing a rifle at him. Covered in mud, bruises and blood, he aimed the gun at Sarat. "She's not going anywhere."

Sarah screamed when Sarat picked her up and held her in front of him as a shield. "I know you want her; don't be stupid," he said, peering past her ear at Rand.

"The only way out is through me." Rand leveled his sights. "If you hurt her, you'll die right here."

Sarat said nothing. He stared at Rand, thinking. He looked closely and noticed that the barrel of the gun was shaking. Yet, it wasn't the gun that was shaking, it was Rand. He smiled and wrapped his hand around Sarah's tiny neck. "Drop the gun or I squeeze."

"If you hurt her, I'll kill you." Rand's face turned to steel. "Then I'll track down everyone you know and I'll kill *them*, parents, brothers, cousins, everyone. And when I'm done, I'll find every person who has ever known you or talked to you."

"You're lying!"

Rand shook his head again and tried to control the shaking. "I don't lie. You hurt her and everyone you have ever known dies; that's a promise. And believe me, I'll have plenty of time to do it."

Sarat looked at Rand nervously. He kept watching as Rand's shaking grew steadily worse, and the barrel increased its bouncing back and forth. *He can't even aim.* Sarat slowly passed Sarah to his left hand and dropped his right down next to his holster.

Sarat glanced down to make sure his gun was still there. When his head came back up, Rand was no longer looking at him. Instead, Rand was looking at Sarah who was staring right back at him. Before Sarat understood what was happening, Rand gave Sarah a tiny nod.

Immediately, she closed her eyes tight, and Rand shot Sarat in his right leg. He howled in pain and dropped Sarah onto the floor just before Rand fired another round into his chest. Sarat's body fell backwards and lifeless onto the floor.

Rand let his gun drop and looked at Sarah who still had her eyes closed. When she opened them, she saw Rand and ran forward, jumping into his arms and burying herself in his neck. She hugged him tightly, and Rand wrapped his muscular arms around her little frame.

She leaned back and rubbed her eyes. "I knew you would come."

"No matter what," Rand smiled back. And for that moment, he felt no pain at all.

With Sarah still in his arms, Rand turned away from Sarat's body. He walked to the overhead camera and yanked the power cord out of the wall.

Several minutes later, Rand peeked around the corner of the small brick house where Sarah had been kept. Walking behind him, she held Rand's hand and tried to look out from under his legs. Rand raised his FLIR goggles and looked out over the open area. The firefight had stopped momentarily, and he could see paratroopers lying in the tall grass. But there were no white shapes for Zahn's men further up the slope. *Where were they?*

What Rand could see was the entrance to some kind of bunker, but there was nowhere to hide between him and it; it was all open field. They could go around, but it would take far too long, even without a six-year-old girl. He looked back up to the bunker. *There was only one way.*

Without warning, Sarah gasped loudly behind him. Rand whirled around to see her astonishment and dropped down onto his knee.

"What is it, Sarah?"

She stood there with her mouth open. "You have a shadow!" Sarah watched as a faint shadow began to envelop Rand, finally covering his entire body. It slowly brightened until it became a bright yellow. "It's yellow!" she cried.

Rand felt a strong, warm sensation deep within his chest. As it grew, it became warmer and warmer and expanded out from his torso down to his arms and legs, all the way to his fingers and toes. Then, all at once, his shaking stopped. He was whole.

Rand hugged Sarah again before looking back up at the dark hill. "We have to get Christine."

Sarah stood before him, still grinning from ear to ear, but her excitement faded almost immediately. Rand's shadow became yellow, but it didn't stop. It continued to change, quickly turning to pink, orange, red and finally *black*.

Christine awoke and gasped through the cold water being thrown on her head. She wiped it from her face and coughed violently, spitting blood onto the wet floor. In a panic and blinded again, she protected her face with her right hand and scooted back against the wall.

"Wake up, you're missing the fun," Zahn's voice echoed from somewhere in front of her.

Christine spit again, not sure whether it was more blood or water this time. "What?"

"Your rescue team has arrived," Zahn replied dryly. "But sadly, they're not doing too well."

She shook her head and peered up at his silhouette. "I don't want to see it."

"Of course you do," he snapped. He reached down, grabbed a fistful of her hair, and pulled her to her feet.

Christine yelled in pain and stood up.

Zahn pulled her across the room and shoved her face toward the wall of monitors. They all showed the outside perimeter now and from different angles. Random muzzle flashes could be seen everywhere as the fight raged. Zahn leaned forward and whispered into her ear.

"These men are your only hope. And they're all dying. How does that feel?"

It felt sickening. She wanted to throw up over what was happening. Christine stumbled to maintain her balance when Zahn pushed her head forward even more.

"Do you still believe?" he hissed. "Do you still think this can be stopped? It can't, and you're going to watch it all happen, with me."

Christine rolled her eyes weakly, trying to look away from the monitors. She fought hard against Zahn's tight grip and managed to turn just enough…when she saw it. She saw it and her eyes opened wide in shock. Sarah was gone! "What did you do?!" she screamed.

A startled Zahn looked around, trying to understand what Christine was screaming about. She was staring at his computer screen. The video feed of Sarah was gone, replaced by nothing but static.

"What happened?" Zahn yelled with bulging eyes. He pushed Christine out of the way and sent her stumbling to the side. Zahn smashed the table with his fist. "Dammit! Who did this?" he screamed. "I'll kill them! WHO DID IT?!"

"I did."

Zahn and Christine spun around to find Rand standing in the doorway, his face white and his body covered in blood. He gave Christine a weak smile and tried to step forward but he collapsed and fell onto his knees, catching himself with his hands on the floor. After a few moments, he leaned his head back, gasping for air. His jacket had over a dozen holes where the bullets had torn into his body and blood now oozed out.

"Rand!" Christine cried. She tried to run to him, but Zahn grabbed Christine and pulled her back.

He looked at Rand curiously. "This is him?" he finally said. His pursed lips turned into a broad smile. "*This is him?*" Zahn burst out laughing. He peered down at Rand who barely managed to keep his knees under him. "This is who *he* sent to protect you?" Zahn laughed again, harder. "The big man must really be in trouble."

Rand swallowed hard. "Sarah?" he said in a weak voice.

Christine opened her mouth to answer when Rand spoke again, louder.

"Sarah?"

The ruck sack on Rand's back began to move. Christine and Zahn watched in stunned silence as his pack shifted again, and Sarah's tiny head popped up over Rand's shoulder.

"You okay?" Rand whispered.

"Yes," Sarah said and climbed off his back. Christine couldn't believe her eyes. Sarah was wrapped from head to toe in Rand's bullet proof vest.

Christine pulled hard, breaking Zahn's hold and running to Sarah who wrapped her arms around Christine. She looked at Rand. *"What did you just do?"*

Sarah answered for him. "We came to get you."

Zahn's laugh was now almost hysterical. "Christ, how much more perfect could this be?" He looked at all three of them as he stepped forward, barely able to contain himself. "A woman who can barely stand up, her great warrior who is about to lose consciousness, and," he tilted his head, "God's newest miracle, right here before me and as pretty as a little flower." He shook his head and continued laughing. "This truly could not be any sweeter!"

With the last of his strength, Rand grabbed Sarah and Christine and pushed them both behind him. He fumbled over his pants and jacket looking for his gun, but it was nowhere to be found.

"This is the icing on my cake," Zahn said as he stood in front of them. "To send all three of you right back to him and at the same time, no less." He looked at Rand who was leaning over and fighting to breathe. "And I'm going to start with you. For as you know, when you die without a soul, you don't go home, ever."

Zahn withdrew his gun from the holster and made sure it was loaded. Satisfied, he let the slide spring forward. "And then our little girl here. Because I want you, Christine, to watch it." Zahn held the gun up and pointed it at Rand.

Rand looked up at the barrel of Zahn's gun as darkness closed in around him. His vision was failing, and he could barely move. After all of this, after everything he'd fought for, this was the way it was going to end.

Quietly, behind Rand and Christine, Sarah slowly stood

up. She looked down at them and stepped forward, putting her little body between Zahn's gun and Rand.

Zahn looked at her curiously. He smirked at the thought of Rand having to be protected by a six-year-old in his final seconds.

"He didn't forget you," she said softly.

Zahn froze. He looked as though he didn't quite hear her. "What?"

She stared up at Zahn who towered over her. "He didn't forget you," she repeated.

The look in Zahn's eyes changed from delight to confusion, and he took a small step back. Without saying a word, Sarah matched him by taking her own step forward.

Zahn nervously looked at the others and then back down at Sarah. "What is she doing?!" he said and took another step backward.

"He never forgot," Sarah said in a hushed voice. She closed the gap again.

Zahn yelled at Rand and Christine. "Did you tell her to say this? Tell her to stop!" He nervously grabbed a small metal table and slid it between them. *It wasn't possible! What she was saying wasn't possible! He was left here; he was abandoned!* He backed up even further away from the table when he saw it, something in Sarah's eyes. He had seen those eyes before, a long time ago, in the young boy Ryan Kelly. His voice began to tremble. "Stay away from me."

He watched in fear as the tiny girl walked around the table and came closer. "He loves you," she said. "He's always loved you."

"No, he doesn't!" yelled Zahn. "He left me!"

Sarah looked at him and shook her head. "He never left you."

Zahn backed into the wall and, in a panic, he pointed his gun at her and pulled the trigger.

Nothing happened.

His finger would not move. Zahn pulled again harder,

but his finger remained frozen. He tried to switch to his left, but his entire hand became frozen, both unable to let go of the gun and unable to fire it. As Sarah came closer, Zahn kept moving away. He looked back at Christine, who was watching and moved next to her, away from Sarah. "Stop her! Tell her to stop!"

Christine said nothing. She only watched in amazement as Sarah continued to approach Zahn completely unafraid. Zahn's composure had suddenly changed. He was no longer a violent monster; he was now a monster who was afraid of a mouse. As Sarah closed in again, Zahn was now pushed into the corner of the room, paralyzed with fear.

Sarah stopped in front of him and stood there quietly. Finally, she whispered, "He wants you to come home."

Christine watched Sarah reach down and take Rand's limp hand in hers. With the other, she reached out and grabbed Zahn's hand. Slowly Rand's body began to glow and his black shadow became visible. The blackness spread from his torso and traveled up his arm to Sarah's hand where it continued through her and into Zahn.

Zahn's body instantly and violently arched backwards, as the blackness slowly enveloped him and his eyes rolled into his head. His jaw tightened and his body began to shake after Sarah let go, letting Zahn fall to the floor still convulsing as if in a giant seizure. Soon, the shaking began to fade, taking Zahn's strength with it. He opened his mouth, gasping for air, just as Rand had.

Finally, his head slowly fell forward, and he stared at nothing. His vision was nearly gone. "I'm going home," he mumbled and tears began to appear in his eyes. "I'm going home."

"Wait!" Christine cried. She scurried across the floor to where he was propped against the walls. "You have to stop the attack! You have to stop the missiles!"

Zahn continued to stare straight ahead. He could no longer see nor hear anything. With the last of his energy, he suddenly gasped. "Oh god, what have I done?" His voice faded into a whisper, "He'll never forgive me."

With that, Zahn's head rolled to the side and he was gone.

62

"NO!" screamed Christine. She grabbed his jacket and shook him hard, but Zahn's body simply slid the rest of the way down the wall to the floor. She looked up at the wall of monitors, some still showing the rioting in China. She moaned and desperately turned back to Rand who lay still behind her. "Rand!" she screamed and grabbed his shoulders. She pulled his head up to hers and brushed his hair out of the way when her left hand felt something: a pulse.

Christine gasped and looked up at Sarah. "He's still alive!"

Sarah nodded, smiling. "He's yellow again."

Two soldiers stumbled into the room with one hopping and leaning on the other. They both looked down at all four of them.

Bazes spotted Rand on the floor and then looked at Christine and Sarah, whom he noted was much smaller than he expected. He then looked at Zahn's body sprawled out with his mouth open. "What happened?"

"Who are you?" asked Christine through swollen eyes.

"My name is Bazes," he nodded at the other man, "and this is Clausen. We came with Rand."

"What the hell took you so long?"

"Those bastards were wearing some kind of cold suits!" growled Clausen. He immediately realized what he had said and looked at Sarah with a guilty frown. "Sorry 'bout that."

Bazes turned and looked around the rest of the room, stopping at the monitors on the wall with the video feeds. "What is this?" he asked.

"Listen to me!" Christine pleaded. "We have to do

something. It's a nuclear attack! The missiles in China are going to go off!"

Bazes' eyes opened wide. "What?!"

"It's a massive virus! The attack on China is some sort of decoy!"

"Dear God." He pushed away from Clausen and hopped on one leg, quickly searching his pants. Bazes found what he was looking for in the right leg pocket and ripped it open, extracting a small satellite phone. He flipped up the oversized antennae and pressed a button.

"It's Bazes. He's dead." He looked back at all the monitors. "And we have an emergency!"

63

Guo Cheng was the Minister of Public Security of the People's Republic of China, which was charged with the security and safety of the entire country. He slowly returned his phone to its receiver and pushed a red button on the base. Less than ten seconds later, his assistant came running into the room. Cheng looked at him urgently. "Get the Prime Minister and the President on the phone *right now*." His assistant bowed and disappeared.

With a deep sigh, Cheng leaned back in his chair and stared at his phone. The call had been from Benecke, head of Homeland Security in the United States.

Before the call, he thought he had enough problems. The riots had escalated, and their only option for stopping the global cyber-attack was to kill all internet connectivity in and out of the country. But it would come at a price. That attack was on the Chinese government only, but to stop it meant stopping all electronic communication and commerce for over a *billion* people. The economic impact, especially in the current economy, was going to be horrific.

That was before Benecke's call. Now what they had to do was much worse, and it was going to be absolutely disastrous.

Ron Tran exited his gate in the Bueno Aires airport along with several hundred other passengers, all arriving on the first wave of morning flights. His inability to sleep on planes left him exhausted, but the excitement of the last three days had kept him awake purely from the adrenaline. He spotted a group of people standing around a giant television and walked quickly to join them.

Something was wrong. He pushed in closer from the back of the crowd and tried to understand what was happening. He couldn't translate the words of the newscasters, but he could see words in Chinese inside a window in the upper left hand corner. China was dark.

A wave of anxiety began to form inside him as he peered harder at the screen trying to understand what that meant, but the Chinese message just kept repeating the same words. *China is dark.*

Suddenly he realized, China was not just offline; China was literally "dark". China had turned off the power for its entire country, all at once. Every single one of its nuclear and coal power plants, over 70 in total, were *all taken offline, plunging the entire country into total darkness.*

Tran shook his head; he couldn't believe it. He instantly thought of Stux2 and China's Command and Control system. The systems, as well as the missile silos, all had back up power, but those were from other plants. With all of the plants offline, there *was no redundant power.* Even the plants that had backup generators wouldn't have enough juice to power the systems and connections all the way back to the country's central command system. *They had stopped it.*

Tran backed up and tried to think. How did it all happen? What did it mean? Where was Zahn? After several minutes, Tran stood up and calmly walked down the giant hallway, blending in with the huge crowd of arriving passengers. As he walked, he calmly unzipped his backpack and slid his laptop computer out. He held it casually in his hand until they passed the next garbage can, where he quietly let it fall in. He then walked downstairs and circled back to the ticket counter.

"I'd like to purchase a one way ticket, please," he said, handing his ID to the agent.

She peered at the card and placed it back onto the counter. "Of course, Mr. Chang. Where are we headed today?"

"La Chinita, Venezuela."

Christine sat on the cold floor, leaning her head against the wall. She had one hand on Sarah who lay asleep in her lap and her other on Rand, who was still out. Bazes sat in a chair nearby watching the video feeds on the wall.

"Did they stop it?" she asked Bazes quietly.

He turned and looked at her, considering the question. "Yes."

She nodded and looked down at Sarah. After a few minutes, she spoke again. "Are you with the government?"

This time, Bazes smiled. "Actually, you can probably say the government is with me."

She wrinkled her brow, unsure of what that meant. "So does that mean you have some authority?"

"Yes."

"I'm wondering if you can help me with something."

Bazes raised an eyebrow. "Such as?"

"There is someone I need the FBI to investigate."

"And who would that be?" he asked.

"I don't know his name, but he's a ranger at Natirar Park in New York."

Three years later…

Kingston Estates was the largest youth house in Kansas City, situated on a sprawling ten acres along the Missouri River and less than fifteen miles from downtown. Lawrence Grayson, Kingston's Director, walked down the large hallway leading out to the main yard. He was proud of the house, and it showed.

"As you can see," Grayson boasted, "this is one of the nicest facilities in the state and we pride ourselves on it. We also place more children than all of the others combined. As "houses" go, the children are fortunate to be at ours."

They turned left and walked down two sets of steps out into the sun. The lawn and surrounding bushes were well-kept and looked as clean on the outside as the two-story building did on the inside. After walking up a small hill, Grayson stopped at the top and gestured to the large field in front of them, where dozens of children were playing. They were all different ages with the smaller children running around together, while the older children clumped and played in smaller groups.

"Mr. Grayson!" one of the smallest boys called, running up to him. He smiled and bent down as the boy approached. "Yes, what is it?"

"I have to go potty."

Grayson turned and smiled with a mild look of embarrassment. "If you'll excuse me, I'll be right back." He grabbed the young boy's hand and hurried off.

Sarah, now nine, quietly stood on the grass scanning

the yard. After a moment, she looked up at Christine and pointed to the far corner. "That's him."

Christine's gaze followed her hand and spotted a young boy just four or five years older than Sarah. With sandy brown hair, he was alone on the opposite side of the field, doing pull-ups on an old rusty bar. He didn't notice them, and as she watched, Christine realized he was not interacting with any of the other kids.

"Are you sure?"

Sarah nodded.

Christine smiled. They had been searching for a long time. She turned to her left. "Well?"

Next to her, Rand watched the boy carefully. After several seconds, he nodded with a satisfied look. "He looks trainable."

Christine smiled again and slipped her hand back into Rand's.

EPILOGUE

Dozens of people leapt from their wagons and carriages, running through the puddles to help. A crowd was beginning to form, and several people darted away to find a doctor, but it was too late.

Dean Kelly sat on the muddy ground cradling the body of his young son in his arms. "My Ryan! My perfect little Ryan!" he cried out over and over, tears streaming down his face. Kelly just stared at his son's pale face, so peaceful and calm, and rocked his still body back and forth.

The pain was overwhelming and unimaginable. His boy was gone. His perfect boy. His little Ryan was so smart and so gifted. Even his father, a man of high intelligence, was stunned at his own son's abilities. Ryan never had to be told something twice. He remembered virtually everything from almost the day he could speak. At the age of ten, he was better at mathematics than any tutor Kelly could find. But what Ryan loved more than anything else was biology. *Now, that was all gone*, Kelly thought to himself. All of Ryan's dreams were gone.

What Kelly did not know was the greatness his son had been destined for, a destiny that would now never come: to become a prodigy like few the 19th century had ever seen. To be the youngest to finish Yale University at thirteen years old; and, to gain a doctorate in medicine by the time he was sixteen.

In the late 1890s, he would have gone on to make numerous biological breakthroughs which would have radically advanced the understanding of the human body. In 1912, after joining the famed Institute for Cancer Research in London, he would have made the greatest contribution of his life: discovering unique cellular characteristics that could later identify and predict mutation behavior.

However, the discovery would go misunderstood for decades until Ryan Kelly's daughter, following in her father's footsteps, would uncover important clues and take it even further. In 1952, she would develop the biological knowledge and foundation for the first prototype: a prototype for a cure of human cancer cells. And less than forty years later, by the end of the twentieth century, cancer would rank just below chicken pox on the list of most dangerous global diseases.

But young Ryan Kelly was gone and his future suddenly erased. Neither his father, nor the rest of the world, would ever know about his discoveries and his gifts to mankind.

God would try again.

ABOUT THE AUTHOR

Michael Grumley lives in Northern California with his wife and two young daughters. His email address is mgrumley@gmail.com, and his web site is www.michaelgrumley.com where you can also find a supplemental Q&A page for this story.

MESSAGE FROM THE AUTHOR

Thank you for reading my second book *Amid the Shadows*. I hope you enjoyed it. If you could please take a moment to leave a review I would be very grateful. As you may know, being a new, self-published author makes it very difficult to compete with the big name authors without book reviews. It's just the way Amazon works, and I have to admit, it sure would be nice to finally make it out of the dimly lit corners of Amazon.

If you do write a review, please email me at the address above and I will forward you a short bonus chapter covering some of Jonathan Avery's mission against the Nazis. I thought it would be a fun way to say "Thank You".

BOOKS BY MICHAEL C. GRUMLEY

BREAKTHROUGH
March 2013

AMID THE SHADOWS
September 2013

Made in United States
Troutdale, OR
01/06/2024

16753775R00192